HERE'S HOW AN UNEMPLOYED
COLLEGE GRADUATE BECAME . . .

A LOGICAL MAGICIAN

HELP WANTED: Logical young man with an open mind and active imagination wanted for highly unusual but financially rewarding career opportunity. Some risk involved. Background in mathematics and fantastic literature advised.

Jack Collins never thought he'd find a job after college. Especially a job that combined his math skills and his love of fantasy.

But then again, Jack Collins never thought that he'd be working for Merlin the Magician—or that he'd be tracking down a savage, ancient demon in the streets of modern Chicago . . .

Well, the ad *did* say "some risk involved."

A LOGICAL MAGICIAN

"Entertaining . . . lighthearted . . . a lot of fun."
—Charles de Lint, *Mystery Scene*

Now the Logical Magician returns—in an all-out war between ancient mythology and modern mathematics . . .

A CALCULATED MAGIC

Ace Books by Robert Weinberg

A LOGICAL MAGICIAN
A CALCULATED MAGIC

A CALCULATED MAGIC

ROBERT WEINBERG

ACE BOOKS, NEW YORK

To my mother, Dorothy Weinberg,
the equal of any mom in this novel . . .

This book is an Ace original edition,
and has never been previously published.

A CALCULATED MAGIC

An Ace Book / published by arrangement with
the author

PRINTING HISTORY
Ace edition / February 1995

Cover art by Peter Scanlan.

For information address: The Berkley Publishing Group,
200 Madison Avenue, New York, NY 10016.

ISBN: 0-441-00144-0

ACE®
Ace Books are published by The Berkley Publishing Group,
200 Madison Avenue, New York, NY 10016.
ACE and the "A" design are trademarks
belonging to Charter Communications, Inc.

PRINTED IN THE UNITED STATES OF AMERICA

10 9 8 7 6 5 4 3 2 1

scientia est potentia
(knowledge is power)

mundus vult decipi
(the world wants to be deceived)

∞

Prologue

That no one ever guessed that Boris Bronsky was nothing more than an unimportant member of the Russian State Department was directly attributable to sixty-three red Xs. The marks were engraved next to the names of those who incurred the wrath of the Soviet premier or the secretary of the Communist Party. The imposing list of his victims served as a grim warning to leave Boris Bronsky strictly alone. In a country where spies spied on spies spying on spies, Boris retained astonishing autonomy. He worked independently, without supervision, without interference, without controls.

Thus, on June 6, when Boris entered a dark alley of a disreputable section of Paris, no member of any secret organization followed. Not that Bronsky ever worried about such matters. He was, in fact, incredibly naive about the inner workings of the KGB and the Secret Service. It never once occurred to him that his own organization would monitor his movements. He probably would have been even more astonished to learn of the nine agents who had disappeared without a trace trying to keep pace with him over the years. But Boris was a man with absolutely no imagination. That, and his total lack of ambition, was why he had been chosen for this position in the first place a quarter of a century before.

His predecessor, Nikoli Valda, equally notorious in his time, had chosen Boris as his protégé after reviewing the records of hundreds of civilian employees working for the KGB. Valda never confided to his young assistant how he had made his choice. Many years later, Boris concluded it was because he was a man of simple tastes, not easily bored. Which was actually closer to the truth than he realized. For though he was respected by a few, feared by many, Boris Bronsky lacked ambition. And that, considering the power he wielded, was all-important.

Among his family and friends, Boris was affectionately nicknamed "the Bear." Standing six feet four inches tall and weighing slightly more than 340 pounds, Boris's resemblance to the animal was quite apparent. A layer of thick, curly brown hair that covered much of his body helped to further the illusion. As did his small, piercing black eyes. Bronsky looked the part of his namesake.

However, according to those who loved him, the title came from Boris's gruff but friendly nature. To his fellow Russians, bears were creatures of the circus—huge, powerful animals without the least bit of meanness in their souls. Bears played with huge balls and buffeted clowns and suffered the most outrageous practical jokes with a seemingly unlimited amount of patience. It was Bronsky's gentleness that earned him the nickname "the Bear."

It was a measure of Boris's skill at keeping his personal and professional lives distinct entities that none of his family knew his other nickname, the one whispered behind his back by his lackeys in the Kremlin. It was a title bestowed in fear, never written down, and known only to a very few. To those in power, Boris Bronsky was "the Permanent Solution."

Elimination of the enemies of the state was Boris's specialty. He was the final resort, the last protocol. Only after the secret police and the KGB had tried and failed was Boris summoned. His was a talent used sparingly and with great deliberation. For once unleashed, Boris Bronsky was relentless, unyielding, unstoppable. No one escaped "the Permanent Solution."

He was, in a sense, one of the last Soviet institutions. In a time of one incredible change after another throughout Russia, he remained a solitary, steadfast, unmoving rock. Sixty-three missions of extermination had been assigned to Boris Bronsky. Of them, sixty-three had ended in the termination of the victim or victims. No one could explain his success. Or dared question his methods. They knew only that Boris never failed. *Never.*

Tonight, he was engaged in mission number sixty-four. At the end of the deserted alley was a single door leading to a basement apartment. As usual, the door was not locked. Opening it, Boris stepped inside. A single light bulb burned above the entrance. It shed just enough radiance to illuminate one end of an old wood table extending into the inky blackness. Set in front of the table was a rickety old chair. As best Boris could tell, it was the same table and chair that had been there on the first of his visits twenty-five years ago.

Boris sat down. His hosts never arrived until a few minutes after he was settled. That, too, was part of the ritual. They came after him and left before him. Never once had he caught a glimpse of them. They moved in absolute silence and remained always in the shadows. Yet he knew immediately when they entered the room. Their smell betrayed them.

Boris's nose wrinkled in disgust. The most liberal doses of perfume could not hide the stink that announced the arrival of his three hosts. It was a pungent, unforgettable smell that somehow reminded Boris of reptiles.

Ignoring the odor, Boris leaned forward, elbows on the table. "I want a man killed. He betrayed his country, Mother Russia. His death is necessary for the good of the state."

"You know our price," said the woman who usually did most of the talking. Her deep, gravelly voice was barely more than a whisper, but it filled the entire chamber. Like her companions, she never offered her real name. Instead, she used a title. "The Retaliator." It fit.

"The money has already been transferred to your Swiss bank account," said Boris, fidgeting in his seat. No matter how many times he dealt with these women, he could not shake the feelings of dread that accompanied the visit. Their very presence frightened him. There was something inhuman about them.

"Detail his crimes," said another woman. Her voice was higher and shriller than her companions'. She took the name "the Rager." Righteous anger boiled through her every word.

"The traitor's name is Sergei Karsnov," began Boris. "He is forty-seven years old, stands one hundred and seventy centimeters, and weighs a little under ninety kilos. He has black eyes and black hair and speaks five foreign languages, including English, perfectly."

"His crimes," interrupted the Rager impatiently. "What were his crimes?"

"Sorry," said Boris, mentally shaking himself. He should have remembered. The three killers didn't care about their victim's appearance. They could learn that from the files he provided them at the end of the meeting. However, for some unexplained reason, they preferred hearing aloud their quarry's transgressions.

"In 1989, working for the Department of Chemical Warfare, Karsnov developed a new strain of the disease anthrax that could be administered by airborne spores. When tested on laboratory animals, the new plague virus proved to be extremely efficient. Unfortunately, Karsnov felt the results were not conclusive without a human sample. So, unbeknownst to his colleagues, he released a tiny sample of the spores in St. Petersburg."

"He poisoned his fellow countrymen to test the effect of a plague virus?" repeated the Rager, sounding properly outraged. "What happened?"

"Exactly what you would expect," said Boris. "Anthrax symptoms are very similar to those of pneumonia but the treatment for one and the other are entirely different. The disease is deadly unless handled properly. Nearly a hundred people died before Karsnov's crime was detected. It took a massive effort by the army and the KGB to stop the spread of the plague. By the time Karsnov was implicated in the crime, the scientist had managed to flee the country."

"And now you want him dead," said the Retaliator. "You want justice for those who died."

"Of course," said Bronsky, knowing he was treading on dangerous ground. The assassins demanded motivation as well as money. In a strange manner, they were highly moral killers. "The blood of their mother, of Mother Russia, demands revenge."

"The rules of the state must be obeyed," said the third killer, who had remained silent until now. Her voice was cold and remote. She was called "the Endless."

"That is the law," said the Retaliator in agreement.

"That is the law," repeated the Rager.

Sighing deeply, Boris nodded. By those words, he knew that the three had taken the assignment. Karsnov was as good as dead.

"You said he fled," continued the Retaliator. "Where did he go?"

"To America, we think," said Boris. "Karsnov has two passions.

A protégé of hard-liners in the Kremlin, he hates the United States with an all-consuming mania. He has spent most of his adult life perfecting weapons to be used against the Americans. With the cold war over and peace between our two nations, we suspect he plans to use the anthrax plague to fulfill his own twisted agenda."

"His other passion?" asked the Endless.

"Karsnov loves to gamble. He plays cards compulsively, for hours, sometimes days on end. The desire to win at any cost engulfs him and sweeps him away. That is why we think he is in America. My colleagues in the Secret Service believe he is in Las Vegas, Nevada. Gambling," he added unnecessarily, "is legal there."

"You have warned the Americans?" asked the Rager.

"Of course not," said Boris. "They would never believe that Karsnov has turned rogue and is working on his own. Like my superiors, they see a plot under every rock. Comrade Yeltsin is in the midst of delicate negotiations for more aid from the United States. One mention of the anthrax plague would destroy any hopes of that mission."

"How did the scientist escape your own KGB?" asked the Retaliator. "Usually they are quite capable of dealing with traitors."

"We are not sure," said Boris. "According to several reliable though not official sources, Karsnov is being aided by an ultrasecret group of Islamic terrorists based in the United States. The group's plans are not known to us, but evidently they want revenge against the United States for the humiliation suffered by Iraq in that war of a few years ago. What better way than to unleash a plague virus on the unsuspecting citizens of a major American city?"

"We have dealt with fanatics before," said the Endless.

"Those same unnamed sources," said Boris slowly, "reported that members of this group, The Brotherhood of Holy Destruction, wielded seemingly supernatural powers. According to uncon-firmed reports, they smuggled Karsnov out of Russia on a magic carpet. I knew it sounded incredible, but I thought it only proper I should mention the story to you."

"We have dealt with sorcery before as well," said the Endless, her voice unchanged. "It exists, but it can be stopped. We shall not fail."

"I'm not worried," said Boris, thinking of the previous sixty-three assignments. The meeting was drawing to a close. There were only a few things left to be done. He reached into the attaché case at his feet. "I brought along Karsnov's files for you."

"And a personal effect?" asked the Rager.

"Of course," said Boris, reaching again into the case. "Karsnov wore this pocket watch for years. In his haste to escape, he left it behind."

Boris put the files and the watch onto the table. Carefully, he pushed them forward into the darkness. Someone picked up the file and then the watch. He could hear it being passed around. Bronsky shuddered in anticipation, knowing what came next. His every encounter with the three mysterious hunters ended the same way.

"*Labe, labe, labe,*" chanted the three assassins in unison, their horrifying voices blending into a monstrous chorus of sound. "*Phradzou!*"

An instant later, an unseen door opened and closed and they were gone. The hunters were off on their mission to seek and destroy.

Boris rose to his feet, scratching his head in bewilderment. Dull and unimaginative, he still wished he understood the purpose of that final burst of noise.

Years before, he had smuggled into the meeting a compact tape machine and had recorded the mysterious words. A KGB language specialist had identified the phrase as ancient Greek and translated it for him as "Seize him, seize him, seize him; mark him!"

The translation left Boris as much in the dark as before. He had no idea what the statement signified or why the three assassins pronounced it at the end of each meeting.

A plain, simple man, not educated in the classics, Boris had never studied the famous Greek playwrights. He had never heard of Aeschylus or his most famous play. Which, all things considered, was probably for the best.

∞

1

Stretching both arms high over his head, Jack Collins inhaled deeply, pulling lungfuls of fresh air into his chest. He smiled. It felt good lolling in bed with no thoughts of rushing off to an early-morning class. After attending college nine years straight, a little laziness never hurt anyone.

Idly, Jack checked the clock by the side of his bed. It was a few minutes after nine in the morning. Under normal circumstances, he would have shaved, dressed, and breakfasted an hour and a half ago. Right about now, he would be greeting the shuffling, half-asleep zombies who constituted his first mathematics lecture class of the day. But times and circumstances were anything but normal.

Jack Collins, graduate teaching assistant in mathematics and logic at the local university, no longer existed. Vanished along with that persona were his dreams of obtaining his doctoral degree and becoming a full-time professor. Instead, in a dramatic change of fortunes, Jack had joined the investment firm of Ambrose and Associates, Ltd., and become a hero. Through his efforts, aided and abetted by a group of unlikely friends and allies, he had saved the world from the forces of everlasting night. And in the course of his quest, met and romanced the most beautiful girl in the world.

The thought of Megan Ambrose, daughter of his boss, Merlin the Magician, made Jack smile. Extremely bright and visually stunning, Megan was everything any man could ask for. That she cared for him was one of those mysteries Jack was willing to accept with no questions asked. After his adventures dealing with Dietrich von Bern, the Lord of the Wild Hunt, master of the monstrous Gabble Ratchets, Jack felt he deserved a few breaks.

Besides, like himself, Megan was a halfling—a child of a supernatural being and a human parent. As such, they were able to communicate with each other in their dreams. It was a talent that had saved Jack's life more than once during the past month, and it had forged unbreakable bonds between him and Megan. Bonds that had led to their engagement and plans to be married in the reasonably near future.

Jack rubbed his eyes, banishing the last remnants of sleep from them. He yawned and blinked several times, trying to focus his vision. Even though it was several weeks since his adventures had first begun, he still had not completely adjusted to seeing the world through a pink haze. The rose-colored contact lenses he wore enabled him to distinguish between normal people and supernatural beings. Humans had auras, clearly visible with the magical eyewear. All other beings, which included trolls, faeries, goblins, witches, familiars, vampires, and hundreds of others, did not.

Mankind shared the Earth with the creations of its own collective subconscious. According to Merlin the Magician, who had spent centuries puzzling out the explanation, this cosmic overmind had the power to turn dreams into reality. When enough people believed that a supernatural being or legendary beast truly existed, it physically came into being. The myths and stories about the creature defined it, from its appearance to the way it thought and acted. Once alive, these creations remained, unaffected by the ravages of age, unless *disbelieved* out of existence. Which rarely ever occurred. By and large, they were merely forgotten.

Immortal and unkillable except by very specific methods, the supernaturals survived long after the belief that brought them into existence had died out. They changed with the times, blending in with their creators, remaining ever true to their original nature. Good continued as good, evil stayed evil, and neutral abided uninvolved and in between.

Thus, Merlin the Magician became a commodities broker,

advising the rich and famous. Cassandra Cole, last of the Amazons, turned into a martial-arts teacher and bodyguard. And barrow trolls became neo-Nazi skinheads.

At first, it had been quite confusing to Jack. But not for long. As a voracious reader of fantasy novels, he found Merlin's explanation of the supernatural astonishing but otherwise quite acceptable. Trained in logical thinking, he found his background in mathematics provided the right answers to supernatural mysteries. It didn't take Jack long to slip into his role as the Logical Magician.

Grinning, he rose from his bed and headed to the bathroom, three steps away. Living in a trailer, everything was close by. To Jack's way of thinking, it was one of the few benefits of such a life. One of the very few benefits.

He was staying in the trailer camp more for protection than for lack of funds. Merlin paid him a very generous salary. Moving out of his college apartment a week ago, he had been terribly tempted to rent a fancy place on Chicago's near north side. Or accept Megan's offer that he share her expensive condo. But as pointed out by his friends, both choices posed clearly unacceptable risks. Jack's life was still in deadly danger. And if he was killed, eternal night would engulf the globe.

Though he had defeated Dietrich von Bern, the Huntsman's mysterious master was still at large. An ancient demigod of incredible powers, it threatened modern civilization. Using his crystal ball, Merlin proclaimed Jack the only one who could stop the entity. It was a duel not yet completed. Until the creature had been found and somehow destroyed, Jack could not afford to relax an instant. Thus, he stayed, surrounded by friendly supernaturals, in a trailer camp in the far western Chicago suburbs.

Megan visited as often as possible, but the cramped trailer provided little room for romance. Nor did their dozens of busybody chaperons, ranging from the Witch Hazel and her familiar, Sylvester, a talking cat, to Simon Goodfellow, a faery changeling who always managed to interrupt at the most inconvenient instant possible. It was enough to try the patience of a saint. And Jack definitely felt anything but saintly concerning Megan.

Wonderfully erotic thoughts about his girlfriend forced Jack to turn the shower water ice cold. Short and slender, with dark hair and sparkling eyes, Megan resembled an elf. Which was probably why Jack originally thought she was entirely supernatural and not merely a halfling. That she was very human and quite passionate, he had discovered only recently. For all of her ethereal charms, Megan could be quite risqué when the time and opportunity presented itself.

After showering and shaving, Jack flung on a shirt, sneakers, and pair of faded blue jeans. A quick glance at the clock told him he had barely enough time to grab a bowl of cereal and milk before meeting Cassandra on the meadow for his self-defense lessons. He grimaced as his muscles mentally groaned in anticipation. These workouts were necessary, but not appreciated. World-saver or not, Jack was a thinker, not a fighter. However, there was no arguing with an Amazon.

Arriving at the tree-lined glade at exactly nine-thirty, Jack was not surprised to find Cassandra there and ready for action. The Amazon was a chronic overachiever. Her back to him, she had started exercising on her own.

Self-discipline was a way of life to the Amazon. She always arrived early and left late. Practice, practice, and more practice filled her life. Cassandra defined dedication—bordering on obsession.

Tall and slender, Cassandra had skin the color of dark chocolate. Her eyes and shoulder-length hair were jet black. High cheekbones and a thin, aquiline nose gave her a fragile, delicate look. Only the whipcord-lean muscles in her arms and shoulders hinted at the true strength she possessed.

In her hands, the Amazon held a thick walking staff. Capped on each end with silver, the stick was covered with exotic markings carved into the wood. Simon had once mentioned in passing something about ancient Greek mottoes. Jack felt sure they dealt with the glory of battle. A mythological warrior woman, Cassandra didn't fight to live—she lived to fight.

Jack watched, entranced as she wove her staff in an intricate series of maneuvers. The wood moved so fast that at times the air whistled with its passage. Cassandra twirled on her toes, graceful as a ballet dancer, as she completed routines designed to kill or maim anyone foolish enough to engage her in combat. Cassandra played rough. When necessary, she was deadly.

"About time you arrived, Jack," declared the Amazon without turning. He was quite positive she had never seen him. But she had known he was there. "You're three minutes late."

"Sorry," said Jack. "How did you identify me?"

"Your breathing, of course," she said. She spun around and planted her staff six inches into the hard soil. "Once you've mastered the fundamentals of self-defense, I'll teach you some basic survival techniques. You make too much noise walking. And you breathe way too loud."

Jack sighed. He didn't recall any of the fantasy novels he enjoyed dwelling on the hero's tedious and painful training sessions. In books, the protagonist was always in perfect shape and a master fighter. Unfortunately, teaching mathematics didn't require any such skills. It was going to be another traumatic morning.

The Amazon smiled, as if reading his thoughts. Mentally, Jack grimaced. Cassandra reserved her grins for days when she planned the most demanding physical torments imaginable. He wondered if it was too late to remember another appointment.

Cassandra took one step toward him when her eyes widened in sudden surprise. Something large and black rocketed over their heads. "Assassins!" screeched the bird. "Assassins!"

Instantly, the Amazon launched herself at Jack. Her right shoulder slammed into his chest, sending the two of them sprawling to the earth. Above them, the clearing exploded with the roar of automatic weapons.

Jack gulped in shock as Cassandra's staff disintegrated into a thousand toothpicks. On the far side of the glade, the greenery vanished, swept away by a steel broom.

"Stay flat," commanded Cassandra and disappeared into the woods. Knowing his limitations, Jack had no intentions of doing anything but.

An eternity passed in less than a minute. As suddenly as it had begun, the gunfire ceased. Still wary, Jack stayed put. At the moment, the ground seemed the safest place to be.

With a flap of wings, a huge raven landed only a few inches from Jack's nose. Intense pinpoint black eyes stared into his.

"All's clear," declared the bird, in a surprisingly deep voice. It spoke with a slight accent that Jack found vaguely familiar. "The babe neutralized the opposition. I spotted three men and she got them all. Tough cookie, that lady."

"How do I know you're telling the truth?" asked Jack. "You could be trying to trick me."

"After warning you of the attack in the first place?" replied the raven. "That doesn't make sense, Johnnie."

Jack groaned. The nickname confirmed his worst fears. The bird squawked with a noticeable Swedish accent. It sounded just like his mother. Who was the only person in the world who still used that particular boyhood title.

"You're Hugo?" guessed Jack, sitting up. He had never been very good at telling his mother's two pet blackbirds apart. "I never knew you could talk."

"I didn't know you were hanging 'round with Amazons," retorted the bird. "So we're square."

Jack groaned in dismay. It had only been a few weeks since his final encounter with Dietrich von Bern and his army of Border Redcaps. He had hoped for a little more rest before returning to the fray. However, this unexpected assassination attempt didn't bode well for the future. Jack had a feeling it was going to be a long day. A very long day.

2

A few seconds later, Cassandra appeared at the edge of the clearing dragging an unconscious man by the feet. A short, powerfully built man with a dark brown beard that covered his face, he was dressed in khaki green combat fatigues. That his head bounced along the ground with solid thumps bothered the Amazon not a bit. Cassandra hated being disturbed during their practice sessions. Jack knew better than to ask the fate of the other two attackers. Sometimes he preferred not knowing all the answers.

"There were three of them," declared the Amazon, dumping the lone survivor a few feet away from Jack. "Each man carried an AK-47 and knew how to use it. For humans, they made remarkably little noise. Lucky for us, your friend here sounded the alarm."

"Humans?" repeated Jack, caught by surprise.

He had naturally assumed their enemies to be supernatural entities. New minions of his sinister foe, sent to eliminate him before he could interfere in the demigod's schemes. Jack stared at the unconscious man with undisguised annoyance. The assassin definitely possessed an aura. He was distressingly mortal.

"What's the story with this clown?" asked Hugo, hopping forward to peer into the man's face. "Disgruntled ex-student?"

"I never saw him before in my life," said Jack. "Besides, math majors don't carry automatic weapons. At least," he added cautiously, "none of my students did."

"Let's wake him up and ask him a few questions," said Cassandra. There was an icy calmness to her voice that made Jack shiver. "If he proves uncooperative, I can break a few of his bones. Slowly. One at a time."

"I can peck his eyes out if you want," added Hugo helpfully. "Haven't done it for centuries, but I think I still remember the technique. It's like riding a bicycle. Once you learn how, you never forget."

"No need to resort to torture unless absolutely necessary," said Jack, turning green. Born of mankind's most vivid imaginings, the supernaturals had a tendency to view everything in terms of extremes. There were no grays for them, only blacks and whites. "The sight of you two should loosen his tongue quick enough."

"Maybe," said Cassandra, sounding doubtful. "Though anyone using an AK-47 isn't going to start talking just because he's threatened by a talking bird." She smiled. "Crushing a few fingers usually starts them babbling."

"Talk first, torture later," said Jack firmly.

"Spoilsport," said Cassandra.

Pulling the man up by his collar into a sitting position, the Amazon slapped him briskly across the face a few times. After a few hits, the bearded man grunted in pain and opened his eyes.

"We failed, huh?" he said, glancing at the trio without fear. "I assume you got the other two and I'm the only one left." The man spat. "Damned bird ruined the ambush. No fair using animals as lookouts. How'd you manage that trick?"

"I'll ask the questions," said Jack, trying to sound tough. "Who are you and why did you try to kill us?"

"I did my best," said the bearded man, talking to himself. He completely ignored Jack's remarks. "The Old Man warned us it wouldn't be easy."

"Old Man?" asked Jack, picking up on the title. "Who are you talking about? Are you with some intelligence agency or something? The CIA? The FBI?"

"Quit babying the bozo, Johnnie," said Hugo, flapping up to the startled prisoner's shoulder. "Let me poke out one of his eyeballs. That will get us some answers."

"Game's over and we lost this round," said the prisoner. "But my reward's earned. I'm outa here. I'm off to paradise."

The instant the man completed the phrase, he slumped lifelessly in Cassandra's arms.

"Hell," said the Amazon, releasing her grip on the prisoner. His body dropped like a sack of cement to the ground. "A poison stick-it note."

"A what?" asked Jack, his gaze still captivated by the dead man. A few seconds ago, the prisoner had been a living, talking being. Now he was lifeless clay. Jack swallowed hard, trying to keep his breakfast down. Despite weeks of heroics, he was not cut out for life-and-death situations.

"A poison stick-it note," repeated Cassandra, grimacing. "It's a recent development in the espionage field. All those spy novels and movies the past few decades rendered the hollow-tooth-with-poison suicide gambit worthless. An easily inserted plastic mouth-piece prevented a captured operator from taking the easy way out.

"Since modern interrogation methods could break even the most hardened or fanatic agent, a new suicide method had to be developed. That's the poison stick-it note. It's a deadly pellet placed directly in the skull. Merely thinking the proper phrase sends the necessary electrical impulses to the brain and releases the toxic chemical. So far, the method has proven to be a hundred percent effective. The only way to stop someone from suicide is to keep him unconscious. Which makes questioning your captive awfully difficult."

Jack rose to his feet. "Great. It was bad enough when I was dealing with a power-hungry demigod determined to conquer the world and turn it into a vast wasteland. Now, for some unknown reason, secret agents willing to commit suicide rather than be questioned by us are looking to kill me. What else can go wrong?"

Hugo glided up onto Jack's right shoulder and settled uncom-fortably close to his ear. The blackbird was surprisingly light for its size.

"Your mother wants to see you, Johnnie," it stated. "She's waiting for you downtown in Merlin's office."

"Mother," said Jack, inhaling a deep breath. He had almost forgotten about her. "She's in Chicago. Not in New Jersey."

"You catch on quick," said the raven sarcastically. "Freda arrived in the city this morning on a business trip. After hearing about your encounter with magic, she wanted to talk to you. Not to mention meet your fiancée. So she sent me to find you. I arrived overhead just in time to spot those thugs creeping through the woods. When I saw the firepower they were carrying, I thought a warning was in order."

"My mother," said Jack again. "In Chicago. At Merlin's office." He paused for an instant. "How did she learn about Merlin? And my experiences with magic? I never said a word on the phone about any of that."

"A little bird told her," cawed the raven. Jack swore the bird was laughing at him. Spreading its wings, Hugo darted skyward. "See you two downtown."

Cassandra's gaze followed the raven until it was out of sight. "Your mother is an animal trainer?"

"Not that I ever knew," replied Jack. "Though I guess it's possible. I recall my father once stating he first met her at a circus."

"A lot of supernaturals gravitated to circuses and traveling shows," said Cassandra. "They provided wonderful camouflage for beings with unusual powers."

"Mom rarely talks about her days as a performer," said Jack with a shrug. "I gather some of her relatives were disturbed when she left the act to get married. Dad just grins whenever I ask and mumbles something about seven sisters being too many for any one family."

Jack scratched his head, trying to sort out his thoughts. "Ever since I realized Mom was the supernatural member of the family, I've been trying, without success, to place her in some mythology. It's not easy trying to associate one of your parents with a legendary character. I never paid much attention to Mom's pet blackbirds."

Cassandra tossed the corpse of the bearded assassin over one shoulder. "Don't worry about it. I'm sure she'll tell you all you need to know. How about changing your clothes? You don't want your mother to see you covered with dirt. In the meantime, I'll take care of the bodies."

"Whatever you say," declared Jack. "I'll meet you at the car in half an hour."

"Sounds good," said Cassandra. Then, before he could wander off, she grabbed him by an arm. Barely exerting any pressure, there was incredible power in the Amazon's fingers.

"Stay alert, Jack," she warned. "If someone wants you dead,

there's a good chance they sent out more than one kill squad. There could be another bunch of assassins back at camp."

"I'll keep my eyes open," promised Jack, feeling very melo-dramatic. "One brush with death a day is my limit."

Walking as quietly as possible through the woods, Jack consid-ered the morning's events. As usual, things were taking place at a much faster rate than he preferred.

In most of the fantasy novels he read, the hero always had long periods of time when nothing happened. That was when the brilliant hero finally put all the facts together and came up with the startling deductions that saved the day. Jack shook his head in disgust. Most of his thinking was done while running from one supernatural menace after another. What little free time he had, he usually spent recuperating or sleeping.

Concentrating, he tried to recall anything else his father had ever said about his mother. They had met when his dad was in Europe on a business trip thirty years ago. Other than the odd match she made with his father—she was tall, busty, and blonde, while his father was short, dark, and slender—he couldn't think of anything the least bit unusual about her. She made a wonderful peanut butter, lettuce, and mayo sandwich; enjoyed working for the family export business; and owned a horse named Flying Feet that she rode once a week on Saturday.

Her two pet ravens, Hugo and Mongo, she kept outside in a special birdhouse in the backyard. They often disappeared for days, sometimes weeks, at a time, but they always came back. Thinking back to his earliest childhood, Jack couldn't remember a time when the birds hadn't been around. He wondered, idly, if his mother was a witch and the birds were her familiars.

Somehow, he couldn't imagine his mom as a witch. Especially not after having met a witch named Hazel who lived in the trailer camp along with her cat, Sylvester. With a mental shrug, he pushed the idea from his mind. As Cassandra had stated, he would learn the truth soon enough. He was nearing his trailer. Time to watch out for strangers.

Fortunately, no one suspicious was about. Jack hurriedly changed into a pair of good slacks and a sport shirt. He also managed to wash his face and comb his hair before heading over to the parking lot where he was to meet Cassandra. After all, though his mother might be a witch or a sorceress or one of a dozen other types of supernatural entities, first and foremost, she was still his mom.

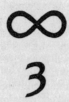

3

Cassandra waited patiently by the side of a 1967 Buick Electra. Piled at her feet were three AK-47 automatic rifles, a trio of mismatched handguns, five knives, over a dozen hand grenades, and several lethal-looking items Jack didn't recognize. The Amazon looked grim. The blood drained from Jack's face.

"Where did the heavy armament come from?" he asked.

"Courtesy of our friends in the woods," replied Cassandra. "This stuff was all I could carry. You should've seen the stuff I left behind. Those characters were walking arsenals. They definitely meant business, Jack. What they lacked in style and grace, they made up in firepower."

"Aren't hand grenades illegal?" he asked, not able to think of much else to say.

Cassandra shrugged. "I doubt if they worried about the police."

Reaching down, she lifted a cloth sack off the ground. Inside it, something wiggled. "I dislike modern weapons," said the Amazon. "Guns are so . . . uncivilized. So I brought along my own secret weapon."

"You're expecting another attack?" he asked.

"They found us at the camp," answered Cassandra. "I discovered a radio transmitter back in the woods. Which probably means that their confederates realize the first attack failed. Chances seem pretty good that they'll try again. I'd be very surprised if we make it to the city without an encounter."

"But we'll be on the highway," he declared. "Nobody fires a gun on a highway."

Cassandra smiled. "Ever hear of drive-by shootings, my naive young friend? Assassins don't worry about breaking city or state ordinances." She patted the mysterious sack, which shook violently under her touch. "Better we're prepared than dead."

Jack nodded unhappily. Cassandra actually appeared quite cheerful. Which was not surprising. As an Amazon, she lived for danger. Violent action defined her existence. The one thing she never walked away from was a fight.

"You think they'll try an ambush on the road instead of waiting till we get to the city?" he asked, opening the door to the Buick.

"If I wanted to kill someone," answered the Amazon, sliding into the driver's seat, "I couldn't think of a better location than the Chicago highway system."

"The traffic is murder," admitted Jack.

"The major roads are always under construction," stated Cassandra, turning the key in the ignition. "There's potholes big enough to swallow a truck. Drivers in this area are the worst tailgaters in the country. Entrance ramps barely exist, making high-speed merges a crapshoot. Everyone drives twenty miles above the posted limit." She grinned. "Who would notice a few guys shooting at each other from car windows?"

"Well," said Jack, settling back in the sedan's lush seat, "at least this car's built like a tank. I remember you saying that when we bought it. And it does have its secrets."

The Buick was no ordinary vehicle. It had been rebuilt inside and out by Fritz Grondark, one of the fabled dwarven mechanics. Already possessing one of the biggest engines ever put in an automobile, the magically enhanced Buick was capable of outrunning anything on the road. Incredibly responsive to its driver's touch, it could make impossible turns and stop in half the time of a normal vehicle. The unmarked condition of its exterior proclaimed that it could not be scratched or dented. Jack wondered if that also meant the car was bulletproof. He hoped so.

Stepping on the gas, Cassandra gunned the car onto the country road that led from the trailer camp to the highway into town. Nervously, Jack kept a lookout for anyone following them.

The first fifteen minutes passed without incident. Jack liked jazz while Cassandra preferred classical music. After much debate, they settled on an oldies station. Weekday traffic was light and they made good time. Cassandra kept their car in the middle lane, maintaining several car lengths between them and any other vehicles. The mysterious sack remained untouched in the back-seat.

"Seat belt fastened?" she casually asked Jack, adjusting the rearview mirror as she spoke.

"Of course," he answered. "Why?"

"It's against the law to sit in the front without your belt buckled," said the Amazon. "Besides, there's two cars coming up fast behind us. I think company's arrived."

Turning, Jack caught a glimpse of a pair of black Cadillacs a half dozen car lengths behind them. There were two men in each car—one driving while the other was in the rear seat. Jack noted they were dressed in the same khaki greens as his earlier attackers.

"If they're pros," said Cassandra, "one car will pull up on our side while the other remains behind. That gives them a second chance if we manage to evade the first attempt."

"Wonderful news," said Jack, slumping in his seat. "Can't we outrun them?"

"Not with this traffic," said Cassandra, waving at the congestion ahead. "There's too many trucks for us to weave safely in and out of traffic. We're moving at a steady fifty. Don't worry. We can take them."

Jack suspected the Amazon was using the heavy traffic as an excuse. She hated running from a fight. No matter what the odds. He only hoped Cassandra's honor wouldn't get them both killed.

The Amazon grunted in satisfaction. "Here they come. The first car is making a move. They're pulling up on your side. Obviously, you're the primary objective, Jack. These guys want you dead."

"Terrific," said Jack. "You have a plan?"

"Of course," said the Amazon. "Something nice and easy and unexpected. Grab the sack. Don't be afraid. There's nothing in it that can hurt you. At least, not as much as a bullet."

Immeasurably cheered by that remark, Jack reached behind him and pulled the cloth bag onto his lap. Something large and active wiggled on his legs. But he was too concerned about the assassins to care.

"Now what?" he asked, terribly aware of the other car's hood only a few feet away from their rear bumper.

"Shooting accurately from a moving car isn't easy, even for trained killers," said Cassandra. "The man in back won't risk firing until they're right on our side. Loosen the string on the top of that sack. Be ready. When I yell, toss the bag out your window. And then duck."

Jack untied the cord on the cloth bag. Putting both his hands beneath it, he waited for Cassandra's command. Behind them, a motor roared.

"Now!" the Amazon shouted, and spun the steering wheel to the right.

Metal screeched against metal as the Buick slammed hard into the black Cadillac. Jack caught a glimpse of the driver of the other car, feverishly fighting to keep his vehicle on the road. Then, obeying orders, Jack hurled the cloth bag out the window. Sending it hurtling directly into the front seat of the other car.

Immediately he ducked, expecting the roar of gunfire. Instead, there came a horrifying scream, the screech of tires, and the sound of steel hitting concrete. Seeing the ghost of a smile appear on Cassandra's lips, Jack slowly straightened in his seat.

"Perfectly executed," declared Cassandra, her gaze fixed on the rearview mirror. "They collided with the cement guardrail on the shoulder. The Cadillac is pretty well demolished, but that's their worry. No other vehicles involved, but traffic behind them has slowed to a crawl. As usual, nobody on the highway can drive past an accident without gawking for a few seconds. By the time their buddies in the following car make it past the scene, we'll be downtown."

"What was in that bag?" asked Jack.

"A snake," said Cassandra. "A nice big one I found in the woods. Not the least bit dangerous, but it sure looked vicious. I thought it might distract the driver at a crucial instant. Guess I was right. Surprising how the coolest professionals are suckers for large, ugly, nasty reptiles."

Jack drew in a deep breath, glad he had not asked Cassandra earlier about the contents of the bag. He was not particularly fond of reptiles himself.

"They were both mortal," he said, as much to himself as his companion. "Neither of them were supernatural."

"I noticed," said the Amazon. "It looks like not all of your enemies are mythological beings. Any idea who the killers might be? Or why they are after you?"

"Unfortunately," said Jack, "I suspect I know the truth. Something the first killer said set off alarm bells in my mind. I think I've finally placed the reference. And I'm not happy about it."

He paused, gathering his thoughts together. The more he considered the clues, the more positive he grew that he had correctly deduced the identity of his attackers.

"You're wrong about the supernatural element," he continued. "The evil mastermind behind these assassination attempts is a particularly notorious mythical being. He's definitely not mortal. The problem for us is that his followers are. They're usually the dregs and lowlifes of society. In these times, that means there could be thousands of them. And most likely, they're all programmed to try to kill me—without any regard for their own safety."

4

They arrived downtown without further incident. However, remaining cautious, Cassandra insisted that they park blocks away from the building in which Merlin's suite was located. Office workers breaking for lunch provided plenty of cover for their entrance to the complex and onto the elevators. Only when they were on the way up to the thirty-fourth floor did the Amazon relax.

"Dedicated assassins are real trouble, Jack," she declared when they were alone on the elevator. "Over the centuries, I often served as a bodyguard for the rich and famous. I worked for both kings and queens and, at times, the masterminds who pulled their strings. In every case, when a group of dedicated professionals decided that their target had lived too long, death proved inevitable. Even the most competent protector, and I was the best," the Amazon stated completely matter-of-factly, "could not stop fanatics."

Jack nodded. "Ever hear the story of Saladin's pillow?"

"No," said Cassandra, a puzzled expression on her face. "I remained in the Far East during the Crusades. I found chivalry repulsive. What about Saladin?"

"I'll tell you shortly," said Jack, as the elevator stopped on Merlin's floor. "First, it's time to face my mother."

Steeling himself for the inevitable, Jack pushed open the door that read, Ambrose Ltd., Investments. As always, a brief smile flickered across his lips as he silently scanned the company motto etched in black letters beneath the title. We Guarantee Your Future. Merlin used the best possible method to back up his investment advice. He studied the future in his crystal ball.

"Johnnie!" Freda Collins's voice had lost none of its earsplitting intensity in the year since Jack had seen her last. As usual, the hug that followed squeezed the last breath of air from his lungs. Jack stood six feet tall, and was slender and dark like his father. His mother matched him in height, but was blonde, blue eyed, and big busted. Many people, seeing and hearing her for the first time, mistook her for an opera singer. Or a lady wrestler.

After crushing his shoulders to a pulp, his mom thrust him an arm's length away. "Still skinny as ever," she declared, with a laugh that shook the room. "Maybe married life will put a little meat on your bones."

Then she paused, catching her first sight of Cassandra, who stood frozen in the doorway. "You?" said Freda, an odd note in her voice.

"You," his mother repeated, this time not as a question, but as a statement of fact. Then she spat out a word in an unknown tongue that sounded remarkably like a curse.

Jack's eyes bulged. In all of his life, he could never once remember his mother swearing. But he never recalled seeing the look of intense emotion that swept across her face as she stared at Cassandra.

"So you refer to yourself as Freda now," said Cassandra, her own voice tight with suppressed feelings. "Quite a change from the old days."

"You are obviously the one called Cassandra," said Jack's mother. "I should have recognized you from Merlin's description. Though I assumed you long dead, food for the ravens."

"As did I of you," replied Cassandra. "Ripped to shreds on some battlefield by vultures."

With a savage howl, Freda Collins flung herself forward. To be met in midair by a screaming Cassandra Cole. Arms locked around each other's shoulders in an unbreakable grip. A few anxious seconds went by before Jack realized that the two women were embracing. And laughing wildly.

"Uh, care to explain what the hell is going on?" he asked,

wondering where Merlin and Megan might be hiding. Not that he blamed them much for keeping out of the way. "I gather you two recognize each other."

"In the good old days," said Cassandra, her face beaming, "we were best of friends. Many were the times we fought side by side, slaughtering anyone foolish enough to cross our path."

"Those were fine times," nodded his mother in agreement. His mom, the one who baked gingerbread men at Christmastime. "The clash of steel, the sweat of battle, the smell of blood, the agonizing cries of the dying."

"Remember the Thirty Years' War?" asked Cassandra. "Fighting with the Swedes against Tilly in Leipzig. Those were violent days, filled with excitement."

"Especially with the bubonic plague killing half the population of Venice the same year," replied his mother. "They wanted to burn you as a witch because of your color. Lucky I was there with my sisters to save you from the fire."

"I paid back that debt during the war between Russia and Poland thirty years later," returned Cassandra. "Those Cossacks had more than a game of kiss and tell on their minds."

"You were a demon," said Freda. "How many did you slaughter that afternoon? Twenty, thirty?"

"Mother," protested Jack, his face turning red. "What are you saying!"

"Sorry, Johnnie," said his mother, not quite succeeding in suppressing a grin. "Different times, different customs. I'm quite satisfied living with your father these days, helping him manage his business. Each age has its noble warriors. In this century, businessmen fight the great battles. But it is fun to reminisce a little about the past."

"Your sisters?" interrupted Cassandra.

"The same as ever. We talk infrequently. They took offense that I left the act to get married. The last I heard, they were touring out west in a rodeo. My ravens spy on them. According to the birds, they continue performing trick riding stunts, forming human pyramids on the backs of horses, and shooting holes in playing cards. The same dull stuff we did for Buffalo Bill."

Jack rubbed his forehead in bewilderment. His mind was overloading with too much data too soon. He spotted Megan edging out of the door of Merlin's inner office. Anxiously, he hurried over to his girlfriend.

"You were expecting this?" he asked, taking hold of her hands. As usual, a tingle of excitement raced through his body from the touch. To Jack, Megan was real magic, pure and simple. The old-fashioned kind.

"Not really," she replied, grinning. "We thought it would be nice to leave you and your mother alone for a few seconds to say hello. Neither of us expected this outburst. Father's hiding behind his desk. What's the story?"

"Apparently Cassandra and my mom are old drinking buddies," said Jack, rolling his eyes in mock dismay. "We know Cassandra is the last of the Amazons. My mother, it turns out, is evidently some sort of warrior maiden."

Megan giggled, as behind them the two women chattered away contentedly. "Your mom reminds me of the lead singer in one of those Wagnerian operas. You know, the sturm-and-drang things featuring Rhine Maidens and Siegfried and the Norse Gods."

Jack opened his mouth to reply, then snapped it shut. He felt a little dizzy. It was either too many dramatic revelations in too short a time or going too long without lunch.

"The two birds that arrived with my mom?" he asked. "They anywhere around? I want to ask them some questions."

"Probably yakking away with Merlin," answered Megan. "I never met ravens who talked so much."

"I'm not surprised," said Jack, opening the door to the inner office. "Let's say hello to your father. This pair won't notice we're gone."

Merlin the Magician nodded a cursory hello to Jack and Megan as the two of them entered the inner chamber. The wizard, an elderly man with weather-browned skin and a long snow white beard, was engaged in a deep conversation with one of the ravens. Hugo and Mongo sat perched on the top of the magician's chair, their yellow claws sunk deep into the leather.

Though he had lived with the birds most of his life, Jack still couldn't tell one from the other. Now that he realized the pair were creations of magic, not nature, he understood their identical nature. The blackbirds had been imagined to life as twin ravens. Mankind's subconscious mind had never given them any distinguishing aspects. Each bird was the exact duplicate of the other.

"Finally made it back," said the raven, not speaking with Merlin. Jack assumed it had to be Hugo. "What took you so long?"

"We encountered some more problems on the highway," replied

Jack. "Besides," he added, unable to resist, "it's not as far traveling straight as the crow flies."

"Crow?" squawked the bird, sounding indignant. "No insults, please. Mongo and I are ravens. We're the most famous ravens in all of mythology."

"I'll bet," said Jack. "Though I'm not sure how the pair of you hooked up with my mom."

"Simple," replied the bird. "Once the priests of the White Christ arrived in the northlands, the Boss realized his days were numbered. Before vanishing, he worked hard providing all of his loyal servants with good homes. Mongo and me always got along real well with your mother so we decided to stay with her. The wolves, Geri and Freki, moved in with your aunt Hannah.

"We stop in to see them once or twice a year. To keep things simple, they pretend now to be dogs." The bird laughed, a bizarre sound. "Big, *big*, dogs, with immense teeth."

"I'm lost," said Megan, "completely, hopelessly lost."

"Merely uninformed, daughter," said Merlin, rising to his feet. "You're lacking the proper information. This fascinating creature has just told Jack that his mother is one of the fabled 'Choosers of the Slain.' Or, as they are called in books today, the Valkyries."

Megan looked at Jack, her eyes wide. "Valkyries as in 'Ride of'?"

"You got it, sister," said Hugo. Beside it, Mongo flapped its wings and cawed out a few barely recognizable bars of the Wagner piece. The screeching hurt Jack's ears. "Freda was a high flier once. She and her sisters tore up the skies on Wings of Horses."

"Then who are you two?" asked Megan.

"Hugi and Mugin at your service, ma'am," said Hugo. The two birds dipped their heads, as if bowing politely. "Trained circus performers, notorious spies and gossips, and onetime companions to the mightly All-Father, leader of the Norse Gods, Odin."

"It's all coming back to me now," said Jack. "Edmond Hamilton and Lester del Rey both wrote novels about ordinary mortals who find themselves in Götterdämmerung, the Twilight of the Gods. So did L. Sprague de Camp."

An avid fantasy fan with a phenomenal memory, Jack's knowledge of legendary and mythological characters came primarily from the stories he had read over the past decade. In most cases, the information he remembered served him better than consulting *Bulfinch's Mythology*.

"Personally, I liked de Camp's *Incomplete Enchanter* the best," declared Hugo. "He portrayed Odin true to character—rude, mysterious, and always brooding."

"Nah," said Mongo. "Hamilton's *A Yank at Valhalla* was tons more fun. He justified everything through super science and the story had a slam-bang finish. They don't write stuff like that anymore."

"You two read science fiction?" asked Jack, bewildered. "I didn't know birds could read."

"We're not ordinary birds, Jack," said Hugo. The raven's piercing black eyes froze Jack with a wicked stare. "Don't you forget it. In the old days, we flew all over gathering information for the All-Father. Each night we landed on his shoulders and described to him what was happening throughout the world."

"*World* meaning the immediate surroundings," interrupted Mongo, sounding slightly sarcastic. "Amazing how the scale of things changes once you escape the limits of the nearby surroundings."

"Whatever," said Hugo, flapping his wings in annoyance. "Give me a chance to explain without interruption, please."

"I'm sure Jack has already deduced the rest," said Mongo. "He's a bright boy. You heard Merlin's narrative how Johnnie saved the world from the forces of darkness."

"Yeah," said Hugo. "But think what he could have done with our help."

The big raven shrugged, not an easy task considering it had no shoulders. "I guess Mongo's right. It ain't hard to figure out the full report. Since we had to spy and then report to the All-Father, we were created with the ability to read and speak."

"But why indulge in fantasy fiction?" asked Jack. "Why not history? Or perhaps westerns?"

"Use your brain, Johnnie," said Hugo. "How many times did you come home from school and find one of your books on the floor with the pages open? Or have a volume disappear for a week or two, then turn up again as if it had never been gone?"

Jack's face turned bright red. "The two of you? Borrowing my books? My *valuable*, first-edition books!"

"Calm down," said Mongo. "We tried to be careful with them."

"Sure we were," said Hugo. "Though turning the pages on those old pulp magazines put a hell of a crimp in my neck. The paper kept crumbling into shreds."

"My pulps?" said Jack, growing more and more agitated. "You turned the pages of my pulps with your beaks? Some of those magazines are sixty years old. They're irreplaceable!"

"Tasted like it, too," said Hugo. Then, seeing the expression on Jack's face, the raven quickly added, "The shreds, that is. The tiny bits of paper that fell off the edges."

Freda Collins chose that moment, as her son started reaching out with both hands to wring the life out of the bird in front of him, to open the door to Merlin's office. "Good to see you're getting acquainted," she declared cheerfully.

"Mother," said Jack, dropping his hands to his sides, "your ravens have been secretly reading my fantasy books for years." His voice trembled with the anger of a true collector. "They put beak marks in my pulps."

"Blame me, Johnnie," said his mother, calmly. "I gave them permission. The birds were bored. There wasn't a lot for them to do the past few decades, now that warfare's changed so much. Reading was their only escape from monotony. Besides, they liked your taste in literature."

"Yeah," said Hugo. "You never heard us complain. Including when you got hooked for a year on those dreadful H. P. Lovecraft Cthulhu Mythos pastiches."

"Besides," said Mongo, "flying around one day we found a used bookstore in the Bronx where there's a complete set of *Weird Tales* in fine condition for sale—cheap. The owner doesn't know a thing about pulp magazines. He'd probably let them go for a song. We couldn't tell you about them before. But now Hugo and me can work as your book scouts. We'll find plenty of bargains. Discovering hidden items is a talent we possess."

"Well," said Jack, taking a deep breath. "I guess I forgive you. But, in the future, inform me what you want to read. That way, at least, I can take the magazines out of the plastic bags for you."

"Deal," said Hugo.

Things quieted down after that. Freda updated Jack on family matters, including the latest scandals, marriages, and deaths. The two ravens provided the embarrassing details. Jack soon realized the birds hadn't exaggerated their skill as spies. They knew the dirt on everyone.

Afterward, Jack was forced to recap in detail his adventures fighting Dietrich von Bern, the Wild Huntsman. His mother and the ravens had heard some of the story from Merlin. But the magician and Megan had been in enchanted sleep for most of the exploit. Jack, with Cassandra's promptings, filled in the rest.

About halfway through the story, Merlin supplied lunch via a teleportation spell to the nearest restaurant. A BLT and a Coke did wonders soothing Jack's temper. As did the admiring comments from both his parent and her blackbirds.

"My son, the world-saver," said Freda Collins, when Jack finished his tale. "Not that I'm surprised. The blood of heroes flows in your veins. Too bad you never learned the identity of the demigod pulling the Huntsman's strings. Hidden enemies are the most dangerous kind."

"So far, even Merlin's magic has proven useless," said Jack. "The demigod stays far enough in the background to be untraceable. It's a mystery that has to be solved sooner or later. But that's the least of my problems. The events of this morning present a much more immediate dilemma. One that has to be dealt with right away."

"This morning?" said Megan, her voice concerned. "What are you talking about?"

"Didn't Hugo mention the assassins?" asked Jack.

"Assassins," said Megan, her eyes flashing dangerously. She turned to the raven. "What assassins?"

"Oops, sorry," said the bird quickly. Obviously, Megan frightened him a good deal more than Jack. "Since the attempt failed, I decided not to say anything till Johnnie arrived and could provide the details himself."

"An assassination attempt," said Merlin, frowning. "That's strange. I recently tried using my crystal ball to predict our enemy's next move. While the results were inconclusive, I saw nothing to indicate it planned any direct violent action against you. At least, not in the immediate future."

"Not one attempt, but two," said Jack. Briefly, he described both attacks and how Cassandra foiled each of them. "In both cases, the killers were mortals, not supernaturals. But I believe behind them stands a particularly fiendish supernatural mastermind."

Jack drew in a deep breath. "No *direct action,* you said. Unfortunately, that doesn't rule out working through a proxy. The demigod is staying safely out of sight and letting another monstrous figure fight its battles. Unlike Dietrich von Bern and his Border Redcaps, this villain uses human henchmen."

"Which changes the rules of the game drastically," said Cassandra. "Mortals aren't bound by the same rules as supernatural entities. And there are so many of them."

The Amazon did not look pleased. Nor did anyone else. "You hinted earlier you knew the identity of this new mastermind, Jack," said Cassandra. "Who is it?"

"I'm not positive about the answer," said Jack, "but everything I've seen and heard so far points to one infamous figure. The actions of the assassins and the few remarks made by our one prisoner before he committed suicide support my theory. Why he is serving our mysterious enemy I don't know. But for some unexplained reason, I've been marked for death by the Old Man of the Mountain."

5

Nobody said anything for a moment. Jack gazed around at his friends and relatives, feeling a mixture of annoyance and astonishment. He refused to believe that they didn't comprehend his predicament.

"Wasn't he the big, white-bearded giant in that Betty Boop cartoon?" asked Megan, a puzzled expression on her face. "The one we watched on TNT with the Cab Calloway sound track?"

"You're being threatened by an animated monster?" squawked Hugo. "That stretches credibility a bit far, doesn't it?"

Jack sighed in amazement. "Aren't any of you familiar with the stories of the Old Man of the Mountain and the Order of Assassins?"

Seeing the blank looks that greeted his question, he knew the answer. Eyebrows knotted in concentration, he stared directly at the two ravens. "I thought you birds knew everything. The old legends said you spied on mankind's doings each day and whispered it that night in Odin's ear."

"A gross exaggeration, I'm afraid," said Mongo. Of the two birds, he had the better vocabulary. "As I mentioned earlier, Johnnie, our range was limited by the imagination of our creators. They never envisioned the true extent of the world. We watched the northlands pretty well, but that was it."

"Besides," added Hugo, "we fly awfully fast, but there's only so much territory you can cover in a day."

"I wish Simon was here," said Jack, shaking his head unhappily. "He'd understand why I'm concerned."

"Where is the changeling?" asked Freda. "He sounds like an interesting character. I'd like to meet him."

"Simon left yesterday for England," said Jack. "He's arranging a transfer to another college. It's a ritual he goes through each year. He won't return for weeks."

A faery changeling, Simon Goodfellow had proven a valuable ally in Jack's battle with Dietrich von Bern. Like all magical beings, Simon had evolved with the times. Centuries ago, he had been the magical child left behind, replacing a baby kidnapped by faeries. In the modern world, he was a know-it-all exchange student who was never at a loss for an answer. True to his nature, Simon always interrupted at the wrong time, grated on his friends' nerves, and generally acted the nuisance. Yet he was also a loyal, brave companion. Jack missed him already.

"If the Old Man of the Mountain isn't the cartoon character," said Megan, patting Jack's hand, "why not tell us who he is?"

"I guess it's not that surprising that none of you heard of him," said Jack. "He comes from a mythology entirely different from any of yours." He glared at the ravens. "Ed Hamilton wrote a story in 1943 for *Weird Tales* that featured the Old Man of the Mountain. He titled it 'The Valley of the Assassins.'"

"We never read it," said Hugo. "The *Weird Tales* were packed too tightly together on the shelves. We tried but couldn't pull them out."

"Thank God for small favors," muttered Jack. "To understand the legend of the Old Man of the Mountain, I have to tell you of the secret society he founded, the Hashashin. Or, as they were called by the Crusaders, the Assassins.

"The name in Arabic literally means hashish addict. The drug was used by a sect of fanatical Shi'ite Moslems during the eleventh century to induce religious visions. The leader of these Hashashin was a brilliant renegade cleric, Hasan al-Sabbah. Less interested in spiritual objectives than material gains, Hasan created what was probably the most successful terrorist organization ever. For his followers were unafraid of death. Without such fear, the Hashashin made the perfect killers. They were willing to die to accomplish their goals. Which usually were missions of murder or extortion.

"The Hashashin were fearless because they knew in serving al-Sabbah they were *guaranteed* admission to paradise. Suffering for a short time on Earth meant nothing if followed by an eternity of pleasure. For, unlike most prophets, al-Sabbah provided his men with a glimpse of the hereafter."

"Nice trick if you can manage," commented Hugo. "How did he accomplish that? Mass hypnotism?"

"Better than that," replied Jack. "The headquarters of the cult was set in a huge mountain fortress, Alamut, located in the mountains of northwest Iran. Thus, al-Sabbah's title, the Old Man of the Mountain.

"In the center of the citadel was a secret garden constructed by the Old Man's servants. Stocked with fruit, wine, and beautiful slave girls, the oasis resembled the Moslem concept of paradise. When a new recruit came to Alamut, he was fed drugged wine which put him to sleep. When he awakened, he found himself transported to Heaven, complete with willing women and bountiful wine. After indulging in a day of pleasure, the naive recruit was returned to the fortress via another dose of drugged wine. Knowing what awaited him in death if he served al-Sabbah faithfully during life transformed an ordinary man into a fearless assassin. Deadly risks meant nothing to them since they knew that paradise beckoned. They were unstoppable."

"I take it these Hashashin made quite a name for themselves?" asked Cassandra.

"The Assassins spread terror throughout the Middle East for the next two hundred years. No one was safe from the whims of the Old Man of the Mountain. From Alamut, he conducted a reign of fear unmatched in history. The mere whisper of his name was enough to cause a panic.

"When al-Sabbah died, one of his followers rose in his position and assumed the title, the Old Man of the Mountain. The murders continued. And, with each death, the cult's power and influence grew."

"You mentioned Saladin?" prompted Cassandra.

"The Crusaders' most dangerous foe made no secret of his distaste for the Assassins. One afternoon, he mentioned to his generals that he was considering an assault on their headquarters in Syria. The next morning, Saladin woke to find an Assassin's knife driven into the pillow next to his head. He needed no other warning. Saladin never mentioned the order again."

Jack paused. "Did you hear someone moving in the outer office?"

"I canceled my appointments for today," said Merlin, "so that we would not be disturbed." The magician's brow wrinkled in annoyance. "Strange, I sense . . ."

Before Merlin could finish the sentence, the door to the inner room burst open and a half dozen men dressed in green combat fatigues, carrying Uzi machine guns, crowded into the chamber.

"Shit," said Hugo.

"Death," replied a tall, bearded man with shaven head. "Death to our quarry and his friends."

Savagely, he squeezed the trigger of his Uzi. Nothing happened. At his sides, his men aimed and fired. Again without results.

"A dampening spell on the office makes gunfire impossible," declared Merlin smugly. "Those weapons are useless."

Snarling with rage, the bearded man slammed his gun to the ground. Angrily, he pulled a huge knife from a sheath strapped to his side. "Now they die!"

"You talk too much, baldie," declared Cassandra. A flawlessly executed spin kick ended with her right foot slamming into the bearded man's jaw. His teeth exploded across the room. His mouth a red ruin, the man fell backward, his eyes wide with shock.

Howling wildly, his followers reached for their own knives. Jack, Megan, and Merlin retreated to the rear of the room, knowing they'd only be in the way. Six normal humans, even trained assassins, were no match for one angry Amazon. Not to mention a slightly out-of-shape Valkyrie and two fiendish ravens.

With a war cry of "For Asgard!" that nearly shattered the chamber's glass windows, Freda Collins hurtled forward at the astonished killers. For a woman her size, she moved with astonishing quickness.

Effortlessly, Jack's mother grabbed two of the men by the neck, raised them into the air, and smashed them together like two bricks. They collided so hard that Jack could hear the sound of their bones breaking across the room. Snorting in disgust, Freda threw the limp pair against the office wall. They collapsed lifelessly to the floor.

Hugo and Mongo made short work of the third attacker. Wings thrashing furiously, they slashed at his unprotected face with their claws and beaks. His head spurting blood, the man collapsed facedown on the carpet. One concluding shudder and he was still. Remembering the raven's earlier remarks about poking out eyes, Jack felt no desire to learn how that luckless individual had expired.

The last two killers actually managed to draw their weapons before Cassandra reached them. That proved to be their undoing. Faced with two attackers armed with knives, the Amazon reacted by instinct alone. Her deadly hands moving faster than the eye could follow, she killed both men instantly.

Jack clenched his fists in frustration. Of the six attackers, only the leader remained alive. Anxiously, Jack glanced at the bearded man, his back pressed to the doorframe. Face white with shock, the assassin surveyed the carnage surrounding him. Bloody lips moved as if in prayer.

"Stop him," cried Jack, but it was already too late. Without a sound, the bearded man slumped to the floor, dead. There would be no learning anything from this group. Jack had a feeling that questioning prisoners was going to prove quite difficult.

6

"Weaklings," said Freda Collins, snorting in derision, staring at the bodies littering the floor. She was barely breathing hard. Daintily, she cracked her knuckles. "Odin would have sent us packing if my sisters and I brought ones such as these back to Valhalla."

Mentally, Jack filed a note to ask his mother someday about her adventures as one of the Choosers of the Slain. It was an intriguing thought, but there were more pressing concerns to worry about.

"What are we going to do with these guys?" he asked. "Explaining their condition to the police might prove difficult."

"No problem," said Merlin, reaching for the telephone. "I'll use a preserving spell on them so they won't decay. There's a friendly giant who often handles heavy moving jobs for me. I'll have him stop by after the building closes and pick up the corpses. He'll dispose of them for a reasonable fee."

Sighing, Jack folded his arms across his chest in annoyance. Nine men had died today and it wasn't close to suppertime. He felt as if he were living in an Arnold Schwarzenegger movie.

"Continue with your story, Johnnie," said his mother. She looked at her watch. "But make it quick. I have a business meeting with Mr. Weissman, the herring importer, in thirty minutes. I dare not be late. It would make your father furious."

Jack shook his head. When the real and the imaginary worlds collided, the real world won. His mom could deal with rampaging assassins without breaking into a sweat. However, the thought of telling her husband that she had fumbled a business deal was an entirely different matter. He hurried on with his explanation.

"There's not much more to tell. In the middle of the thirteenth century, the Assassins made the fatal mistake of killing two envoys under truce." He glanced at the two ravens. "Seabury Quinn wrote a story about the murders. He titled it, 'The Gentle Werewolf.'"

"Never heard of it," said Hugo. "Another one from *Weird Tales*, I bet."

"Right," said Jack. "In any case, the order was crushed by its enemies and Alamut was destroyed. Few if any members of the cult survived. But by that time it didn't matter. The Old Man of the Mountain had achieved legendary status."

"I understand," said Megan. As Merlin's daughter, she was quite familiar with her father's theories about mankind's collective subconscious mind. "People refused to accept the Old Man's death. Someone with that name ruled the cult for two centuries. Only an inner circle knew that it was not the same person. Tens of thousands of people in the region considered him immortal. In time, their belief created a supernatural being with the uncanny powers described in legends. As in the case of Dietrich von Bern, the actual human died but later returned as a creature of myth."

"Dozens of novels have been written in the past fifty years postulating that the Order of Assassins has survived to this day," said Jack. "There might be more truth to those books than the authors imagined. These attacks on me seem to demonstrate that the cult is still in operation." Jack paused. "Which means that the Old Man of the Mountain is alive and well and living somewhere in America."

"Sorry, dear," said his mother, gathering him up in her arms for another bone-crushing hug, "but I've got to leave. You can tell me the rest later. I'm taking you and Megan out for dinner. A little celebration for your engagement. Hugo knows where. You birds stay here with Johnnie till then. Assist him in any way possible. But stay out of trouble."

His mother stormed out of the office, her face aglow with the joy of a Valkyrie about to engage in battle. Jack wondered how Mr. Weissman would cope with his mother. Then he remembered his father's deft handling of equally enthusiastic salesmen. Maybe his mother was right and today's businessmen were the real dragon slayers.

"She acts like we're not trustworthy," said Hugo, his feathers ruffled.

"Freda always makes it sound like we encourage violence," added Mongo.

"Well, Jack," asked Cassandra, interrupting the two birds, "what's the plan?"

"Yeah, boss," said Hugo, flapping his wings. "Who do we kill next?"

Jack grimaced. "No more violence," he declared, trying to avoid staring at the bodies on the floor. Instead, he found himself looking at one of the Uzis dropped by the assassins. It served as a grim reminder that the killers intended murdering everyone in the office, not just him. Shedding innocent blood was not one of their primary worries.

"Unless necessary," he added, knowing he was opening a Pandora's box by using such language with supernaturals. They bent definitions easier than politicians. "And I mean, absolutely necessary."

"We must somehow learn where the Old Man of the Mountain makes his headquarters," said Merlin, stroking his beard thoughtfully. "He is the only one who can put an end to these attacks. Though persuading him to do so might prove difficult."

Cassandra smiled. It was not a pleasant smile. Even the two ravens appeared shocked. "Give me a few minutes alone with him," she said softly. "I'll show him the error of his ways."

"Hold on," said Jack, raising his hands for silence. "We're ignoring one important fact. The demigod behind things isn't merely concerned with killing me. It plans to rule the world. There has to be another reason it contacted the Old Man of the Mountain than my demise. We have to discover that scheme and defeat it as well."

"Sounds simple enough to me," said Mongo. "I love complicated webs of intrigue. Where do we start?"

"Searching the pockets of our intended executioners might be a good beginning," said Megan. "I know professionals aren't supposed to keep clues in their pockets. But it never hurts to check."

As expected, none of the men carried any identification.

However, a tattoo on one assassin's shoulder served equally well.

"'I love Las Vegas,'" read Jack, astonished. "I find it hard to believe that any respectable murderer would have his hometown tattooed on his body."

"These losers weren't top-notch professionals, Jack," said Cassandra. "I'd rate them fair at best. Maybe the Old Man of the Mountain has been experiencing difficulties recruiting new members for the order."

"Maybe," said Jack. "But I still suspect it might be a trap."

"Who cares," said Megan. "If that's where the Old Man of the Mountain has his headquarters, that's where we want to go. Trap or no trap. We don't have much choice, do we?"

"Nope," said Jack unhappily. "No choice at all."

7

Roger Quinn looked at the blemishes on his elbow and shuddered. There were five of them, evenly spaced around the bone. Dark marks, the size of dimes, they closely resembled the fingerprints of a child or a very small adult. That, of course, was impossible. No one's touch caused skin to brown and age like old parchment. At least, no one human.

"I'm at a loss to explain them, Mr. Quinn," said Dr. Philips, frowning. "I've never seen their like before. It's as if your flesh in those five spots is decaying at an unnatural rate. Nothing in my experience relates to selective tissue degeneration in such a selective manner. With your consent, I'd like to do some more tests."

Roger shook his head. "No, thanks. You're the third skin specialist I've consulted." There was a note of quiet desperation in his voice. "The others ran all the tests imaginable. They took samples of skin tissue from my elbow and analyzed it for weeks. The results were identical in both cases. Absolutely nothing."

"You have no idea what might have brought about this condition?" asked Philips. "You're a scientist. Maybe an experiment went wrong?"

Roger grimaced. "I work with computers, doc, not chemicals."

Wearily, he pulled on his shirt and began buttoning the buttons. He should have known better. No doctor living could help him with his problem. They were bound by conventional teachings. It never once occurred to any of them that they might be dealing with a manifestation of the supernatural. In reality, Roger needed an exorcist, not a specialist.

Unfortunately, finding a real ghost breaker in modern California was no easy task. There were plenty of spiritualists in the phone directory, offering assistance in everything from love potions to fighting demons. They came in all nationalities and religions, both sexes, young and old, black and white. Only one common thread bound them all together. Each and every one of them was a fraud.

Financed by one of Roger's numerous secret bank accounts, a team of private detectives investigated the background of all of the self-proclaimed psychics. Not surprisingly, most of them turned out to be well-known con men or women, whose only talent consisted of making their clients' money disappear.

Those few spiritualists who checked out clean, the detectives visited. The investigators offered huge sums to anyone capable of demonstrating actual psychic powers. Despite hugely extravagant claims of great and miraculous powers by each individual, none of them was able to perform any actual feat of black magic or sorcery.

After weeks of fruitless searching, Roger fired the detectives. He was still convinced that supernatural beings with amazing powers existed in the real world. He knew it for a fact. Sooner or later, the investigators would have found the right one. Unfortunately, Roger didn't have time to spare.

"You'll stay in touch?" asked Dr. Philips as Roger rose from the examination table. "If those blotches grow bigger, we could try radiation therapy."

Roger grimaced. "I doubt if I'll be back. I'm off to Las Vegas tomorrow. Hopefully, the answer to all my problems lies there."

"Las Vegas?" said Philips. "I didn't know there were any major cancer clinics located there."

"There aren't," said Roger. "I'm going there to see an old man about his payments on a mountain."

"I'm afraid I don't understand," said the physician, sounding puzzled.

"Neither do I," said Roger, heading for the door. "But that's not unusual. I rarely do anymore these days. Mere mortals are not privy to the secrets of the Gods."

"Whatever you say," declared Philips, shaking his head. He obviously thought Roger was slightly demented. "I'm an agnostic myself."

"So was I," said Roger. "Once."

Stepping into the street a few minutes later, Roger squinted in the harsh sunlight. According to the city directory, there was a travel agency located within two blocks of the physician's office. He glanced down at his watch. The doctor's appointment had lasted six minutes longer than he anticipated. However, he had allowed an eleven-minute margin of error in his schedule. His day was proceeding pretty much according to plan.

Roger was meticulous to a fault. A computer programmer for twenty years, he believed in exactness. Each morning, he mentally outlined his schedule for the next twenty-four hours in fine detail. Once decided, he maintained that routine no matter what happened. Though most people thought Roger was slightly crazy, he considered himself the soul of logic.

A tall, thin man with a scraggly beard and thinning brown hair starting to gray at the temples, Roger appeared to be nothing more than the usual California computer jock. His sloped shoulders and intent, slightly glazed glare reinforced that image. Few people realized that he was president of one of the most powerful consulting firms on the West Coast. And none of that select number knew the secret of his success.

Five years ago, Roger had been a computer hacker working for a minor software company in Silicon Valley. Smart but not brilliant, his obsession with exactness had lost him jobs with most of the major firms in the computer industry. Thus, he struggled in obscurity, earning a salary barely enough to cover the high cost of living in California.

The big change in his life came the night he attended a New Age séance. Convinced by the event that the occult existed, Roger spent weeks investigating spells necessary to raise demons. He soon concluded that black magicians, unwilling to reveal their closely guarded secrets to others, deliberately changed their invocations when committing them to print. It was as if the spells had been published in code, without a key. But medieval sorcerers had not taken into account the greatest code breaker of all time—the modern computer.

Less than a month after attending the séance, Roger raised his first demon. Soon he was making his talent pay, in a manner never considered by earlier sorcerers.

An unexpected talent for deception made Roger extremely rich. Quitting his job, he set himself up as a business consultant, specializing in correcting problems no one else could solve. Using black magic, he summoned a host of minor fiends and sent them out on missions of industrial espionage. Invisible to all but their master, the devils proved extremely capable agents of destruction. And they cleverly disguised their efforts so they appeared to be the result of accidents or employee blunders.

Needless to say, Roger's corporation displayed an uncanny ability to spot and eliminate such troubles. Within a short time, his firm had earned the reputation as the company that solved problems no one else could handle. Within months, Quinn Enterprises had risen to national prominence in the consulting field. After a year, there were company offices in major cities throughout the United States. And there was talk of expanding overseas.

Much of the work handled by the firm was routine and required no supernatural intervention at all. His competent and capable staff handled those matters. Roger reserved his demonic allies for special efforts.

The invisible creatures made wonderful spies. They eavesdropped on confidential conversations and copied confidential documents with ease. Knowledge was power and Roger knew the secrets of most of the major corporations in the country. From such information came even greater wealth. But too much was never enough, and Roger wanted still more. It was a path that led to disaster.

Seeking more powerful allies, one night Roger attempted to raise one of the demon princes of hell from the Bible. Unfortunately, he forgot that the names of most of the major devils from the New Testament were based on the titles of ancient pagan gods. Instead of raising a demon, Roger summoned the Crouching One, Lord of the Lions, a long-forgotten Babylonian deity.

Not subject to any of the usual binding spells, the demigod frightened Roger. When it was accidentally freed from the magic circle holding it prisoner by an unexpected earth tremor, the being proved to be more trouble than he could handle. Roger reluctantly found himself serving the Crouching One in the demigod's quest to rule the world.

At the door to the travel agency, Roger once again muttered a silent prayer to whatever powers existed that kept the Lord of the Lions confused about the power of direct dialing. The ancient god still did not understand the modern world. Otherwise, it might realize that making reservations to Las Vegas didn't require Roger taking an afternoon trip downtown to a travel agency.

At times, these brief moments of freedom tempted him with the thought of escape. A quick drive to the airport and he could be in another country in a few hours. Roger strongly doubted that the Lord of the Lions would be able to locate him once he was a thousand miles away. He had plenty of money in bank accounts easily accessible throughout the world. His nemesis was woefully ignorant about branch banking. Still, two factors prevented Roger from acting.

The first, and most important, were the marks on his elbow. The five spots were the fingerprints of the demigod, placed there when he first summoned the creature to the material plane. Roger remembered watching objects wither and age, then turn to dust, after being touched by the Crouching One. His was a grip that killed.

At present, the Lord of the Lions needed him, and thus the spell of dissolution was held in check. Roger suspected any attempt to escape would result in the magic taking effect. He had no desire to be reduced to a pile of ashes.

Secondly, the Lord of the Lions planned to rule the world. He was a ruthless, ambitious god. Forgotten and unworshiped for thousands of years, the demonic being possessed little of its original powers. Still, it schemed and plotted a return to greatness.

Recognizing its limitations dealing with the modern world, the Lord of the Lions had promised Roger tremendous rewards for his help. Assuming that the promises of a part-God, part-demon could be trusted. Roger doubted the Ancient One's word—but the thought of being absolute ruler of the United States tempted him more than he liked to admit. For there was the real possibility that the Lord of the Lions might prevail.

The demigod's first attempt at restoring its powers had nearly succeeded. A massive human sacrifice in Chicago had been thwarted at the last minute by a college mathematics student named Jack Collins, aided by several supernatural creatures.

Collins had used logic and modern technology to defeat the powerful sorcery of Dietrich von Bern, Master of the Wild Hunt, and servant of the Crouching One.

To Roger's surprise, the Lord of the Lions accepted the setback with equanimity. Good always arose to battle evil. If the Crouching One symbolized darkness, then Jack Collins and his friends, under the guidance of Merlin the Magician, represented the light. The demigod had engaged in such battles before. It was confident, in the end, night would triumph over day. Roger wasn't so positive, but his opinions didn't matter. At least, not yet.

As he pushed open the door to the travel agency, Roger wondered for the dozenth time why the Crouching One wanted to go to Las Vegas. The demigod had offered no explanation for its command and Roger knew better than to ask. The Lord of the Lions acted in strange and mysterious ways.

As he explained his needs to the woman behind the desk, Roger mentally shrugged his shoulders. At the moment, the Crouching One was in control of events. Roger accepted that fact for now. But it didn't mean he wasn't planning to change things in the future.

Ever since raising the Lord of the Lions, Roger had schemed to gain mastery over it. For all of its age and knowledge, the demigod possessed the personality of a strong-willed child. Roger felt sure, given enough time, he could use psychology to influence the Crouching One's ideas. Lately, growing impatient with his servitude, he had begun investigating another method of attack. What could be summoned by black magic could be controlled by black magic. Or so Roger reasoned. All he needed was some time alone with his computer. And the black magic texts in his library.

Jack Collins had been quite useful in that respect. The longer Collins and his friends held the Crouching One in check, the better. The Ancient One had a one-track mind. Worrying about the Logical Magician, it ignored the ambitions of its assistant. Roger smiled. His scheme was nearly complete. Another few days and he would once again be in charge.

Arrangements for the trip took three minutes less than Roger estimated. He had six minutes to spare before returning to his mansion and the Crouching One. That gave him plenty of time to make the world a bit more difficult for his boss. He looked around the office, and noticed a bunch of flyers and cards about Las Vegas.

"Would you mind if I take one of these?" he asked the travel agent, reaching for a postcard.

"Of course not," said the woman. "Planning to inform friends of your upcoming visit? I have some postage stamps if you need one."

"Thank you," said Roger, sincerely. He scribbled a short note and address on the back of the card. "I appreciate the courtesy."

"No trouble," said the agent. "I'll put the card with our outgoing mail."

The woman glanced at the name and address. "Jack Collins, Chicago. A close friend of yours, Mr. Quinn?"

"We've never met," said Roger, rising from his chair, smiling. "But I'm sure we will. Soon. Quite soon."

8

"Are you positive my mother wanted you to bring us to this place?" Jack asked suspiciously several hours later.

"Trust me, boss," said Hugo. "I know it don't look like much on the outside. But wait till you step indoors. You'll be surprised. I promise."

Jack looked at Megan and shrugged. "What do you think?"

They were on a deserted side street on Chicago's near south side. Big, old buildings, most of them warehouses, crowded the block. None of the structures appeared less than a hundred years old and all were in a state of near collapse. Of them, only one had a doorway that opened to the street. A solitary light burned above the entrance. On the side of the door was a small metal sign reading Members Only.

After a brief trip to Megan's condo on the near north side, where they had changed into appropriate clothes for a fancy dinner, they had taken a taxi to the address given them by Hugo. The raven flew ahead, promising to meet them at the club. Mongo had remained at Merlin's office, discussing philosophy with Megan's father.

"Well," said Megan, "considering our location and the lack of traffic, I suspect finding a cab might prove to be difficult. And there's no way I plan to start walking anywhere in this neighborhood. It'll be getting dark soon. Better inside than out here. Besides," she added cheerfully, "what can happen to us in there?"

"That's what I'm worried about," replied Jack. He stared at Hugo. Jack regretted leaving Mongo behind. Of the two, the other raven seemed a great deal more reliable. Hugo was more than a bit flaky.

"Okay, bird," he said, finally coming to a decision. "Megan's right. Standing out here won't do us any good. Lead on. I just hope that after centuries your fabled memory hasn't started slipping."

"About time," said the raven, and flapped over to the door. Hovering, it pecked the wood paneling hard three times. "Open up in there. It's me, Hugo Odinsbird, with two friends. We have reservations."

A few seconds passed and then, soundlessly, the door swung back, revealing a pitch black tunnel. "Enter," declared a low, gently mocking voice. "And welcome."

Gathering a deep breath, Jack took Megan by the hand and crossed over the threshold. For an instant, darkness overwhelmed them. Then, as if emerging from an air lock, they found themselves in a brightly lit, lavishly decorated foyer. A few steps ahead, waiting at a narrow podium, stood an elegantly dressed maître d'. Behind him were a pair of immense oak doors, decorated with intricate carvings.

"Mr. Collins and Ms. Ambrose, I believe?" asked their host. "Right on time." He looked closely at them, then around them. "I was told to expect a pair of ravens as well."

With a loud squawk, Hugo came flapping through the black portal. "Damn," said the bird. "I hate those warp doors."

"They are a nuisance," said the maître d', "but they operate quite effectively in keeping out the riffraff. Only those who belong can pass through. Where is the other fowl?"

"The second bird is busy tonight," said Jack. "We're it."

"Excellent," said their host, and snapped his fingers. Seemingly out of nowhere, a slender young woman, dressed in a stunning pink outfit that left little to the imagination, appeared. "Ms. Vesta will show you to your table."

Behind him, the huge oak doors swung wide. "I'm off," declared Hugo, and went flying through the opening. "See you inside."

"Typical," said the maître d', the slightest sneer crossing his lips. "Birds are so impatient. The rest of your party is waiting on the second level. Have a good evening."

"Thank you," said Megan, flashing a smile at the host. As they followed Vesta into the next room, she leaned close to Jack and whispered, "Watch what you're thinking, buster. Remember, I can eavesdrop on your dreams. And there'd better not be any pink cutie floating around inside your head tonight!"

"Who, me?" asked Jack, trying to sound insulted. "You know you're the only girl I dream about."

"Keep it that way," whispered Megan ominously. Then, in a normal tone of voice, she continued, "This place is huge. It's the size of the railroad terminal."

She wasn't exaggerating. Laid out on three levels, the nightclub was immense. There were hundreds of tables scattered in haphazard fashion around a wide dance floor. On the stage behind it, a jazz group was playing background music, while a trio of beautiful, dark-haired women softly crooned a song in a language Jack didn't recognize. Somehow, it sounded vaguely familiar.

"Don't listen too closely," warned Vesta, noticing the direction of Jack's interest. "Those girls aren't any ordinary vocal group. They're the sirens. Supernaturals are immune to their lure. But with mixed blood, you're not."

"The sirens?" repeated Megan, excitement in her voice. "Then this must be the Chaos Club."

"Of course," said Vesta, weaving a path between the tables. "Where did you think you were?"

Jack, anxiously trying to ignore the sirens' song, exchanged glances with Megan. "The Chaos Club?"

"Father's mentioned it to me several times," said Megan, "but he's refused to take me here. The old geezer dislikes being surrounded by supernaturals. Claims whenever he comes here, the patrons always want him to perform magic tricks. Merlin *hates* using sorcery for entertainment. He thinks it trivializes the art."

Jack's eyebrows narrowed, trying to make sense of Megan's ramblings. After a few seconds, he thought he understood. "You mean, this is a nightclub specifically aimed at supernatural entities. A sort of Gavagan's Bar or Callahan's Saloon for mythological beings?"

"Precisely," said Megan. "Weren't you listening to what I just said?"

"The Pied Piper is performing on the bandstand tonight," added

Vesta, smiling brazenly at Jack. She winked. Her expression made it quite clear that if Megan was annoying him, she was definitely available. "Pan's scheduled to sit in for a couple of sets later on. He really swings."

"The patrons are all supernaturals," said Jack, his gaze sweeping across the club. Other than the absence of the auras that identified them as mortal, everyone in the nightclub appeared terribly ordinary. Which was not very surprising. Survival in the modern era for the supernaturals meant blending in with their surroundings. They evolved and adapted to the times. "And the staff as well?"

"Sure," said Vesta. "A consortium of gnomes and leprechauns own the place. Diogenes handles the bookkeeping, while Hercules works as the bouncer. With him around, we never have any trouble."

"Who's the maître d'?" asked Jack, fascinated by the girl's matter-of-fact listing.

"That's the Comte de Saint-Germain," said Vesta. "Despite those novels written about him, the count's no vampire. He is quite mysterious, though, and quite sophisticated. And he knows *everybody*."

She ascended a short flight of steps leading to the second level, revealing quite a bit of white thigh. "I'm a wood nymph," she continued, gazing at Jack in disconcerting fashion. "From the golden age of Greece."

"I met some of your cousins at the mall a few weeks ago," said Jack without thinking.

"Yes," said Vesta, her voice sultry enough to melt butter. "So I heard."

"Me too," said Megan, jabbing an elbow into Jack's ribs.

Jack turned red. The mall nymphs had proved to be delightful if exhausting company. Dedicated to the practice of free love, as often as possible, they were not the type of girls you mentioned to your fiancée. Especially if she had an intense jealous streak—like Megan.

"Here at last," said Vesta cheerfully. Waiting for them at a large table were Freda Collins, Cassandra, and Fritz Grondark. Dressed in a pinstripe suit coat that barely stretched across his massive shoulders, the dwarf tugged unhappily at the gaudy tie laced around his neck. Hugo loitered by the floral centerpiece, nibbling at the greenery.

"About time you arrived," grumbled the bird. "I'm starving."

After seating Megan, Vesta pulled back Jack's chair. As he took his spot, her hands grazed across his back. "If you ever lack for company," she whispered, "think of me. I'm available."

Standing, she nodded pleasantly to the entire company. "Bryan will be your server tonight. He'll be here shortly with your menus. Enjoy your dinner."

"Charming young lady," said Freda after Vesta departed. "That's one of the nicest things about the Chaos Club. The help here always seems so anxious to please."

"I'll say," declared Jack, wiping beads of sweat off his forehead.

"I took the liberty of ordering us all champagne," said his mother, standing. She raised her glass. "I'd like to propose a toast. To Jack and Megan. Happiness today, and forever after."

They drained their goblets and Jack kissed Megan. The touch of her soft lips banished any thoughts of nymphs from his mind. There was only one woman for him, and she was sitting by his side.

"I, too, would like to honor the lucky couple," said Cassandra. Jack noted that their empty glasses were once again filled to the brims. Magic did have its uses. "To a long life, many strong children, and a clean death in battle."

"Bravo," said Fritz Grondark, banging a huge fist down on the table for emphasis. Fortunately, the furniture at the Chaos Club was built to withstand punishment. "Well said."

Grinning, the dwarf dug into the pocket of his suit. "I made these special for you," he declared. Pulling out a small ivory box, he handed it to Jack. "Go ahead. Open it."

Jack, with Megan peering over his shoulder, did so. Inside the box were two gold rings. Each band consisted of a pair of twined serpents. Their eyes glowed red with tiny rubies.

"For your wedding," said Grondark proudly. "Handmade from Alberich's gold. I made a similar pair for Siegfried and Brunhild." The dwarf coughed self-consciously. "These, of course, aren't cursed."

"I'll drink to that," said Jack. The champagne went down incredibly smoothly.

"Merlin politely declined my invitation to the festivities," said Freda, with a sniff of indignation revealing her thoughts on the matter. "Witch Hazel and her familiar, Sylvester, sent their regrets but could not attend due to a Witch's Sabbath. They asked me to wish you their best."

"Enough chattering," said Hugo, having eaten most of the floral display. "When do we order dinner?"

"This looks like the waiter now," said Jack. A handsome young man, dressed in a tuxedo, bustled over to their table. Quickly and efficiently he handed them all menus.

"Glad to have you dining with us tonight, friends," he declared. "My name is Bryan and I'll be your server. The special for tonight is nectar and ambrosia, served Greek style. I've sampled it earlier and there is no question our chef has come up with food fit for the gods."

"Sounds wonderful," said Cassandra. "I'll have that."

"Not to my taste," said Fritz Grondark. "You still serve that two-pound T-bone with all the trimmings?"

"The Erisichthon special," replied Bryan, grinning. "Few order it and fewer finish it. But I'm willing to bet you'll do it justice."

"Mead for me," declared Freda. "And boar's flesh for my raven."

To his relief, Jack discovered the extensive menu included numerous specialties fit for human consumption. "I'll have the shrimp scampi. With a baked potato."

"Very good, sir. And the lady?"

"The whole Maine lobster, please," said Megan, smiling innocently at Jack. "I love the sound their shell makes when I crack it open."

Mentally, Jack swore never to look at another woman again. He valued his life and health too much to dare cross Megan.

"Thank you," said Bryan. "I'll return in a few minutes with your salads and some bread."

"No dressing on mine," cawed Hugo. "But lots of croutons. I love croutons."

"To be sure," said Bryan, and departed.

"I never imagined a place like this existed," said Jack, his gaze sweeping around the restaurant. The Pied Piper and the sirens had long since left the bandstand. They had been replaced by a solitary saxophone player. A short, stocky figure dressed in baggy pants, with a thick brown beard and long, curly hair, he had to be Pan. The noise of the room drowned out his music but Jack thought he caught a few bars of "Yakkety Sax."

"Is there a restaurant like the Chaos Club on the East Coast?" asked Megan.

"Of course," said Freda Collins. "In the heart of New York City. It's called the Immortals Palace. The food and drink aren't nearly as good as here. Minos owns the Palace and he's a tightwad. He waters down the mead and . . ."

Freda suddenly stopped speaking. She clenched her jaws shut. Eyes narrowing to pinpoints, the Valkyrie folded her arms across her chest. Jack, quite familiar with his mother's moods, recognized a storm brewing. As did Hugo.

The raven swung its head around in a circle, searching for the cause of Freda's anger. Halfway through the motion, the bird froze in a complete stop. Three figures were approaching their table. "Oh hell," Hugo declared, "it's him."

Him, whoever he was, was a tall, slender man with a narrow face and thin, thin cheekbones. His glowing black eyes matched his slicked-down black hair. Bloodless lips, curled in the vague semblance of a smile, creased an otherwise white face. He wore a black suit with white shirt and black tie. There was a harsh coldness to the man that chilled Jack's blood.

He walked slowly, arrogantly, like a king making his way through his subjects. Following him, a few steps to the rear, were the two biggest men Jack had ever seen. Seven feet tall, with shoulders nearly as wide, they were built like walking walls. Shaggy white hair, white beards, and glazed white eyebrows defined them. They were creatures of ice and snow and eternal night. Though they wore conservative business suits, they should have been dressed in the skins of animals.

"Frost giants," muttered Fritz Grondark. "I knew I should have brought my monkey wrench."

"There's nothing to worry about," said Freda Collins, her voice taut with emotion. "Even they know better than to risk the anger of Hercules. Besides," she added, with a harsh laugh, "Loki keeps them on a tight leash."

"Loki?" said Jack, caught by surprise. "But I thought the Norse Gods vanished with the advent of Christianity in the northlands."

"The evil one accompanied the Gods on many of their adventures," said Freda, "but his parents were frost giants. When belief in the White Christ banished the Aesir, Loki remained—to plot mischief against mankind."

"Obnoxious bastard," added Hugo. "He deals in illegal weapons these days. Sells guns to whoever can afford them. I'm surprised to see him in the States. Usually he's in the Middle East. And lately in Eastern Europe. Maybe Mongo knows something. Remind me to ask him later."

"Quiet," said Freda. "He approaches."

Lips pursed as if in deep thought, Loki strolled around their table, not stopping until he reached Freda's chair. The frost giants took positions behind Cassandra and Fritz Grondark. The two hulking monstrosities exuded cold. They were like walking snowmen. No one paid the least attention to Jack or Megan.

"Freda Valkyrior," said Loki, his voice surprisingly mellow. "Long time no see."

"Not long enough," snapped Freda. "What do you want, trickster?"

"Want?" replied Loki. "Why should I want anything? Enjoying the fabulous mead available only at this fine establishment, I spot an old acquaintance. I felt it my duty—nay, my privilege—to come over and say hello."

"How touching," said Hugo, hopping to Freda's shoulder. "Seen the kids lately?"

According to Norse mythology, Loki was the father of three bizarre offspring. One was the Fenris Wolf, destined to swallow the sun during the Twilight of the Gods. Another, the Midgard Serpent, had grown so gigantic that it circled the world beneath the sea, clutching its tail in its mouth. The third, his daughter, Hel, was born so ugly that she was given domain over Nifflehelm, the land of the dead. Jack suspected Loki did not like being reminded of his children.

Astonishingly, the man in black laughed. "Ah, the ever-humorous Hugi. Still performing tricks in the circus with your idiot twin brother? Too bad the All-Father isn't around to hear your jokes. I'm sure he would have been quite amused."

Squawking with rage, Hugo launched himself at Loki. But the bird never reached his target. Moving with shocking speed, the frost giant behind Cassandra reached out with both hands and grabbed the raven by the neck.

"Should I crush his head, master?" asked the snowman, his white eyes glistening with excitement. "Should I?"

"No, you fool," gasped Loki, angrily. He was having trouble breathing because Cassandra's left arm was wrapped around his

throat. The Amazon's other hand held the point of a steel dagger
to the trickster's right eye. "Release the bird."

"Yes, sir," the giant said, and dropped Hugo to the table. "Sorry,
sir."

With a whisper of steel, the knife in Cassandra's hand disappeared. Releasing Loki, she stepped over to Megan's side. Smiling
her most dangerous smile, she nodded politely to Loki. With a wry
grin of his own, he nodded back.

"Nicely done," he remarked. Then he turned to the bemused
giant. "The next time I tell you to watch the Amazon," he said, his
voice colder than ice, "watch the Amazon.

"Actually, Freda dear," continued Loki, acting as if nothing had
happened, "I came over to meet your famous son."

"Me?" said Jack, as all eyes turned in his direction. "Why me?"

Loki chuckled. It was not a pleasant noise. "Several times
during the past century, I found it necessary to employ Dietrich
von Bern. While not without his faults, I always found him quite
competent. That any mortal, even one of your ancestry, could
defeat him as well as one of the Great Beasts, astonished me. I had
to see for myself what made you special."

The Norse deity stared directly into Jack's eyes. Mortal's gaze
met immortal's and held. For an instant, neither figure moved.
They remained frozen in place, as if communicating by thought
alone. No one at the table dared make a sound, afraid to disturb the
strange scene taking place before them. A minute passed. Another.
Then, gradually—very, very gradually—Loki started to tremble.
His body started to shake, not with fear, but with relief.

"You don't have an answer," he declared, his voice quivering
with emotion. "Not even a Logical Magician can accomplish the
impossible."

"Perhaps not," said Jack quietly. "But I don't give up very
easily. I'll find a solution."

Loki chuckled harshly and shook his head. Eyes glowing, he
stepped back from the table. Hands on his hips, he rotated his head
slowly, taking in everyone sitting at the table. His thin lips curled
in a sneer of disdain. He was arrogance personified.

"Follow your champion," the man in black declared, "and be
damned. He cannot succeed. You are stupid fools."

Yet for all of his sarcasm, there was a note of doubt in the Norse
deity's voice. Something troubled the trickster. Worry lines

clouded his forehead. Despite his statements to the contrary, something he had seen in Jack's eyes frightened him. Badly.

The trickster's gaze darted from one frost giant to the other. "Attend me, you fools. We are done here. I have learned all I needed. We are leaving at once."

"But, master," said the giant posted behind Grondark, "what about smashing their bones . . ."

"Shut your mouth, you animated icicle," shouted Loki. For the barest instant, the laughter was gone, revealing beneath it an unspoken fear. "The plan has changed. No reason for us to waste effort on these churls. The Old Man of the Mountain will deal with them. They are his problem, not ours. Come."

Whirling about, Loki strode for the exit. Back stiff, he never once turned around. Shaking their heads in bewilderment, the two frost giants hurried after him.

"I'm glad that's over," said Fritz Grondark, rising to his feet. Clutched in one hand was a massive hammer. "Not my monkey wrench," he declared apologetically, "but if push came to shove, I thought it might do the trick. I never go anywhere without some sort of protection. To be honest, I wasn't sure the past few minutes if I was going to need it or not. That Loki speaks in riddles."

"Yeah," said Hugo, straightening out its feathers with its beak. Otherwise, the bird appeared unharmed. "First he tells us we're a bunch of dumb jerks. Then, he races out of here faster than snow melting in the desert. Does Jack amuse him? Or scare him six ways to Sunday? It doesn't make any sense to me. Anybody care to explain? I'm one bemused fowl."

"Loki possesses the power to see into a man's soul," said Freda, staring oddly at her son. "He can read the truth to any question he asks. What secret concerns him, Johnnie? And, more important, what is your answer?"

"Loki wondered if I knew how to kill a god," replied Jack. "He read in my thoughts that I didn't. That's what made him laugh. Until he caught the rest of my deliberations."

"The rest?" repeated Megan.

"I don't understand how to defeat a god," said Jack, smiling grimly, "but I have a theory. That's what scared Loki. I do have an idea. A very interesting idea."

9

"I refuse," said Freda Collins, a few moments later, as Bryan served their salads, "to let that lout, Loki, spoil our celebration." She raised her champagne glass. "Drink up. In Valhalla, we never worried about the morrow. We lived only for the moment."

"Yeah," said Hugo. "Eat, drink, and be merry. You know the rest. Typical dumb Norse credo."

"Bird," said Freda evenly, "I can wring your neck as easily as the frost giant. And Cassandra would probably lend me a hand."

"Listen," said Jack, anxious to escape the squabbling, "the band's playing a slow number." He pushed back his chair. "Megan and I love to dance. We'll be back before the main course is served."

Except for a few older couples, they had the dance floor to themselves. Jack eased Megan about, enjoying the sensation of holding her close. Her head resting on his chest sent his pulse racing.

"Calm down, handsome," she declared, giggling, "or you'll get us arrested."

"Not here," said Jack. "Morality seems to be one of the few human traits not adopted by the supernaturals. They are totally without shame."

"So I've noticed," said Megan.

"It's not their fault," said Jack. "Remen.ber, they're creations of mankind's collective subconscious. Thus, they embody all of humanity's suppressed dreams and desires. A common fantasy among both men and women is a nonviolent encounter with a sexually aggressive partner. The supernaturals can't help acting the way they do. We're the ones who programmed them that way."

"Well, keep your hands to yourself where nymphs are concerned," said Megan. "Those women are well beyond the aggressive stage. They've evolved into predators. And to them, you're a particularly choice cut of beef."

"A fact," said Jack truthfully, "that never ceases to amaze me. I'm neither particularly handsome or exceedingly muscular. Beautiful ladies never treated me like a sex object before."

"Push your own analysis a step further," said Megan, snuggling even closer. "Humans have always dreamed about romantic liaisons with legendary characters. Encounters that featured the visionary playing the lead role. Those thoughts were, in turn, embedded in the basic character of supernaturals. The nymphs don't want rugged barbarians. They want the men whose imaginings created them. In other words, guys like you."

"Thanks," said Jack. "I think."

"Don't pout," said Megan. "I find you quite handsome and very desirable. And I'm not pre-programmed."

"Very desirable?" asked Jack.

"Very," said Megan, running her fingers slowly along the back of his neck. Her touch sent shivers running down his spine.

The song ended and reluctantly they returned to their table. Fortunately, during their absence, all disagreements had been settled peaceably. Freda and Cassandra were reminiscing about old battles while Hugo regaled Fritz Gröndark with bawdy tales about the sex lives of elves. A few moments after Jack and Megan resumed their seats, Bryan arrived with the main course.

The food was superb. As promised, it was a memorable meal. Though Jack found it somewhat disconcerting watching Hugo ripping and swallowing chunks of boar flesh only inches away from his own plate. Nor did it help when halfway through their dinner, the bird belched, then declared loudly, "The only thing lacking is a pint of blood to wash down the grease."

"There's Cartaphilus, the Wandering Jew," said Megan, trying to point out some of the notables to Jack as they ate. "He plays chess with Father once a month. Under a pen name, he writes travel books."

Hercules, when spotted wandering close to the bandstand, resembled a professional wrestler. The distinguished cut of his tuxedo could not hide the bulging muscles in his chest and arms. He nodded pleasantly to Cassandra when she waved.

"One of the few men I admire," admitted the Amazon. "He's always treated me with respect."

"The good-looking blonde at the front table is Elaine, the Lady of the Lake," continued Megan. "Father's known her for hundreds of years." She lowered her voice so only Jack could hear her. "I think she and Arthur were more than just good friends, if you catch my drift. Dad refuses to discuss the subject. He's a stick when it comes to gossip."

Over strong coffee and mints, talk turned from celebrities to more serious topics.

"Loki can't be trusted," said Freda, draining her cup in one gulp, "but I doubt if he will interfere in your mission. Though he pretends otherwise, the trickster is a coward by nature. Despite his laughter, you frightened him here tonight, Johnnie. Whatever his involvement with these matters, I believe he will remain inactive until a clear winner emerges."

"He did mention the Old Man of the Mountain," said Cassandra. "Which confirms your suspicions. Now we know for sure who our enemy is."

"Our current enemy," corrected Jack. "Still lurking somewhere in the background is our primary foe—a demigod from the dawn of civilization. It's the one we have to defeat to save the world."

"The Ancient Ones were created without weaknesses," said Cassandra, a note of apprehension in her voice. Supremely confident in her own abilities, the Amazon feared no mortal or supernatural opponent. However, an actual god presented a unique challenge. "Their worshipers believed them immortal and inde-structible."

"As was the All-Father," said Freda Collins. "Under one name or another, he existed from the end of the ice age till the coming of the White Christ. Yet, in the end, the priests vanquished Odin and the Aesir without engaging in a single battle."

"They were disbelieved out of existence," said Jack. "The first commandment specified 'Thou shall have no other gods before me.' As Christianity spread across half the world, the passionate beliefs of its worshipers wiped out the pagan gods. With so many people believing they did not exist, they couldn't. They vanished into the outer darkness."

"Until some imbecile summoned one back to our world," said Megan. "Forcing us to battle a pagan demigod intent on reestablishing its rule over mankind."

"But why doesn't this first commandment still work?" asked Hugo. "Nobody believes in the Ancient Ones these days."

"Exactly," said Jack. "Nobody believes and hasn't in hundreds of years. The first commandment lost its power once the last of the pagan gods disappeared. Ordinary people stopped disbelieving because there were no longer any false gods to deny. That's our problem. Understand?"

"No," said Hugo. "Call me a birdbrain, but I'm still lost."

"The Ancient One returned to our world not through belief but by magic. As a god, ordinary sorcery doesn't work against it. It can be banished only through disbelief. But we're the only ones who know it exists. And it takes thousands if not millions of people to disbelieve it to limbo."

"So you first gotta convince a bunch of bozos to believe in this god," said Hugo, "then persuade them to not believe in it any longer." The bird paused, then shook its head in a very humanlike gesture. "Good luck."

"Now you understand why Loki laughed," said Jack. "It's a complicated situation."

"You'll find the solution, honey," said Megan, patting Jack's hand. "Father has complete faith in you. And so do I."

"Whatever happens," said Cassandra, "you can count on me. An Amazon's loyalty never wavers."

"I don't make friends easy," declared Fritz Grondark, "but like Cassandra here, when I make them, I stick with them. That's the dwarven code."

"With friends like these," said Jack's mother, "how can you fail." She grinned. "Of course, being your mother, I have to say that."

"You guys talk too much," said Hugo. "That's why I liked the All-Father. He never spoke without a purpose."

"He was a rather taciturn individual," said Freda. "I never once recall hearing him laugh. Ragnarok weighed heavily on his mind. And it was hard for him to concentrate in Valhalla, considering the hall was always filled with a noisy bunch of drunken heroes."

"It wasn't his style," said Hugo. "Odin disliked senseless chatter."

Glancing at Megan, Jack raised his eyebrows in mock astonishment. His fiancée giggled. One thing they agreed upon was that all supernaturals loved to talk. Dream creations, they were brash, impulsive, melodramatic, and bold. And rarely silent for more than a few seconds. It was part of their nature.

"I could talk all night," said Freda Collins, as if reading her son's mind, "but I have an early flight to catch tomorrow morning. Mr. Weissman placed a big order with the company. I need to return home to supervise its delivery."

"Damn and double damn," said Hugo. "Just when things were getting interesting here."

"Don't worry, bird," said Freda, signaling Bryan for the check. "I've decided to leave you and Mongo here with Jack. He needs all the help he can get."

"Hey, great news," the bird said, and hopped onto Jack's shoulder. "I love a good fight. Especially the mop-up afterward. You know, examining the bodies . . ."

"Stop," said Jack, "before you get started." He looked at his mother. "I appreciate the offer of the ravens, but are you sure you can manage without them?"

"Manage?" said Freda with a laugh. "After centuries of listening to their advice, a few weeks without their croaking will be like returning to Valhalla."

"It's settled then," said Hugo. "We're part of the team." Flapping its wings, the blackbird launched itself into the air. "Wait till I tell Mongo."

Staring at his mother as she counted out money for the bill, Jack wondered if the whole dinner hadn't been planned to reach this exact conclusion. Knowing his mom, it seemed quite possible. Mentally, he shrugged his shoulders. Though Hugo had a bloodthirsty streak equal to Cassandra's, he found the bird otherwise entertaining company. And Mongo as well. Working with them should prove to be an interesting, if not unique, experience.

10

Sitting on the sofa in the living room of Megan's apartment, Jack felt free for the first time in weeks. Tonight, the world would survive without him. The Logical Magician was taking a break.

Using the TV remote control, he casually channel-surfed, looking for an old movie to watch. He didn't particularly care what, as his mind was on other things. Specifically, Megan, indulging in a bubble bath, after which she promised to change into something "comfortable." The way she pronounced the word when they returned to her dwelling curled Jack's toes.

To his surprise, upon leaving the restaurant, Cassandra insisted that he spend the night in Megan's apartment. She felt he would be much safer there. Normally quite Victorian in her attitudes, the Amazon was more concerned about possible Assassin ambushes at the campgrounds than Jack's moral responsibilities. Megan, slightly tipsy from the champagne, had enthusiastically agreed it was a good plan. Her hand, resting on Jack's thigh the entire ride back to the building, made it quite clear that she liked the scheme for several reasons.

Merlin owned the entire apartment complex. Megan occupied the penthouse on the roof, which could be reached only by a private elevator. With Cassandra stationed in an empty apartment

directly across from the building entrance, Jack seemed absolutely
safe from attack—other than one planned by an amorous young
lady.

Sighing, then sipping on a can of Coke, he decided that life
wasn't so bad. He was young; in good health; engaged to a
stunning, sexy, wonderful woman; and defending the world
against the powers of darkness. He was definitely, as the ancient
Chinese curse decreed, living in *interesting times.*

"Oh, Jack," cooed Megan, from the far side of the room, "time
to turn off the TV."

Slapping the set's power button, Jack turned and froze. Megan
stood by the sliding door leading to the outdoor patio of the
penthouse. The bright moonlight shone like a spotlight on her
stunning figure. She was dressed in a long, flowing red silk
dressing gown. The material was so fine and thin that it was
almost transparent in the light. Beads of sweat exploded across
Jack's forehead and his mouth turned incredibly dry.

Chuckling, Megan spun around on her toes, raising her hands
over her head like a ballerina. "Like it?" she asked, knowing
exactly the effect her display was having on him. "I bought it
special just for you."

"Very n-n-nice," he managed to stammer out. Awkwardly, he
climbed to his feet. "You're the most beautiful woman I've ever
seen."

"And you're seeing quite a bit of me tonight," said Megan,
giggling. She pulled open the door to the terrace. "Let's go outside
on the patio. There's a nice breeze this time of night. Sometimes,
when I can't sleep, I sit outside watching the stars. This building
is the tallest in the area, so no one can see up on the roof. It's an
island in the sky. We'll be completely, totally alone out there.
Completely alone. At last. The two of us."

"The two of us," Jack repeated, gulping. Math majors, including
ones who had saved the world once, were not used to dealing with
aggressive women. Especially very attractive aggressive women
wearing very little who obviously had romance and seduction on
their mind. Gathering his courage, Jack decided it would be an
important learning experience. Trying to act casual, but knowing
the glazed look in his eyes betrayed him, he stumbled after Megan
onto the patio.

Megan sat on a large cushioned glider in the center of the patio.
Surrounding her was a bright garden of red and white carnations.

She patted a spot close by on the cushions. As if in a dream, Jack sat where instructed. Fresh from her bath, Megan smelled sweeter than any flower. Quite naturally, she wrapped her arms around his neck. They kissed. A long, lingering kiss. A promise of more to follow.

"You must be awfully hot with so many clothes on," she murmured a few minutes later as they paused to breathe. "It's such a warm night out on the patio."

"It is quite warm," said Jack, nodding. He was sweating profusely, though definitely not from the heat or humidity. He tugged at the collar of his shirt. "I'll take off my shirt."

"Let me," said Megan. Bending her head, she kissed him gently on the neck. Her fingers played with the top button of his shirt. Opening it, she kissed him at the top of his chest. "I'll bet you've never been undressed by a woman before."

Jack knew better than to answer. There had been that wild incident with the mall sprites a few weeks ago. But since they were supernatural beings and thus, technically, not actually women, they might not qualify. He quickly decided silence was the better part of valor. Instead, he let himself drift happily into a nirvana-like state of physical pleasure. His breath quickened as Megan's lips sank lower and lower.

Megan, her own breath coming in short, intense gasps, was fumbling with Jack's belt, when they were unexpectedly interrupted.

"Nice technique," declared a deep, booming voice from the corner of the patio farthest from the door. "At least, for a human."

"Son of a bitch," said Jack, struggling up from his half-reclining position. His shirt dropped to the ground. "Can't I ever be seduced without interruption?"

Next to him, Megan, her features flushed with passion, swung around and glared at the intruder. "Who the hell are you? And how did you get on my patio?"

"Not who," said Jack, casting a meaningful glance at the inside of the apartment. He had a strong premonition they were no longer safe on the open patio. Megan was too angry to notice. "But what?"

The speaker was shaped like a man but was definitely not human. Eight feet tall, with neon red skin, he was immensely broad at the shoulders and incredibly narrow at the waist. His head was the size of a pumpkin, with long, pointed ears and a bare trace of a nose. Growing increasingly concerned, Jack noted that their visitor's legs vanished into wisps of smoke. He had no feet. His arms, folded across his huge chest, were as long as the tentacles of an octopus. And ended in hands with four fingers instead of five.

"You're a genie," said Jack, finally placing the being. "Like the one in the Disney cartoon."

"Great flick," said the supernatural. "I loved it. Saw the movie twenty times. That Robin Williams is great. But I'm no genie. They're dweebs. I'm an Afreet. I'm a lean, mean, fighting machine."

"How interesting," said Jack. He laid a hand on Megan's shoulder. "Don't you think it's time we went inside, good-lookin'? Wearing that outfit, you'll get chilled."

About to make a caustic remark, Megan caught the expression on Jack's face. For the first time since the appearance of the Afreet, she seemed to realize their precarious situation. The genie had not come to her patio to discuss animation. It was there for a purpose. Being a creature of Arabic mythology directly linked it with the Old Man of the Mountain.

"I am getting chilly," she declared, pulling her dressing gown tightly closed. "And it is getting late."

"Later than you think," said the Afreet. Before either of them could move, the creature reached out with both hands and grabbed Megan by the shoulders. Effortlessly, it raised her ten feet into the air.

"You're light as a feather," the entity declared. "Thank Allah for small favors."

"Put her down!" Jack yelled. The Afreet ignored him. Desperately, Jack looked around the patio for some sort of weapon. The best thing he could find was a three-pronged hand shovel. Waving it wildly, he charged the neon demon.

"Sorry, Charlie," said the Afreet, rising into the air, a struggling Megan clutched close to his chest, "but I'm running a little late. No more time to talk. Don't worry about the girlfriend. She'll be safe with me. You know what they say about flying. It's the safest method of travel."

"Take me," cried Jack. "I'm the one you want, not her."

"Nope," said the Afreet, so high now that it was no more than a red dot in the moonlight. "The boss told me to get the babe. And I got her. Stick close to the phone, buddy. You'll get a call from us. Sooner than you think. Bye-bye."

With a whoosh like the noise of a jet airliner taking off, the Afreet disappeared. Jack clutched his head in despair. Megan was gone, kidnapped by an Afreet. Most likely she was a prisoner of the Old Man of the Mountain, one of the vilest villains in all history.

Cursing, Jack picked his shirt off the ground and reentered the penthouse. The Afreet had said to stay close to the phone. He planned to do exactly as commanded. At the moment, it didn't seem like he had much choice.

∞

11

The call came an hour later. Jack had contacted Cassandra immediately after entering the apartment. She, in turn, relayed the bad news to Merlin and Jack's mother. All of them, and the two ravens, assembled shortly afterward in the penthouse, to impatiently await the phone message and make plans. When the telephone finally rang, it was almost anticlimactic. Placing the speaker on its loudest setting, Jack picked up the receiver.

"Jack Collins here."

"Good evening, Mr. Collins," said the caller. The supernatural being spoke without the slightest trace of an accent. His tone was surprisingly mellow. He talked with the quiet self-assurance of a gambler holding a fistful of aces. "Men call me Hasan al-Sabbah, the Old Man of the Mountain."

"I find that hard to believe," said Jack. "The original leader of the Hashashin never waged war against women. He fought his battles with men. The Old Man of the Mountain, in his own fashion, was a man of honor."

"As am I," declared al-Sabbah. "I sent my Afreet to merely kidnap your fiancée, not harm her. She arrived here a short while ago in perfect health. Ask her yourself."

There was an instant's silence on the phone. Then, to Jack's immeasurable relief, Megan's voice filled the room.

"Jack? Is that you?"

"I'm here, sweetie. Are you okay?"

"I'm fine," said his fiancée, "other than having a miserable headache. My ears kept popping whenever the genie flew over a mountain. He's not very good at controlling air pressure."

Megan paused. "That damned Afreet loved old movies. The entire trip he regaled me with impressions of his favorite stars in their best roles. He did everything from Bogart discussing the water in *Casablanca* to Cagney's death scene from *White Heat*. It was terrible."

"I understand," said Jack, realizing what Megan left unsaid. With Hasan al-Sabbah close at hand, she had to watch her words carefully.

"Keep the faith, honey," said Jack. He wanted to say a great deal more, but not with an audience present. "I'll rescue you. Somehow."

Silence again, then al-Sabbah returned on the line. "Ms. Ambrose is safe and unharmed, Mr. Collins. As my guest, she will be treated like visiting royalty. In fact, her quarters will be heavenly. And, within a week, at the conclusion of certain business transactions that need not concern you, she will be returned unsullied."

The Old Man of the Mountain paused. His pleasant voice grew cold. "I must apologize for the inept assassination attempts by my followers. Acting on the advice of several business associates, I foolishly delegated a team of Hashashin to ensure your non-interference in an upcoming . . . transaction. I suspected any mortal capable of dealing with Dietrich von Bern was more than a match for my recruits. But my client insisted, and the customer is always right.

"Three attempts and three failures convinced my patrons they were wasting their money and my time. Freed to follow my own instincts, I decided that kidnapping your sweetheart was the solution to our problems. Please do not disappoint me by playing the hero."

Jack grimaced, knowing what came next. The routine never varied. By their very definition, supernaturals followed certain basic behavior patterns. It was part of their nature. All of them talked too much. They explained their reasons for every action. Villains, like al-Sabbah, always began by flattering their opponents. Then, afterward, came the threats.

It was terribly predictable. Jack felt as if he had become part of a cliché-filled manuscript. Unfortunately, Megan's life depended on his outwitting the script. And for all of his melodramatic poses, Hasan al-Sabbah was a very dangerous opponent.

"If you insist on meddling in my affairs," declared the Old Man of the Mountain, "your beautiful lady love will suffer the consequences. I believe you understand my method of conditioning the faithful. The routine, with minor variations for modern times, remains remarkably similar to that I employed centuries ago. Heavily drugged men are easily fooled by willing houris and low-level magical effects. The treatment provides me with assassins willing to do anything to achieve their heavenly reward. The only problem is that the coarse, brutal thugs I am forced to recruit lately are oftentimes extremely harsh with the nymphs in my gardens. *Very harsh,* Mr. Collins."

The blood drained from Jack's face. "You're not threatening to put Megan . . ."

"She is a beautiful woman," said al-Sabbah slowly. "Exactly the type of female reputed to inhabit paradise."

"You fiend," said Jack, his hands clenched into fists. "You dirty rotten monster."

The Old Man of the Mountain laughed, a high-pitched cackle that barely sounded human. "Of course," he declared. "I am no more and no less than what humanity made me. Don't blame me for your basest instincts, Mr. Collins. Blame mankind."

Jack drew in a deep breath, calming himself. "A week, you said?"

"Seven days," said al-Sabbah. "Remain in Chicago that time and she will be returned to you unharmed. You have my word. Disobey me and her blood will stain your hands."

"How do I know I can trust you?" asked Jack. "Von Bern made lots of promises. And he broke every one of them."

"A man in my profession requires a spotless reputation, Mr. Collins," said al-Sabbah, sounding slightly miffed. "No one wants to deal with an assassin who lies. My word is my bond. Once given, it is never compromised."

"I guess I have no choice," said Jack.

"Correct," said al-Sabbah. "You have no choice at all. Goodbye, Mr. Collins."

Hands shaking, Jack replaced the receiver on the telephone. Folding his arms across his chest to steady his nerves, he turned to the others. "Well, what do you think?"

"Word or not," said Cassandra, "I don't trust him."

"Whatever he is planning," said Merlin, "it bears directly on the fate of our civilization. The Old Man of the Mountain must be stopped."

"As long as Megan remains in al-Sabbah's power," said Freda, "his hands are locked around your throat. There's nothing to stop him from squeezing them shut."

"Guys like al-Sabbah only understand one thing," said Hugo. "Force. Negotiating is seen as a sign of weakness. Your mom's right. The Old Man's a snake. The only way to deal with a snake is to bite off its head."

"For all of his remarks about returning Megan unharmed," said Mongo, "I noticed that al-Sabbah offers no guarantees about your safety afterward. Villains of his nature strongly believe in protecting their back. To them, the only good enemy is a dead one. And you can be sure he considers you his enemy."

Jack nodded. "I expected to hear nothing less. As legendary heroes, you refuse to compromise with evil. It's against your basic nature. On the other hand, being strictly mortal, I've spent my entire life learning how to make compromises. Up to a few weeks ago, I would have readily agreed to all of the Old Man's conditions. But since then, I've learned some valuable lessons. Ones that will hopefully help me formulate a plan to defeat al-Sabbah and rescue Megan."

"Meaning what?" asked Merlin. "Remember, Jack, Megan's my only daughter. I want her back. Unharmed."

"Me, too," said Jack, his features grim. "That's why we can't make any deals with the Old Man of the Mountain. Al-Sabbah can't be trusted. Outwitting him is the only way to save Megan and protect mankind. Which is why understanding how the Old Man of the Mountain thinks is so incredibly important. We have to devise a scheme that will catch him by surprise. And he's a master of deceit."

Pausing to gather his thoughts, he slipped into his basic lecture mode. Old habits died hard, especially after years of graduate school. "Humans are unpredictable. That's because they make decisions based on emotions as well as logic. Despite the best efforts of social scientists, no one yet has been able to accurately predict how different people will react to the same situation. Identical experiments yield conflicting results. That violates the fundamental tenets of the scientific method. Thus, traditional hard-science practitioners such as chemists and physicists refuse to think of psychology as a true science. The basic rules of cause and effect don't work when applied to people."

Drawing in a deep breath, Jack continued. "However, supernaturals aren't human. Created by mankind's shared subconscious mind, they obey specific rules. Though you have plenty of latitude in your everyday actions, you can't violate certain basic defining characteristics. Each of you, in your own fashion, acts logically." Jack grinned. "Which means that someone trained in mathematics can predict how you will react to specific events."

"Big deal," interrupted Hugo. "So you knew in advance we'd all reject al-Sabbah's demands. Maybe you actually guessed what the Old Man of the Mountain was going to say. What's it matter? Megan's still his prisoner. I don't see you predicting her free."

"Not yet," said Jack, "but give me time. The Old Man of the Mountain has a league of assassins and an Afreet on his side. That's an awful lot of firepower to overcome. As I said before, the only way for us to defeat al-Sabbah is by outthinking him. Using logic is the answer."

"Well," said his mother, "if anyone can do it, you're the one, Johnnie. Didn't Merlin call you the Logical Magician?"

Jack nodded, the weight of the world once again slipping onto his shoulders. He only hoped that Merlin wasn't wrong.

Defeating Dietrich von Bern had been a major struggle. He had an uneasy feeling that the Old Man of the Mountain was going to be a much more difficult opponent. And sooner or later he was going to have to face the demigod behind the scenes. A god that, by definition, couldn't be killed.

∞

12

An hour later, after much fruitless discussion leading nowhere, they finally broke for the night. Jack desperately needed rest. The supernaturals, created without mortal frailties, could function for days without sleep. But he was only human.

"Tomorrow," he declared, yawning. "We'll finalize plans tomorrow morning."

He hugged his mother. "No reason for you to stay around for another day. Don't worry. I've got everything under control. It's my job, remember. I'm the Logical Magician. Give my best to Dad."

"I've always let you make your own decisions, Johnnie," said his mother, "and I'm not planning to change now. Do whatever's necessary to rescue Megan." Reaching out, she ruffled Hugo's feathers. "Use the ravens. They possess incredible powers, even if they do talk too much. And if you find yourself in desperate straits with no possibility of escape, send them looking for help. They won't fail you."

Minutes after everyone had departed, promising to meet the next afternoon in Merlin's office, Jack collapsed onto Megan's bed. Alone. It was definitely not the scenario he had envisioned only a few short hours ago. Totally exhausted, he barely managed to kick off his shoes before drifting to sleep. The last thing he heard was Hugo asking Mongo, "What did she mean about us talking too much?"

He didn't dream. A fact that unsettled him the next morning as he chewed on a piece of toast. One of the benefits of being born the child of a supernatural was the ability to communicate in dreams with other halflings. Especially Megan. Not hearing from his fiancée frightened Jack. An active imagination and a steady diet of splatterpunk horror novels read during the past year suggested too many unpleasant explanations. Gulping down a Coke, he expressed his fears to the two ravens.

"You're probably worrying about nothing," said Mongo. "Any powerful magical being can blanket dream transmissions fairly easily. The Old Man of the Mountain isn't stupid. He wants to keep you in the dark about his whereabouts and his actions. His Afreet is probably keeping Megan's sleep messages bottled up tight."

"That sounds logical," said Jack, feeling slightly relieved, "though completely misguided. Megan already passed along the important information last night. She did it during our phone conversation." He paused. "Still, I'd feel a lot better if I knew for sure the extent of the genie's powers."

"No problem," said Hugo. "I'll fly over to the library and do some research. Meet you at Merlin's office in an hour."

With a loud caw and a flap of wings, the raven was gone. Jack blinked. Somehow, Hugo exited the apartment without opening a window. The Afreet wasn't the only magical being possessing unusual talents.

"How did he do that?" Jack asked Mongo.

"Do what?" replied the raven, busily pecking at a bowl of Cap'n Crunch cereal. The birds exhibited a voracious and extremely non-discriminatory appetite. "This stuff tastes great. Why didn't your mother ever buy it?"

"It's loaded with sugar," said Jack. "Bad for your teeth. Though, in your case, I guess it doesn't matter. You didn't answer my question."

"Question?" said Mongo, delicately peeling a banana with one claw. Any minute, Jack expected the bird to start making French toast. "What question?"

"How did Hugo depart with all the windows closed?"

"Easy," said Mongo, eyeing a box of graham crackers. Hopping over to the package, the raven peered at the list of ingredients. Obviously it was checking to see if the wafers contained sugar. Cawing happily, it ripped the top off the carton. Fortunately, Megan maintained a well-stocked kitchen cabinet. "We know the secret of flying through solid objects. Spying for Odin required us to master a lot of tricks."

"But that violates the fundamental laws of the universe," said Jack.

"Nonsense," replied Mongo. At long last, the bird seemed finished with breakfast. "Atoms consist primarily of space. The total mass of electrons, neutrons, and protons is negligible. Hugo and I merely manipulate our physical structure so that the atoms of our bodies slip through the atoms of the opposing barrier. It's simple."

Jack frowned. "I was terrible at physics," he said. "That's why I went into logic." His eyes narrowed. "Where did you learn about atomic structure?"

"Asimov wrote a column on the subject in one of your digest magazines," said Mongo. The bird quickly changed the subject. "Don't you think we should be heading downtown? Merlin's probably wondering what's keeping us."

"Okay," said Jack, rising from his chair. "But the next time I visit my parents' home, I plan to check all of my magazines for beak marks. God help you birds if I find any."

Fifteen minutes later, they departed for Chicago's Loop. Mongo flew on ahead, scouting the route. Cassandra, armed with a half dozen throwing stars, assorted knives, and a wire garrote wound about her wrist, drove their car. The Amazon was feeling mean and hunting for trouble. Though there was nothing she could have done to prevent Megan's abduction, Cassandra felt personally responsible for its taking place. The expression on her face was enough to keep any would-be assassins at bay. She was not a happy Amazon.

Merlin, Witch Hazel, and Fritz Grondark awaited them at the magician's office. As did Hugo and his twin. And an unusual postcard.

"It came with the morning mail," said Merlin, handing the photo card to Jack. "Though it was addressed to you, I couldn't help noticing the message. Which prompted me to pull out my crystal ball and attempt a reading. Hazel helped, as did Sylvester."

The witch's familiar meowed loudly. "I hate predicting the future. It hurts my eyes peering into that stupid glass."

"But you see things better than we do, dearie," said Hazel. A bent, old crone with scraggly white hair, she looked every bit the witch she was. Appearances were deceptive, though. Hazel was a good witch, and a valuable ally in the battle against the forces of evil.

Jack studied the postcard. One side consisted of a color photo of one of the newest hotels in Las Vegas. On the reverse was scribbled a short note. "Hope to see you at the big auction next week." The cryptic statement was signed, "An old friend."

"Your crystal ball didn't reveal who sent this message?" Jack asked, knowing the answer in advance. "Or why?"

"Of course not," said Merlin. "However, focusing on the card, Sylvester stared into my magic sphere. That's when he caught a glimpse of a room filled with people, both human and supernatural. Their attention was fixed on a small, hairless man dressed in white robes, holding a glass vial in one hand. Standing behind him was a huge neon red figure."

"The Afreet," said Jack, "and the Old Man of the Mountain. Any idea what he was offering for bid?"

"Not a glimmer," replied Sylvester. "The vision lasted only a second. Sorry, Jack."

"No need to apologize," said Jack. "Combining your information with what I already surmised gives us a pretty clear picture of what's taking place. And when."

"It does?" said Cassandra. "I must have missed something somewhere. Would you care to explain?"

"Yeah," said Hugo. "Add me to the list of lost souls. It seems awfully likely that the postcard's a trap. Or a phony lead designed to lure you away from the real action."

"I doubt it," replied Jack. "Especially in view of the clues Megan passed on to me last night over the phone. During the famous scene in *Casablanca* where Bogart discussed the water, the characters directly referred to the city being located in the desert. Just like Las Vegas. And when Cagney died at the end of *White Heat*, he screamed, 'Top of the world, Ma.' "

Jack held up the mysterious postcard. "Notice the name of the hotel on the front of our letter. The Seven Wonders of the World Hotel and Casino. I'm willing to bet a fistful of silver dollars that

the Old Man of the Mountain has his headquarters in the
penthouse on the top of that resort."

"But who sent the card?" asked Cassandra.

"I'm not positive but I'm willing to venture a guess," said Jack.
"Remember, the ancient demigod behind all of these schemes
didn't return to our world on its own. Someone had to call it back.
Perhaps that individual did it entirely by accident. Who knows the
actual circumstances? In any case, this card seems to indicate we
have a friend in the enemy camp."

"Maybe," said Hugo. "But I wouldn't trust my feathers to
anyone fooling around with spells dealing with the Ancients.
Summoning a demigod to the real world ain't the same thing as
making pudding. Nobody with a noble heart tries something like
that in the first place. Not without a reason. Get my drift? This
character ain't lily white."

"Agreed," said Jack, "but we can't ignore the facts. Hasan is
holding Megan prisoner in Las Vegas. He's doing it to prevent us
from interfering with an auction he's holding within the next
week. I'm not sure how the demigod fits into this whole scenario.
It might be working behind the scenes. Or it could merely be a
participant in the bidding. In any case, I can't see any way to avoid
the obvious. We have to attend the event as well. Megan's fate, and
possibly that of civilization, depends on it."

"It sounds like the plot of a horror novel," said Hugo. "I
remember the cover blurb of one published a few years ago.
'Gavel-to-gavel terror where the bidding is for your soul and all
sales are final.' It was called *The Devil's Auction,* but I'll be
damned if I can remember the author's name."

"Who cares?" said Jack. "These horror authors write a book or
two, then disappear. They never amount to much. We need to
make plans, not talk about old books."

"I'm going," said Cassandra, in a voice that brooked no
discussion. "I have a score to pay back to that Afreet and his boss.
Besides, you'll need someone to guard your back against the
assassins. And I'm the best one to do it."

"My beak and talons are yours to command," said Mongo.

"Mine too," said Hugo. "Blood's good for the digestion. Plus,
your mom would never forgive us if we let you get hurt."

"If you need the services of a dwarven mechanic," said Fritz
Grondark, "I'm willing and available."

"To save my daughter's life," declared Merlin solemnly, "I will do whatever is necessary." He paused. "Defeating an Afreet will require powerful sorcery."

"You can say that again," cawed Hugo. "I ransacked the mythology section at the Chicago Public Library downtown for information about genies. It's a nice place. Too bad they spent so much money on the building they couldn't afford to buy any new books. Volumes I beaked through were at least twenty years old. Fortunately, legends don't change over the centuries."

"Would you care to share with the rest of us what you discovered?" Jack asked sarcastically. There were no short remarks or replies with supernaturals. Saying yes or no took five to ten minutes.

"Be glad to," said Hugo, completely unaware of Jack's impatience. "The facts ain't particularly comforting. Afreets are the meanest and most powerful genies of Arabian mythology. Creations of fire and air, they exercise control over both mediums. They can fly, call up storms, and set objects ablaze. Though Afreets normally appear slightly larger than a man, because of their gaseous nature, they can assume nearly any size. They can swell up as big as an elephant or shrink down to the dimensions of a bug. Fortunately, as with most extremely powerful elemental spirits, they have the brainpower of a dinosaur."

"Any other weaknesses?" asked Jack.

"That's the really bad news," said Hugo. "Damned genies don't have many. They're nearly indestructible. Glass frightens them. They refer to it as 'frozen fire.' According to most legends, Afreets can't escape from a properly sealed glass bottle."

"Logical," said Jack. "Glass incorporates fire, air, and sand, all major factors of their existence."

"*Properly sealed* is the problem, Johnnie," continued Hugo. "King Solomon imprisoned most of the genies in bottles, then buried the receptacles in the desert sand. He trapped them in the vessels by impressing his magic signet ring into the wax covering the container's mouth. Nothing less will work. You need King Sol's ring to cage this baby, and that ring disappeared two thousand years ago."

"Terrific," said Jack, gloomily. Closing his eyes, he drew in several deep breaths. Mentally, he recited the fundamental theorem of calculus to steady his nerves. Finally, he opened his eyes and looked around at his companions.

"I refuse to give up before we start. Things look grim, but they looked pretty bad when we fought Dietrich von Bern and the Border Redcaps. Yet we defeated him and a Great Beast as well."

"Couldn't we use the same modern devices that defeated those fiends against the Old Man of the Mountain?" asked Cassandra. "Hasan sounds equal in evil to the Wild Huntsman."

"Unfortunately, different cultures perceive certain behavior in entirely different manners," said Jack. The same idea had flitted through his mind earlier and he had dismissed it after a few minutes' thought. "The Old Man of the Mountain is not thought to be a villain in Middle Eastern mythology. Like death, he's neutral. The Assassins kill for religious beliefs or profit. In either case, that's not considered a sin. Hasan and his servants are immune to our original weapons. We need other devices to overcome them."

"Sounds pretty challenging to me," said Hugo. "Considering that the Old Man of the Mountain is supposed to be immortal. Genies can't be killed, only imprisoned. And there's always the question of how to disbelieve out of existence a demigod nobody believes exists in the first place."

"Mere details," said Jack. "The one thing to remember is that if supernatural beings evolve with the times, then the methods of dealing with them have to change as well. We're going to use modern logic to win this war."

Feeling slightly more confident, Jack rose from his chair. A dozen ideas crowded into his head. Several he rejected immediately as taking too much time or being too risky with Megan's safety at stake. But a number of others offered real promise. Everything depended on the situation in Las Vegas.

"This mission is going to require use of everyone's particular talents," he declared. "I'm going to Las Vegas as soon as possible. Cassandra will accompany me for protection. The ravens will come along to act as our spies. The rest of you are going to stay here."

He raised his hands to quiet their protests. "No complaints. Too many of us traveling would attract attention. There's no question that the Old Man of the Mountain knows too much about me. There's probably a bunch of his agents spying on my every move. The only way to fool them is to create a magic doppelganger to take my place. The three of you working together can handle that spell. In the meantime, Cassandra and I can disguise our features and bring the battle right to our enemy, catching him by surprise.

My plans aren't certain yet, but without your cooperation, they're doomed to failure."

"You're the boss," said Fritz Grondark, shrugging his massive shoulders. "Dwarves are team players."

"I can't say I like being left behind when Megan's safety is concerned," declared Merlin. "But I know you will do everything possible to save her."

"Woods witches can't fight worth a damn anyway," said Hazel. "Brews and potions are what me and Sylvester do best. We're with you, as always, Jack."

Moving with inhuman speed, Cassandra reached into her boot, withdrew a needle-thin stiletto, and thrust it into the floor. The steel blade quivered from the force of the blow as she spoke. "I pledge my life and my honor to this quest. We shall not fail."

Jack licked his lips. The Amazon had a dramatic manner of stating her objectives.

"Hopefully," he said, "we'll achieve our aims with a minimal amount of violence." The barest hint of a frown crossed Cassandra's features. The Amazon preferred the direct, bloody method of settling difficulties. "But," Jack continued grimly, "if it means we wipe out Hasan's entire league of Assassins to rescue Megan, so be it. The Old Man of the Mountain has pushed us around long enough. It's time we did some shoving of our own."

∞

13

"Every man in this airport is *staring* at me," Cassandra whispered to Jack, eight hours later. "I can see the lust in their eyes. I doubt if I would draw this much attention if I was completely naked."

"Exactly," replied Jack, grinning. Though he probably felt closer to the Amazon than any other of his supernatural friends, she was so insufferably prim and proper that it secretly amused him to see her squirm. Cassandra was dressed to kill, and the gaze of every man, and most women, in the Las Vegas airport was fixed on her. "The best disguise is misdirection. If the Old Man of the Mountain has spies in the terminal, you're the last person in the universe they'd peg as an Amazon warrior."

"If one more man winks at me," said Cassandra, her voice quivering with emotion, "I will die of shame. After," she promised grimly, "first ripping out his eyes and shoving them down his slimy throat."

"Calm yourself," said Jack. "We're near the baggage claim. Once we locate our luggage, we'll take a cab to the hotel. You'll be out of public sight. At least, for a little while."

Cassandra gasped. "You don't expect me to wear clothing like this getup for our entire stay here? That's unthinkable."

"Better revise your thinking," said Jack, cheerfully. "In Las Vegas, Cassandra Cole doesn't exist. In her place is Saman'ta Jones, high-priced companion to millionaires and jet-setters. Besides," he declared, unable to resist a small dig, "I think you look very sexy."

Cassandra wore a full-length, lycra-spandex white cat suit. It hugged her curves like a second skin. A half dozen strategically placed cutouts revealed large patches of her chocolate-colored skin. The incredibly tight outfit clearly revealed her underclothes consisting of a tiny thong bikini and no bra. Five-inch spike-heeled boots and a three-inch-wide black leather belt completed the ensemble.

Her jet black hair was braided in the latest style, and dabs of color tinted her cheeks and eyelids. Gold chains around her neck clinked and jangled as they walked. And her fingers were capped with long white fingernails.

"I worried you might have a hard time with those heels," murmured Jack as they rode the escalator down to the baggage claim. Under normal circumstances, the Amazon was a few inches taller than he. In boots, she was nearly a head higher. "But you're managing them without effort."

"In my career as a professional bodyguard, Jack," said Cassandra, "I've had to attend more than my share of state functions undercover. Wearing fancy clothes isn't as unusual for me as you might think. Dressing like a high-class hooker is the problem."

"You could be wearing worse," said Jack, then wished he hadn't. Packed in their suitcases were outfits that made the Amazon's current attire look tame. *At least*, Jack reflected, *keeping Cassandra fighting mad wasn't going to be difficult.*

Merlin's money, connections, and magic had smoothed their path to Las Vegas. Their new identities, and the clothes to match them, came from an unnamed but very secret agency that specialized in deception. Their features had undergone slight but significant changes, courtesy of one of Witch Hazel's bitter potions. The wood witch guaranteed the results for a week. There was a harsher edge to Jack's appearance and a softer one to Cassandra's. The modifications were just enough so that the two of them were completely unrecognizable to anyone but their closest acquaintances.

Jack, dressed in a perfectly fitting dark pinstripe suit, was Gordon Green, an extremely wealthy and equally mysterious investment broker. In the inner pocket of his suit he had discovered a bank directory listing his accounts in several major investment firms. According to the entries, Mr. Green was worth well over $50 million. The billfold in his other pocket contained fifty crisp one-thousand-dollar bills. Merlin had money to burn.

Cassandra, despite her vocal and continual protests, became Saman'ta Jones. Getting the Amazon to wear the outrageous outfit selected for her by the deception bureau had been a major battle. Her screams of indignation had nearly shattered Jack's eardrums. Persuading her that she couldn't bring her weapons along on the trip had been the real challenge.

Reservations in one of the most expensive suites at the Seven Wonders of the World Resort proved to be no problem. Nor had there been any hassle purchasing first-class plane tickets for the two of them. Merlin the master sorcerer could work miracles on command. And when magic failed, money talked.

Once arrangements were finalized, the two ravens had been sent on ahead to do some preliminary scouting. "We fly at Mach three when necessary," Hugo told them when asked. "Lucky our feathers aren't real, otherwise they'd fry."

A big, burly black man, standing nearly seven feet tall, awaited them at the luggage area. Dressed in a chauffeur's uniform, he held a white cardboard sign with the name "Mr. Green" scrawled across it. It took Jack a few seconds to remember that was his name.

"I'm Green," he stated. "This is Ms. Jones, my secretary."

Jack noted with some trepidation that the driver didn't possess an aura. Another supernatural. Lately, his entire existence seemed to be defined by legendary beings. He glanced at Cassandra. She shrugged, clearly signaling she had no idea of their chauffeur's true identity.

"Glad to meet you," said the big man, his voice rumbling like thunder. He nodded to Cassandra, his gaze lingering for a moment on her outfit. The smile forming on his lips died when he saw the Amazon's expression. "I'm John Henry. But you can call me Big John. Most people do."

Jack shook his head in disbelief. He had never considered that songs might generate enough belief to bring their characters to life. Evidently, they did.

Big John handled their four heavy bags as if they were weightless. He guided them outside, to a huge white stretch limo. "Make yourself comfortable. The Seven Wonders is on the other side of the city. It's about a half-hour ride. There's a full stocked bar if you care for a drink. And a TV set."

Jack settled into a plush seat and poured himself a Coke. Adjusting to the good life wasn't very difficult. Next to him, Cassandra wrenched off her boots with a grunt of relief.

"I thought John Henry died of a broken heart after battling a steel-driving machine?" said Jack, as they cruised along the highway. It seemed unlikely that the hero of a folk song could be evil, and Jack was curious about the being's origins.

The driver chuckled. "Rose-colored contact lenses, huh? I heard they existed but never met anyone wearing them. Pretty neat." He paused for an instant, then continued, "You got me mixed up with the wrong character. My namesake perished just as you stated. I'm the hero of that Jimmy Dean song, popular in the late 1950s. He never actually killed me, and in a sequel song, an old girlfriend rode into town and rescued me. So many people believed it was a true story, I came to life."

Big John sighed. "The Delta Queen left years ago. She abandoned me to pursue a career as a backup singer for Motown. With the mines shutting down all over the country, I moved to Vegas for the sun. Hacked a cab for years. Finally I earned enough money to buy a limo and start my own business. Type of people that come to this town enjoy traveling first class. At least the ones heading to the hotels. Returning to the airport, they take a cab.

"It's a pleasant existence. Nobody messes with a man my size. And it sure beats the hell out of being buried at the bottom of a cave-in."

They chatted about life in the gambling capital for the next twenty minutes. Big John knew nothing about other supernaturals in the city. An easygoing giant, he was content earning a living and sampling the world's basic pleasures. That he had been created by a hit song becoming part of modern urban folklore set Jack's mind reeling.

If Big John existed, what other modern folk legends might also walk the Earth? There were numerous books detailing common urban myths. It was quite possible that many of the unusual characters they described had been given life by mankind's collective subconscious. Jack found the concept both exciting and disturbing.

The lobby of the Seven Wonders of the World Resort was the size of a naval shipyard—a large naval shipyard. As they deposited their luggage with a bellman, Big John warned, "Don't forget to get a map of the hotel when you check in. People have been lost for days searching for their room. Good luck. Win big."

"Holy Athena," whispered Cassandra as they slowly strolled past row after row of slot machines that lined the path to the front desk. She nodded her head at a huge white marble statue in the southwest corner of the immense atrium. "That's a perfect copy of the statue of Jupiter by Phidias. I saw it at Olympia two thousand years ago."

"Whoever built this palace didn't spare any expense," replied Jack softly. "I wonder who he used to design the exhibits."

Taking Cassandra firmly by one elbow, he steered her to the registration center. Standing still and gawking at the scenery established them as tourists, not high rollers. While there were several thousand people in the lobby, not one of them was paying any attention to the incredible decorations. Pips, grapes, cherries, oranges, and dollar signs were the only things that interested them.

"That's a re-creation of the Great Lighthouse of Alexandria," murmured Cassandra as they continued past a hundred-foot-tall refreshment center. "In the northeast, on a direct diagonal from Jupiter, stands the Colossus of Rhodes."

"No need to question where they put the rest of the sights," said Jack, as they stepped up to a vacant window at the registration desk. Behind the check-in center was a huge map of the entire complex. It listed each of the seven wonders and prominently displayed their location.

Quite properly, the Tomb of Mausolus, King of Caria, was one level beneath their feet. Instead of serving as an elaborate mausoleum, the floor contained dozens of boutiques, shops, and video game arcades. It was a mini–shopping mall for the entire resort complex.

Restaurants were located at the fabulous Temple of Diana at the rear of the casino. A sign posted at the desk proclaimed it served "food fit for a God at prices designed for mere mortals."

The outer buildings containing all of the guest chambers were designed in the shape of pyramids. The higher one's elevation in the structure, the more expensive the room. Jack was not particularly surprised to learn their quarters were at the apex of Khufu's Tomb, an exact replica of the Great Pyramid of Giza.

"The Hanging Gardens of Babylon are to the rear of the hotel," their bellman informed them twenty minutes later, as he turned on the lights of their suits. Big John hadn't lied about the size of the complex. Without a guide, they would never have found the room. The resort was the only hotel Jack had ever visited that featured moving sidewalks. And needed them.

"That's also where the golf range and tennis courts are located," continued the bellcap as he deposited their luggage on racks in the huge bedroom. "At night, they feature a big fireworks display there that you can see from this window."

"Incredible," said Jack, examining the well-stocked refrigerator in the parlor. After the long walk from the lobby, he needed a Coke. Reaching into his wallet, he pulled out a fifty and handed it to the bellman. "This place exceeds my wildest dreams."

"Yes, sir, thank you, sir," said the bellman, grinning, as he made the bill disappear. He glanced at Cassandra and rolled his eyes. "Not that you're in need of any other physical delights, sir. However, in case you desire to sample a truly unique experience, you might make confidential inquiries at the desk about the Eighth Wonder of the World. It's only available to the highest rollers. From what I've heard, it's like visiting paradise."

"Thanks," said Jack, his heart thumping like a trip-hammer. "Maybe I will." He ushered the bellman out of the room. "I appreciate the thought."

Once the man had left the room, Jack turned to Cassandra. "Paradise on Earth? I believe we've just confirmed that the Old Man of the Mountain makes his headquarters in this hotel. Now the fun really starts."

∞

14

Stretched out on several wide cushions strewn across the floor, Roger reflected on how much he disliked sitting on cushions on the floor. However, he wisely refrained from expressing his opinions. The two entities present with him in the chamber were not in any mood to discuss his discomforts. In life, there was a time to speak and a time to remain silent. This was definitely one of the silent periods.

They were in a huge throne room, fifty feet square, forty feet high, decorated lavishly in ivory and gold, on the top of the Seven Wonders of the World Resort. The ceiling consisted of a gigantic mosaic of colored glass, effectively filtering the sunlight into a rainbow that ended on the only chair in the chamber—a massive obsidian throne, decorated with leering white skulls. Seated on the chair was the master of the complex, the Old Man of the Mountain. Pacing back and forth in front of him was Roger's boss, the Lord of the Lions. The two were in the middle of a particularly heated disagreement.

Neither figure's voice was raised in anger. Instead, they spoke softly, almost in whispers. It was all a matter of style, Roger concluded. The Old Man of the Mountain and the Lion Lord were very similar in nature. When their tempers rose, their voices dropped. Only the icy coldness of their tones indicated their true feelings. And the flurry of blue sparks that cascaded off the Crouching One's forehead as he walked.

"Explain to me again," said the Lord of the Lions, his catlike features twisted with rage, "the purpose of this . . . auction."

"I've delineated the reasons behind my decision several times already," said the Old Man of the Mountain. Thin almost to the point of emaciation, he wore a simple white robe belted by a black drawstring at the waist. His face resembled that of a skeleton, with dark, brooding eyes sunk so deep into his skull that they were barely visible. His thin, bloodless lips barely moved as he spoke. The menace in his voice was unmistakable. "Business is business. We had no contract."

"Contract?" said the Crouching One. "Gods do not enter into covenants with murderers and assassins. We select our servants with great care and much deliberation."

The Old Man of the Mountain laughed and glanced at Roger. "An impressive choice," he declared sarcastically. "Obviously, this specimen possesses numerous talents not readily apparent to my humble, untrained eyes."

"Mock me at your peril," said the Lord of the Lions. "My wrath makes nations tremble."

"*Made* nations tremble," corrected the Old Man of the Mountain. "You controlled great powers forty centuries ago. Death and destruction bowed to you then, not now."

"They will kneel at my feet again," said the Crouching One. "As will the entire world. Others, in the past, have underestimated me. Do you dare risk my displeasure?"

A flicker of indecision crossed the Old Man's features. Rising from his throne, he walked silently across the room to a solitary wood table holding the only modern convenience in the entire chamber—a telephone. Lifting the receiver, he asked a single question.

"Any word from the fat one?"

The Old Man of the Mountain paused, intent on the reply. After a few seconds, he nodded. "Call me if there is any message," he commanded, "no matter when."

Replacing the receiver, he turned to the Crouching One. "As I explained earlier, this resort cost several billion dollars to build. When the Chinese forced me to flee Tibet, I had to leave most of my riches behind. Unable to finance the necessary special features of this new mountain hideaway through normal channels, I then had to deal with the American supernatural underworld. Most of the money I borrowed came from a source that made even me shudder. This loan shark was a monster created by today's fears and frustrations and was ruthless beyond measure. I hated dealing with him, but I had to have a new base of operations to survive.

"Normally, my assassination ring generates enough income to pay off any debt without much trouble. However, over the past few years, terrorist organizations have glutted the marketplace with cheap killers. Quality work no longer matters. Dictators and despots instead prefer bargain rates over craftsmanship. Thus, I find myself in financial difficulties."

Roger groaned. He had heard this story three times in the past hour. While he sympathized with the Old Man of the Mountain, the Lord of the Lions was right. A deal was a deal.

He shifted his shoulders as if trying to dislodge an imaginary weight. It felt as if some sort of bird stood close to his neck, its talons digging into the muscles of his chest. But nothing was there. Roger attributed the discomfort to muscle cramps brought on by lying on the cushions.

"The notes come due next week. I need a great amount of cash in a very short time. My underworld contact is not very patient. Holding this auction is the answer. With the number of parties interested in obtaining the Russian's services, I should easily raise enough money to satisfy my creditor."

"You kidnaped Karsnov at my command," said the Crouching One. His narrow fingers curled into fists. Blue sparks circled his forehead. Roger steeled himself for a new outburst. "I was the one who informed you of his plague virus."

"Agreed," said the Old Man of the Mountain. "However, the Brotherhood of Holy Destruction provided the necessary manpower to effect the rescue. My Afreet and my magic carpet transported him out of Russia. And Loki's network spirited him from Europe to America."

The Old Man of the Mountain smiled. To Roger, the Assassin lord looked like a snake about to swallow a rabbit. "Each of you has a legitimate claim to the Russian. Whoever is willing to pay the highest price will have him."

"Have you no respect for the ancient God of your people?" said the Crouching One, a note of desperation in its voice. "I reigned in Babylon for a millennium. Surely that must mean something to you?"

"Not a thing," said the Old Man of the Mountain. "As a true member of the faith, I have no God but Allah. I owe no loyalty, none whatsoever, to the Ancient Ones."

Regaining his throne, the Old Man of the Mountain spread his arms in a conciliatory gesture. "Please do not misunderstand me. I am only trying to be fair to all the parties concerned."

"And make yourself a tidy sum in the meantime," retorted the Lord of the Lions.

The Old Man of the Mountain shrugged. "I am an honorable man," he declared, "but I am in business to make a profit. The auction stands as stated. If you want the Russian, you must bid for his services."

The Crouching One sputtered in impotent rage. Roger could sense the demigod's frustration. Four thousand years ago it would have blasted the Old Man of the Mountain to dust for his impudence. But it was nearly powerless in the modern world. There was nothing it could do but complain.

It might be a good time to change the topic, Roger decided. When frustrated, the demigod spent hours bitterly whining about the lack of respect it commanded. After suffering on the cushions, Roger was in no mood to endure the ranting and ravings of his tedious master.

"You have Karsnov well guarded?" he asked. "And what about Jack Collins? Don't underestimate him just because he's a human being."

"The Russian is safe in a private gambling room above the casino," answered the Old Man of the Mountain. "He loves to play cards. I have kept him entertained with blackjack and poker since his arrival. Nearly two dozen of my best men stand guard, inside and outside the chamber. No one, mortal or otherwise, can reach him. He is absolutely secure."

The Old Man of the Mountain sneered. "As to Mr. Collins, I have effectively neutralized him. My Afreet has stolen his lady love and she is our prisoner in Paradise. There she stays until after the auction. He dares not interfere or she will suffer the consequences. My agents in Chicago report on his every movement. And even if he wanted to strike against me, he has no idea where to begin searching."

Leaning back on the throne, the Old Man of the Mountain

folded his hands across his stomach. "Collins thinks that events come to a climax at week's end. He has no idea that the auction takes place tomorrow evening. By the time the fool learns otherwise, it will be too late."

The Old Man of the Mountain yelped in sudden pain and swatted the air in front of his face with his hands. "By the Prophet's beard," he swore. "It felt as if something pecked me on the nose."

Muttering to himself, the Old Man of the Mountain gently rubbed the tip of his proboscis. The skin beneath his fingers was bright red.

"Probably a bug," said Roger, stifling a laugh. Neither the Old Man of the Mountain nor the Crouching One knew of his postcard to the Logical Magician. Nor of his own scheme. Learning the correct pronunciation of al-Sabbah's name provided the last bit of information to complete his formula. The two overconfident entities were destined for several rude shocks very shortly. Roger felt brazen enough to register one more warning, positive it would be ignored. "Von Bern constantly misjudged Collins. He was a dangerous opponent. With a number of powerful allies."

"Von Bern was a fool," said the Old Man of the Mountain. "He deserved his fate."

The Old Man of the Mountain clapped his hands three times. As if by magic, a dozen scantily clad women appeared from unseen doors, each carrying a tray full of food. Soft music, from an unseen band, filtered through the throne room. Roger groaned. It was the start of another one of the Old Man's interminable banquets. More cushion time. His sore muscles shrieked in protest.

"Hasan al-Sabbah is the master of cunning and deceit," the Old Man of the Mountain declared, reaching for a piece of fruit. "No one thwarts my wishes. No one. Not even a Logical Magician."

15

Sprawled across the immense king-size bed that dominated the master bedroom, Jack watched Cassandra unpack and examine her weapons. The Amazon had refused to travel completely unarmed. A half dozen razor-sharp miniature Lucite throwing stars had been concealed in her boots, and her broad belt held a handful of curare-tipped darts. However, her real arsenal made the trip in their bags.

With practiced hands, Cassandra pulled apart a folding steel luggage cart. In seconds, she disassembled it into a pair of needle-thin stilettos and a garrote. Extending the legs of a seemingly innocent camera tripod to their full length, the Amazon screwed the pieces together to form her favorite weapon—a silver-tipped fighter's staff. Other than their clothing, everything in the suitcases bore a dual purpose, usually connected with death and destruction.

"I should have most of my equipment ready shortly," the Amazon announced, trying on a pair of brass knuckles. "When do you want to start exploring the premises?"

"Not until Hugo and Mongo find us," said Jack. "I promised the ravens I'd wait for them to show up."

"Like this?" asked Hugo, appearing as if by magic on Jack's right shoulder.

"Or this?" said Mongo, popping out of thin air on Jack's left shoulder.

"Very neat," said Jack, mentally trying to force his heart to stop skipping beats. He noted that Cassandra clenched a dagger in either hand. The ravens had caught her by surprise as well. "How do you manage this trick?"

"Simple," said Hugo, flapping his wings as he spoke. "We control the power to make ourselves transparent. It's like turning yourself invisible but better. We can see each other, but nobody else can."

"Working as spies for Odin, we needed the talent," said Mongo, staring at Jack's head. "Would you mind if I whisper this stuff in your ear? It would really bring back memories of the good old days."

Jack shuddered, imagining the raven's beak puncturing his eardrum. "Maybe another time," he declared. "For now, speak aloud. Cassandra also needs to hear what you two learned. I assume you found out something interesting, thus the dramatic entrance."

"You bet," said Hugo. "We located the Old Man of the Mountain right away. It wasn't difficult. Mongo suggested we search for the most lavish place in the complex. Needless to say, that's where Hasan makes his headquarters. It's on the roof of the main resort. Top of the mountain, so to speak. You'll never guess who we found the Old Geezer arguing with?"

"You're right," said Jack impatiently, "I'll never guess. So tell me."

"The Ancient One," said Mongo. "The demigod we thought was behind this entire mess."

"*Thought?*" asked Jack. "You mean it's not?"

"Well, it was," said Mongo. "But it's not anymore. Hasan has taken control of things."

The bird paused and looked at Jack's ear again. Jack shook his head. "Maybe," said Mongo, "we should start from the beginning."

"Good idea," said Jack.

Thirty minutes later, the two blackbirds finished relating the entire conversation that had taken place in the Old Man's throne room. The ravens proved to be excellent reporters, describing each participant in detail and repeating their conversations verbatim. By the time they finished, Jack had a thorough understanding of what was happening. He didn't like it one bit.

"You didn't happen to learn who this Karsnov character is?" he asked. "Or what they meant when they spoke of his plague virus?"

"Actually," said Mongo, "I spent a few minutes afterward chatting with some of the birds perched outside the hotel. You'd be surprised how much information you can learn from the locals."

"Yeah," said Hugo, "and I flew over to the nearest library and reviewed the *New York Times* for information on Karsnov. Wish they made microfiche readers for birds. It strained my eyes reading the film without magnification."

Jack blinked at this latest revelations of the two blackbirds' miraculous powers. His mother had been right. The ravens were incredible. But at the moment he was more interested in the results of their inquiries than how they were conducted.

"Well?" he asked impatiently. "Well?"

"The *Times* identified Karsnov as one of Russia's leading experts on chemical warfare," said Hugo. "Evidently, he got into big trouble a few months ago when the government learned he conducted unauthorized biological warfare experiments on Russian citizens. It involved an airborne strain of anthrax plague that killed several hundred innocent people. According to the newspaper, Karsnov vanished without a trace one step ahead of the KGB."

"Only to turn up here shortly afterward," said Mongo. "Safe and snug with his new patron, the Old Man of the Mountain. And it sounds like the Russian is up to his old tricks. The birds outside tell me that there have been a dozen mysterious deaths in Las Vegas the past few weeks. All of them have been reported as resulting from pneumonia. Which is the way anthrax plague is usually misdiagnosed."

"An anthrax plague?" said Jack. "That's insane."

"Depends on your point of view," said Cassandra. "Loki deals in arms. What better weapon to offer your clients than a deadly plague virus that can't be identified or stopped? It's the ultimate killing device. You can wipe out the entire population, leaving their buildings, possessions, and raw materials untouched. Remember all that talk of the neutron bomb years ago. This plague satisfies all the necessary requirements and it's much more subtle. You can wage war without the enemy knowing a battle is taking place."

Jack shivered. Cassandra painted a convincing if terrifying scenario. "What about this Brotherhood of Holy Destruction?"

"Fanatic Muslim fundamentalists intent on destroying the United States," replied the Amazon. "I've heard of them. They believe that the end justifies any means. They've vowed revenge against the United States for the actions taken against Libya and Iraq. Can you think of a more diabolical plan than to poison the water supply of Las Vegas with a slow-acting version of this plague virus? Tourists from throughout the country come to the city for short visits. Within weeks, the entire country would be swept up in an outbreak of the disease. Millions would die before an antidote could be found."

"Dare I inquire what the Ancient One wants with this formula for disaster?" whispered Jack.

"Oh, we know the answer to that riddle," said Hugo. "As soon as we entered the throne room, Mongo and I recognized your mysterious demigod. He rose to power during the same period when Odin first emerged as a Teutonic forest deity. Mongo and me, we never forget a face. Especially a mug as ugly as the Crouching One's."

"That was the nickname his worshipers in Babylon gave him," said Mongo. "He was the most feared god in prehistory. Most humans called him Lord of the Lions, because his head resembled that of a giant cat. But his proper name was Nergal. He was the Ruler of the Underworld, god of death and destruction, pestilence and . . . *plague*."

$$\infty$$

16

Jack digested this latest revelation in silence. Battling a nameless demigod from prehistory was difficult enough. Learning that the entity was the Babylonian god of death didn't make life any better. Jack knew next to nothing about Nergal, other than the fact that the god had been so feared that its name had been appropriated by early Christians and given to one of Satan's lieutenants in the New Testament. Briefly, he wondered if perhaps a confusion in names had served as the entity's passport into the material world. It hardly mattered. Nergal was back, and Jack had to deal with him.

"It's seven o'clock," he declared. "Later than that for us, considering the time change. Let's head over to the restaurant and eat dinner. I'm starving."

"Me too," said Hugo. "Flying that fast takes a lot out of you. I can eat a horse."

"Ditto," said Mongo. "Though I doubt if they include horse meat on the menu. Damn."

"We'll try the buffet," decided Jack. "You two make yourself transparent and stay unseen and unheard. Cassandra and I will take extra food and you can eat off our trays." His voice grew stern. "Try practicing a little restraint. We don't want to draw any attention to ourselves."

"No problem," said Hugo. "Nobody will notice anything unusual. Cross my feathers and hope to die. Not that it matters. Everybody's gonna be staring at Cassandra."

The Amazon glowered at the raven. She had changed garments, but as expected, the new outfit suited her temperament no better than the previous one. She wore a hand-beaded silk evening dress, cut low across her breasts and with a keyhole back that descended down to her waist. The top half of the dress was defined by a pattern of white beading, while the skirt portion consisted of an overlapping sequence of black iridescent sequins. Black stockings with a snake design around each ankle and five-inch heels completed the ensemble.

"One lewd remark, bird," Cassandra said, her voice deathly calm, "and we will learn if you can speak without a beak."

"Stay cool," said Jack. "If we start arguing among ourselves, we'll never free Megan. And save civilization."

"I'm not sure a culture that extols women who dress in such a manner deserves saving," Cassandra declared through clenched teeth, as they made their way to the elevators.

The buffet, when they finally arrived there fifteen minutes later, was awe-inspiring. A standard feature at Las Vegas hotels, the one at the Seven Wonders had to be the most elaborate offering of food Jack had ever seen. Almost a hundred feet long, it offered nearly every type and style of food imaginable. Hugo, an invisible presence perched on Jack's shoulder, murmured, "I wonder if they stock boar's flesh? Sure looks possible."

Boar's flesh was not available, but there were more than enough choices for the raven. Jack found his plate soon filled to the brim, between his and the bird's selections. Cassandra, directly in front of him on line, suffered the same fate. Finally, sounding slightly exasperated, the Amazon whispered to her unseen companion, "One more item and the plate will crack from the weight. Enough. We can return for seconds."

"Same applies to you," said Jack.

"Okay," replied Hugo, its beak resting on Jack's ear so only he could hear its words. Jack marveled that Odin had remained sane for centuries enduring such conversations. "Hey, there's a chef slicing roast beef at the end of the line. I love roast beef. Please, just a piece or two."

"Last item," Jack said, and stepped up to the carving table.

"What would you like, sir?" asked the chef, a portly middle-aged man, his face wreathed in a perpetual smile.

"Three slices, very rare," declared Hugo loudly, before Jack could open his mouth. "As bloody as possible."

The chef's eyes bulged in amazement. Shaking his head, he bent to carve the meat.

"I'm a professional ventriloquist," Jack declared quickly. "Didn't mean to frighten you. I often forget myself and speak with my mouth closed."

"Oh, sure," said the chef, laying the red beef on top of Jack's plate. "No problem." The man's smile returned. "You're good. Really good. Never saw your lips twitch."

"Practice," said Jack modestly. "Years of practice."

Sighing with relief, he left the chef and hurried over to the booth where Cassandra waited. "Do that one more time," he muttered to the raven, "and I'll let Cassandra skin you alive. In fact, I'll hold you down while she does it."

"Sorry, boss," said Hugo. "The sight of that bloodred meat drove me crazy. It won't happen again."

A plump middle-aged blonde waitress took their drink orders. Jack, who normally avoided alcoholic drinks, was sorely tempted to drown his troubles in bourbon, but settled for his usual Coke. Coping with his allies as much as his enemies required a clear head.

"Something more exotic for the lady?" suggested their server, eyeing Cassandra's outfit with a critical eye. "Perhaps a screwdriver? Or a Bloody Mary?"

"A Bloody Mary?" whispered Hugo. "That sounds intriguing."

"No, thank you," said the Amazon, calmly. Jack silently thanked the heavens above for Cassandra's restraint. It wasn't till later that he noticed her fork bent into a horseshoe. "I prefer fruit juice."

"I'll return in a minute with your drinks," said the waitress. She stared with wide eyes at the huge mounds of food on their plates. "Enjoy your dinner."

As soon as the woman left them alone, they set to eating with all the gusto of travelers who had only dined on airline food that day. By the time the waitress returned, their plates were wiped clean.

"My," she remarked, "you were hungry. Feel free to take seconds. And leave some room for the dessert bar in the corner."

Placing a glass of fruit juice in front of Cassandra, the woman shook her head in amazement. "Incredible that you can maintain such a stunning figure with so healthy an appetite. I merely look at rich food and gain weight."

"Exercise," declared the Amazon. "Frequent workouts help keep me in shape."

"I'll bet," said the waitress, her expression making it quite clear what sort of workout she thought Cassandra meant. "Don't forget the big magic show at nine tonight, folks. It takes place in front of the atrium Lighthouse. You don't want to miss it. The tricks they perform using laser technology and holograms are incredible. The red genie, in particular, is a real crowd pleaser. You'd swear he's alive and not just a special-effects creation."

"A red genie," said Jack. "Sounds fascinating." He pulled a twenty out of his wallet. Establishing a reputation as a big tipper wasn't difficult in Las Vegas. "Thanks for the advice."

"Thank you, sir," said the waitress. "Enjoy the show."

"A red genie," said Cassandra, once they were alone. "That can only be the Afreet."

"My thoughts exactly," said Jack. "Though why the Old Man of the Mountain would use him in a magic show to entertain hotel guests is beyond me."

"People come to Las Vegas for the glitz and glamour," said Cassandra. "According to the birds, the Old Man of the Mountain owes a fortune on this palace. He needs to attract big crowds. A spectacular show is one method of doing that."

"We have twenty minutes till show time," said Jack. "We can walk to the Lighthouse in five. Anyone care for a quick dessert?"

"Sugar?" inquired Mongo. "Do you think they'll have lots of things with sugar?"

Jack nodded. "I'm sure they will."

Smiling, he wondered how his mother would cope with two chocoholic ravens. It was not a subject dealt with in great detail in the *Elder Edda*.

∞

17

They arrived at the Lighthouse five minutes before showtime. A crowd of several hundred people filled the open space before a raised stage. Cassandra, smarting from the knowing smirks she had encountered all evening, forced her way to the front, dragging Jack after her. He knew better than to try arguing with the Amazon. Besides, he wanted to be in a position to watch the Afreet's performance closely.

Though Jack's knowledge of physics left much to be desired, he had survived four semesters of the subject as an undergraduate science major. He retained a reasonably strong sense of the laws that governed the physical universe. While not a big fan of hard science fiction, he had read most of Asimov, Niven, and Clarke. Combining his knowledge of science fact and science fiction, he hoped to discover a new method of trapping a genie. It was that or find King Solomon's ring. And Jack doubted he could find the relic by tomorrow evening.

The show started promptly on the hour. A flash of lights, a blaze of laser lights, and a stage magician dressed in a turban and bright purple burnoose appeared seemingly from nowhere. Working with several extremely scantily clad assistants, the man worked through a dozen standard illusions. He was an adept performer, but he was only the warm-up act for the real star of the show, and both he and the audience knew it. The applause he received was polite but reserved. The crowd impatiently waited for the genie to make its appearance.

Drums rolled, the footlights dimmed, and the magician's bountifully endowed helpers disappeared into the wings. The wizard stood alone at center stage, his face bowed, his hands hidden in the folds of his voluminous robe.

"Years ago," the magician intoned in a deep voice that rolled out across the audience, "an old antique dealer sold me this lamp for only a few dollars."

A narrow spotlight focused on the bronze oil lamp, perhaps a foot long, that the speaker had pulled out from his burnoose. Carefully, the magician placed the prop on the floor in front of him.

"Never did I guess," he declared, "that this was the very lamp that once belonged to Aladdin. Not until that fateful day"—and the man reached out and brushed his fingers against the bronze— "that I first rubbed my prize."

The crowd, including Jack and Cassandra, gasped in astonishment. A thick red mist emerged from the lamp's mouth. It curled like smoke twenty feet over the magician's head. Slowly, as the background music swelled, it solidified into an imposing figure of a man floating on air.

"Behold," said the magician, his voice ringing with emotion. "Behold the genie of the lamp!"

With a whoosh, the bright red figure zoomed over the audience, zigzagged across the entire length of the atrium, touched first the head of Jupiter, then the torch of the Colossus, and finished its trip by circling the Lighthouse three times before coming to a landing right next to the waiting magician.

"Ladies and gentlemen," the wizard proclaimed, "brought to you by the magic of The Seven Wonders of the World Resort, LOA Laser Technology, and OMM Computers, I am pleased to present to you, George the Genie."

The Afreet, dressed in loose-fitting trousers, an open vest, and a fez, otherwise appeared exactly the same as the figure Jack had seen the previous night. Grinning, he waved to the crowd, then bowed. The audience broke out in thunderous applause.

"Notice how he exaggerates his motions slightly," Cassandra

whispered to Jack. "It helps maintain the illusion he's only a creation of electronic gimmickry."

The magician clapped his hands three times. Two huge men, dressed in loincloths, emerged from backstage carrying a massive cinder block between them. Setting it down on the stage, they hastily stepped to the side.

With a laugh, the genie floated over to the concrete slab. Laser lights flashed red and green as the Afreet hoisted the block into the air and effortlessly crushed it into powder. A gust of wind, provided by an offstage fan, sent a mist of powder drifting over the crowd. The applause was even louder than before.

Next, the genie bent an iron bar in half. Then it allowed itself to be pierced by a spear, a sword, and finally, a chainsaw. It was all very flashy and, to Jack, quite frightening. Hugo was right. The Afreet was incredibly powerful and without any visible signs of weakness.

"LOA—League of Assassins," Jack whispered. Onstage, the genie, on orders from the magician, underwent a series of incredible transformations. It changed in rapid succession into a lion, an elephant, a bee, and then finally, into a duplicate of the magician himself. "OMM—Old Man of the Mountain. Not very subtle, are they?"

"Do they need to be?" asked Cassandra. "Ordinary mortals are willing to believe anything involving modern technology, Jack. But try to convince them that magic exists, and they'll laugh in your face."

"The world's a cynical place," Jack said, then froze. Every muscle in his body tightened into knots. It was as if he had been suddenly struck by lightning. Or by the answer to a question that defied normal reasoning.

"Jack, are you okay?" asked Cassandra, shaking him gently by the shoulder. Onstage, the genie had vanished back into the lamp and the show was coming to a close. Already the crowd was dispersing. Unable to speak, he nodded slowly as the brief moment of epiphany faded away.

"Yeah," said Hugo, perched invisibly on his shoulder. "What's the story? For a second, you turned white as a ghost."

"I'm fine," said Jack. "In fact, I feel great. I'll explain later."

"Watching the genie give you any ideas?" asked Hugo.

"Not particularly," Jack admitted, as they wandered among the slot machines. "Anything capable of flying that fast and changing his shape that easily won't be imprisoned by ordinary methods."

"Then you'll have to think of an extraordinary method," said Cassandra complacently. "You always do."

Jack grimaced. Dealing with a myriad of supernatural entities, both good and evil, made life difficult enough. Raised by his parents to have confidence in his own abilities, he refused to admit defeat no matter what the circumstances. Thus far, through sheer determination and more than a bit of intelligence and luck, he had managed to overcome the forces of darkness. However, the absolute, blind faith in his abilities exhibited by his friends and allies unnerved him.

Jack wished he shared Cassandra's optimistic belief in his talents. Unlike the heroes in most of the Swords and Sorcery novels in his collection, he couldn't hack and slash his way through the enemy hordes. Outwitting his foes, not outfighting them, was his only hope. So far, it had proven to be a forlorn hope at best.

∞

18

They returned to their suite to change clothes and plan their next moves. While Cassandra sorted through her suitcase, searching for something she considered fit to wear, Jack made a phone call to Chicago. He relayed in abbreviated form to Merlin much of what the ravens had learned. Story told, he requested that the magician conduct a quick investigation of complex financial records. Afterward, they discussed several specific actions to be taken if Jack's hunches proved to be true. Seconds after Jack finished the conversation, the Amazon emerged from her room clad head to foot in black leather.

"Now this garment is more like it," said Cassandra, as Jack put down the receiver. He whistled in a combination of appreciation and bewilderment.

"If you think men aren't going to notice you in that outfit," he declared, "you're crazy."

The Amazon wore a one-piece soft-leather cat suit. The only break in the shiny material was a metal zipper that extended from her neck to waist. With matching gloves and boots, Cassandra could have stepped out of the pages of any of a dozen superhero comic books.

"Let them stare," she said. Whirling about on one toe, she

lashed out with her other foot in a deadly karate kick. The air seemed to vibrate from the force of her blow. "Dressed like this, I can fight."

Out of her boots came the Amazon's stilettos. In a continuous fluid motion, she flipped the two blades into the nearby wall. "There won't be any plague if the Russian suffers a fatal accident," she declared, pointing at the twin knives gleaming in the lamp-light. "I specialize in causing necessary accidents."

"The same thought occurred to me," said Jack, "but only as a last resort. There are two more pressing problems. First, I require an invitation to this auction. Not attending would be a disaster. Even if you eliminated Karsnov, we have no guarantee al-Sabbah doesn't already own a sample of the plague virus and would put that up for bid instead.

"Second, if Megan is being held prisoner in the Old Man's version of Paradise, I need to discover its location. The sooner we find and extricate her from his minions, the better I'll feel. If we make an attempt on the Russian's life with her in al-Sabbah's power, she'll suffer. I can't allow that to happen."

"You have a plan, I assume," said Cassandra.

"The solution to both problems," said Jack, "is to attract the Lord of the Assassins' personal attention. I've been thinking about the conversation the ravens heard this afternoon. While he never mentioned the source of his loans, he did refer to a flourishing supernatural criminal underworld. Merlin confirmed my own suspicions as to the figure in charge. Based on what I've discovered, I think using the right approach with our buddy, Hasan, will work miracles."

"And if you're wrong?" asked Cassandra.

"I mastered the process of thinking quick under pressure during my years on the college debate team," said Jack. "If I draw a blank with al-Sabbah, I'll switch to another story. I know it's not the best approach, but it's the only one we've got. With the auction tomorrow evening, we're running out of time."

Cassandra scowled. The Amazon preferred the direct approach. Given the chance, she'd opt for an old-fashioned fight to the death over subterfuge and deception. However, she was intelligent enough to recognize that Jack's proposal was their only viable scheme.

"How are you going to gain admittance to Hasan's presence?"

she asked. "I doubt if he's very accessible. Especially for a complete unknown."

"We'll do it the old-fashioned way," said Jack. He pointed to the two ravens, trying to open the door of the suite's refrigerator using their beaks. "With the unseen coaching of our feathered friends, I'm going to win a small fortune gambling. Once the stakes hit the stratosphere, al-Sabbah will come running."

"Did you mention gambling?" asked Hugo, its beak wedged beneath the door handle of the icebox. Mongo stood beside him, trying to force open the lock. "I love gambling."

"Me too," said Mongo, its voice muffled by metal. "In Valhalla, we rolled the bones endlessly."

"Used real bones, I bet," muttered Jack, pulling out a new outfit for the night's adventure. Like Cassandra, he needed to dress properly for the role he intended to play.

Groaning in protest, the door of the refrigerator clicked open. Instantly, both blackbirds darted inside. "Hell," echoed Hugo's voice, "there's no chocolate bars in here."

"I'll buy a box of them for you later at the souvenir shop," said Jack, as he tucked a solid black shirt into charcoal gray pinstripe pants. Next came a thin white tie, the suit coat, and a pair of sparkling black shoes. "After we complete our sting."

Nodding in approval, Cassandra reached into the flower basket and pulled out a white carnation. She stuck it into the jacket's lapel. "Perfect," she declared. "You look like you stepped right out of an old gangster movie."

"Spiffy," commented Hugo. "You wanna tell us how we're going to help run this scam."

"Simple," Jack said, and outlined his ideas to the attentive ravens. For a change, they listened quietly, then, when he was finished, made several useful suggestions. In ten minutes, they had everything arranged.

"I love it," said Hugo, transparent on Jack's right shoulder as they headed for the main casino. "This reminds me of the time we tricked Surt, the fire giant, into thinking he was haunted by the spirit of his first wife. What a laugh! He was afraid to eat for a week. Too bad that story never made it into the *Elder Edda*. It's a lot funnier than that hokey tale about Thor's visit to the frost giants."

"Pipe down," said Jack, glancing around to make sure no one

was staring at him. "I can't use that ventriloquism line a second time. Speak so only I can hear you. Is Mongo nearby?"

"Right over your head," announced the other bird from a spot directly above Jack's left ear. "Once you find a seat at the poker table, I'll fly around to the other players as needed."

"Okay," murmured Jack as he walked into the atrium. Cassandra kept pace several steps to the rear, seemingly relaxed and at ease. Appearances were deceptive. The Amazon was primed and ready for battle.

"Hugo's right," continued Mongo softly. "Our adventures with Surt were much funnier than that stupid story about Thor."

"Tell me another time," said Jack, searching the room for the high-stakes poker game. He finally located it, directly in front of an all-purpose cash station. Though it was nearly midnight, the table was crowded with people.

"There's a minor-class sorcerer stationed on the floor," said Cassandra as they strolled over to the game. "Checking to make sure no one is using magic to alter the odds or fix the cards. Since the birds aren't directly influencing the deck, you're fine."

Like most mathematicians, Jack had played cards throughout college. He started with hearts as a freshman, progressed to double-deck pinochle in his sophomore year, and finally succumbed to duplicate bridge for the rest of his undergraduate stay. In graduate school, the game changed to poker. Possessing a near-photographic memory and excellent card sense, Jack played to win. Cards were not a social event but war, and he believed in taking no prisoners. He rarely lost, but he had never played against professional cardsharps before. Nor had he ever gambled for thousands of dollars on each hand.

Before entering the game, Jack studied the flow of the cards for ten minutes. The table consisted of a big man, a young attractive blonde woman, and a middle-aged male dealer playing five-card stud. A small crowd of people stood behind them, watching the action.

The woman, good looking and flashy with diamonds, sat to the dealer's left. In draw poker, it was the worst position, but she seemed not to care. Her card playing left a great deal to be desired. Quick to fold, she was too easily bluffed. She squinted at the cards like they were her enemies. The blonde had too much money and not enough brains for no-limits draw poker. Five red and five blue chips sat in front of her. Stationed directly behind her were two dangerous-looking young men, dressed in dark suits and wearing sunglasses.

The big man, who referred to himself constantly in third person as "Tex Wilson," sat directly across from the dealer. A hearty, red-faced individual, he was dressed in a cowboy shirt open almost to his waist and smoked a big cigar. He talked much too loud and placed big bets. However, Jack noted that Wilson knew exactly when to drop out when things looked bad, and that he rarely lost a hand in which he wagered heavily. The drink at his side, Jack suspected, was more likely ginger ale than whiskey. Ten red and eight blue chips made up Tex's bankroll. Huddled close behind him, several well-endowed women dressed in attire that made Cassandra's outfits look like schoolmarm stuff squealed with pleasure each time the red-faced man won.

The dealer, like most professional card handlers, played a calm, conservative game, relying on the odds, an unlimited bankroll of chips, and the other players' mistakes to keep him ahead. He dealt the cards with a slow, steady rhythm and appeared slightly bored by the whole proceedings.

A half dozen other men and women, evidently tourists, watched the game in respectful silence. Oddly enough, the males eyed the bimbos clustered around Tex while the females tracked the chips. Different fantasies, he concluded, for different folks.

Finally, Jack decided there was no postponing the inevitable. Signaling to Cassandra, he stepped over to the table and seated himself in the empty chair on the dealer's right. On his shoulder, Hugo murmured in his ear, "Mongo's set in position. Let's take these suckers for a ride."

"Deal me in," said Jack. He pulled out a thick billfold from his suit pocket. "How much are chips?"

"Five hundred on the red," said the dealer, "a thousand for the blue. Red for the ante. Jacks to open, otherwise no deal. No limit on bets."

Nodding his agreement to the rules, Jack reached into his wallet and counted out fifteen one-thousand-dollar bills.

"Kinda young to be playing a man's game, sonny," said Wilson as each player put a red chip in the center of the table. "Sure it ain't past your bedtime?"

Jack gave no indication he heard the big man's words. Several years before, he audited a mathematics course that he was grading for another professor in the department. None of the students in the class realized that Jack was the person actually marking their homework and tests, not the teacher. Listening to their constant complaints after class about the professor's harsh scoring, Jack developed a remarkably impassive expression. His was the perfect poker face.

Calmly, he picked up his cards. He held a pair of sixes. "Three tens for the dealer," whispered Hugo. The ravens communicated by a complex series of prearranged wing signals. "Lady's holding a pair of queens. Possible flush for big mouth."

Playing cautiously, Jack dropped out of the first three hands. Knowing the other hands meant nothing without the right cards.

The fourth hand he pulled a pair of aces, best on the table. After the blonde and Tex both passed, Jack raised a red chip. Everyone matched his bet.

Fate handed him a third ace while filling in Tex's queen high with two more ladies. The other two players dropped out immediately, but Wilson stayed with Jack for two raises. Jack dared not play too aggressive. Not yet. Still, he took Tex for three thousand dollars.

"Junior finally won a hand," Tex declared loudly, taking a swig of his drink. "Beginner's luck."

"What makes you think I'm a beginner?" said Jack calmly, reaching for the next hand. "Only a fool insults a man he knows nothing about."

"Where'd you hear that, sonny?" snarled Wilson. Jack felt sure the man's anger was mostly show. Tex bluffed on the table and off. "Watching the Ninja Turtles?"

Jack merely smiled and studied his cards. The hand was garbage, as were the next three. Tex Wilson crowed as he won back most of the money he lost to Jack without a fight.

"Cards are running pretty poor," muttered Hugo as they paused for drinks. Jack asked for a Coke. Chortling, Tex ordered scotch and soda. Watching the red-faced man closely, Jack saw him slip the waitress a twenty. There might be soda in Wilson's glass, but there would be hardly any scotch. Despite his rude behavior and insults, the gambler was stone-cold sober.

Hugo's shocked whistle almost caused Jack to drop the next hand. Staring at the cards, he felt a little shaken himself. He held two pair—aces and eights. It was the infamous "dead man's hand" dealt to Wild Bill Hickok shortly before he was shot in the back.

"Cassandra's right behind you," said Hugo, as if reading Jack's mind. "You're high. Big Mouth's holding jacks and fives. Beauty queen's sitting with a possible straight, either end. The dealer has a possible flush."

Jack opened boldly with a blue chip. Two pair always looked great but rarely paid off. The odds of drawing a full house were eleven to one. The chances of his opponents filling their hands were much better than his. But many gamblers refused to risk money on straights or flushes. Tonight both of his opponents and the dealer matched his bet.

No one said a word as they each discarded one card.

"Blondie's drawn her straight," declared Hugo. The young woman's hand tightened on her cards and a small smile flashed across her face. She was not very good at concealing her pleasure, which might suit her other activities but not her card playing.

"Big Tex picked up a third jack," croaked Hugo. "That gives him a full house, knave high."

Praying to Pierre Cardan, the father of probability theory and a notorious gambler, Jack lifted his card. Hugo collapsed on his shoulder, nearly dropping into his lap. Carefully, Jack inserted the ace of hearts into his hand.

"Dealer sucked up his flush," said Hugo, returning to position. Bucking odds of several thousand to one, all four players had pulled the card necessary to make their hand. And Jack was sitting with the winning combination.

Betting proceeded at a rapid clip. The dealer, knowing the relative shortcomings of his flush compared to what the others might have drawn, dropped out first. The blonde, not as smart, finally quit when she ran out of chips to continue. Only Jack and Tex remained. Finally, with more than thirty thousand dollars in the pot and Wilson out of chips, Jack called.

"Full house, jacks high," declared the red-faced man, reaching for the chips. Wilson was sweating profusely. He knew that if Jack had continued to bet, he would have been forced to cover to remain in the game.

"Sorry," said Jack, calmly, laying down his hand. "Full house, aces high."

"Son of a bitch," said Wilson, shaking his head in astonishment. "Son of a bitch."

Strangely enough, it wasn't Wilson who was the most disturbed. A professional gambler, the big man knew poker was risky business. Instead, it was the blonde sitting next to him who exploded.

"Two full houses and a straight in the same hand," she screamed, her voice shrill. "Bullshit. It can't happen. This game's fixed."

"What'd you want us to do, Mona?" asked one of the woman's two bodyguards. A .45 automatic loomed large in one of his hands. His companion, gaze fixed directly on Jack, was likewise armed.

"They cheated me," said the blonde. "Find out how."

"Lady," said the dealer, his voice trembling, "we run an honest game here. It's the law."

Behind him, Jack sensed Cassandra tense. He assumed she was preparing to cope with the two thugs. It wasn't until he noticed the man in the plaid suit that he understood the real reason for her concern.

"Is there a problem here?" asked the newcomer. Though man-sized and dressed in blue plaid, there was no hiding the Afreet's neon red features. Reaching out with blurring speed, he plucked the revolvers out of the hoodlums' hands.

"Sorry, but firearms are not permitted in the casino," the genie declared. Politely, he handed each of the gunsels a lump of solid metal that a second before had been their weapon.

"I was robbed," said the blonde, no longer shrill.

"Ronald?" asked a second newcomer. Dressed in a white suit, with white shirt and white tie, he was so thin he resembled a skeleton. His gaze swept around the table, lingering for a second on Cassandra before continuing on. His thin, bloodless lips barely moved as he spoke.

"Strictly legit, Mr. Hasan, sir," said the dealer. "There was an unusual run of cards, that's all. Neither gentleman complained. It was the lady who made a ruckus."

The man in white focused his attention on the blonde. She seemed to shrink in the chair as he stared at her. "You have visited our establishment many times, Mrs. Adams. Please do not force me to deny you further entrance. I believe an apology is in order."

"Oh yes," said the blonde nervously. Hastily, she rose to her feet. "I'm sorry. I truly am. The booze went to my head. It won't happen again."

"Thank you, Mrs. Adams," said Mr. Hasan. "Good night, Mrs. Adams."

"Good night, good night," said the blonde and half walked, half ran from the table, her two bodyguards trailing behind like frightened puppies.

"Excitement's over, folks," said the Afreet. "Drinks, as always, are on the house."

Quickly, Jack rose to his feet. Hasan and the genie were already walking away. "Cash me in," he told Cassandra, as he flipped the dealer a red chip, "and deposit the money in a safe-deposit box. I'll see you later."

Anxiously, he hurried after the man in white. His whole plan of action depended on the next few minutes.

"Mr. Hasan," he called, "can I have a word with you?"

The Old Man of the Mountain, for Jack knew he could be no one else, turned. As did the genie, who showed no signs of recognizing Jack. "Yes? Do I know you?"

"No," Jack said, and mentally crossed his fingers. "But you know my boss. He sent me here to observe your auction."

"Auction?" repeated the Old Man of the Mountain, his voice no longer friendly. "To what event do you refer, Mr . . . ?"

"Green," supplied Jack, preparing for his biggest gamble of the night. "The auction taking place tomorrow evening, Mr. Hasan, involving a certain Russian."

"Who is your boss, Mr. Green?" hissed the Old Man of the Mountain, sounding remarkably like a snake. A very deadly snake.

"He has many different names," said Jack slowly, "but most people just call him *The Man*."

∞

19

Hearing that name, the Old Man's features underwent a startling transformation. His white cheeks paled yet further, until not a bit of color remained. The sneer on his lips changed to a sickly grin. The harshness disappeared from his voice, replaced by an alarming false heartiness.

"My apologies," he declared, taking Jack by the arm. "Please don't be offended by my lack of manners. I had no idea. Usually, *The Man* sends the One Without a Face to inform me of his wishes."

"No problem," said Jack, wondering who the One Without a Face might be. It was the least of his worries at the moment. Al-Sabbah on his one side, the Afreet on the other, they were heading across the casino to the registration area. "Where are you taking me?"

"My office, of course," said al-Sabbah. "We can speak in privacy there. I assume you came about the loan?"

"There is the question of payments," said Jack, trying not to say too much or too little.

"I fully understand *The Man*'s concern," said al-Sabbah. Reaching the main desk, he signaled to one of the clerks to admit them through a gate at the end of the counter. An unmarked door in the rear wall led to a luxuriously furnished office.

"Would you care for some liquid refreshment?" the Old Man of the Mountain asked, dropping into a large armchair behind an oak desk. There was a fully equipped bar in the rear of the chamber. "My Afreet is an accomplished bartender. I, of course, do not consume alcohol."

"A Coke will be fine," said Jack. He wondered if the two ravens were with him or Cassandra. It didn't matter. He was on his own for this encounter.

The Afreet handed Jack his drink and took up a position behind al-Sabbah's chair. Standing there motionless, it could have been a statue carved from red neon.

"My obligation with your boss comes due next week," said the Old Man of the Mountain, leaning forward on the desk. "Is there a problem?"

"Nothing in particular," said Jack, sipping his drink. "Though there have been rumors. . . ."

"Lies, lies, lies," said al-Sabbah passionately. "Untruths spread by my enemies." The Lord of the Assassins paused, regaining his composure. "There were unexpected cost overruns involving construction. Nor did anyone, including my most trusted sooth-sayers, expect this accursed recession to last this long. However, business has increased dramatically the past few months. I anticipate no problem meeting the terms of our agreement. Especially with the additional funds generated by the auction tomorrow evening."

"Care to explain?" asked Jack.

"A wise businessman seizes opportunity by the throat," said al-Sabbah. "The resurrected Ancient One, Lord of the Lions, alerted me to the value of the renegade Russian scientist. With the aid of the Brotherhood of Holy Destruction, I rescued Karsnov from otherwise unavoidable execution and brought him here. However, instead of lending his talents to either party, I decided to put his services up for auction. Though complaining bitterly about my betrayal, both parties agreed to participate. As has Loki, representing certain unnamed Eastern European powers. The bidding should be fierce. And the returns quite profitable, for both me and your employer."

"I hope so," said Jack, trying to recall classic hard-boiled movie dialogue, "for your sake. *The Man* sent me here to act as an observer. Nothing more. He likes to keep an eye on his investments. I assume you have no objections to my attending the auction?"

"No," said the Old Man of the Mountain. "Of course not. *The Man*'s wishes are my own."

"Good," said Jack, nodding. "The boss will appreciate hearing that."

He put down his glass. "The Russian is safe?"

"Absolutely," said the Old Man. "He rests in a heavily guarded suite on the floor above us. Would you care to meet him?"

"Why not?" said Jack. If the situation grew desperate, any information he could provide Cassandra about Karsnov's location would be invaluable. "How do we get there?"

"Follow me," said the Old Man of the Mountain. Leaving his office, they walked over to the statue of Jupiter. Behind it was a single elevator. There was no call button on the wall, only a numeric keypad.

"This leads to my private sanctum upstairs," declared al-Sabbah. "It can be accessed only by entering the proper security codes."

The Old Man's nose wrinkled in disgust. An odd expression swept across his face. "Do you notice a strange odor in the air?"

Jack sniffed. "Funny. It smells like the reptile house in the zoo."

"My thoughts exactly," al-Sabbah said, and hurriedly punched in the correct numbers. The elevator doors slid open. The smell inside the lift was nearly overpowering. There were three buttons on the inside control panel. The Old Man of the Mountain punched the middle one.

Silently, the elevator rose to the second floor. Not sure what to expect, Jack was relieved when they stepped out into an empty office much like the one they had left only a few minutes before. The only difference was a pair of smoked-glass doors situated behind the oak desk. The same reptilian smell greeted them as they moved forward.

"Where are the guards?" asked al-Sabbah, not expecting an answer. "They know better than to desert their posts."

"They are not here," declared the genie, peering behind the desk. Jack breathed a sigh of relief. He had half expected the Afreet to find the receptionists' bodies stuffed into the desk drawers. With supernaturals, anything was possible.

"Where did they go?" asked Jack. "What happened to them?"

"I do not understand," said the Old Man of the Mountain, his tone apprehensive. "They have strict orders to allow no one other than myself onto this level. This elevator offers the only access to the floor. A surprise attack is out of the question."

"But," added Jack, unnecessarily, "they're gone."

"The whole floor is quiet," said al-Sabbah. The level was silent as a tomb. "With thirty of my men stationed here, there should be some noise. Something is wrong."

Face contorted with worry, the Old Man of the Mountain barked out a string of commands in Arabic to the Afreet. Instantaneously, the genie transformed into a cloud of red smoke, its empty clothes crumpling to the floor. Mistlike, the entity seeped through the narrow opening separating the glass portals.

"I am very sorry," said the Old Man of the Mountain, turning to Jack, "but I am afraid you will have to leave us for the moment. Something quite unusual has taken place here. I sent my assistant to investigate, but I fear that I cannot guarantee your safety if you remain. Explaining your demise while in my company to *The Man* could prove to be embarrassing. Would you mind returning to the casino?"

"Not at all," said Jack, hoping he did not look as green as he felt. "I was sent to observe, not interfere."

"Thank you," said al-Sabbah. "I appreciate your understanding." The Old Man of the Mountain paused. "Perhaps you would care to sample the delights of Paradise? It is designed for relaxation and delight. A visit there might erase the ugly memories of this unfortunate episode."

"I have heard a number of interesting stories about your heaven on Earth," said Jack.

"You would honor my establishment if you accept my invitation," said al-Sabbah. "A small party of special guests depart at twelve noon. Meet them at the elevator behind the statue of the Bronze God. A visit lasts three hours. You will return long before the auction. That, for your information, is scheduled to take place tomorrow at ten in the room directly above this chamber."

"See you then," said Jack, stepping back into the lift and pressing the button for the ground floor. He felt as if he were leaving the scene of a real-life Stephen King movie. The entire time spent in the reception office he had been waiting for Jason to jump out from behind the desk swinging a chainsaw–butcher knife. Saving the world was difficult enough without having to traffic in blood and gore. Jack preferred his fantasy much lighter. Without genies, assassins, or inexplicable disappearances.

20

Roger groaned in frustration. Of all the resorts in the world, why did they have to stay in one that contained a replica of the Hanging Gardens of Babylon? Though it was long after midnight, the Crouching One showed no signs of leaving the elaborate arboretum. Instead, the Ancient One insisted on wandering to and fro along the maze of pathways, reminiscing about old times. Roger, who had heard most of the demigod's stories dozens of times before, was bored to tears. And though he prided himself on how little sleep he needed, he was tired and ready to call it a night.

The Crouching One, unfortunately, required no rest at all. Gods never slept. Normally he treated Roger's request for rest as an annoying but necessary habit. Tonight, captivated by his surroundings, the Lord of the Lions wanted company. Which meant Roger.

"I am amazed at the accuracy displayed throughout this reconstruction," said the Crouching One, bending over to smell a black orchid, a rare breed that opened only in darkness. "According to those encyclopedias I read, a complete description of the Hanging Gardens no longer exists. I wonder how the Old Man of the Mountain managed to find one?"

Roger almost answered, then thought better of it. In a brief exchange with al-Sabbah earlier in the day, the Lord of the

Assassins mentioned that Gilgamesh, the immortal Babylonian hero, designed the entire resort. It was a name best kept hidden from the Lord of the Lions. He and Gilgamesh had clashed in the past.

The Hanging Gardens consisted of a square tract of land four hundred feet on each side. Built as a series of low-rising terraces, there were hundreds of varieties of plants and trees contained in its confines. Dozens of winding trails and narrow paths cut through the vegetation, preserving the natural beauty of the grounds. In the one concession to modern agriculture and Nevada heat, the entire four acres were watered by a vast system of automatic sprinklers.

"Nebuchadnezzar built these gardens to please his wife Amyitis," said the Crouching One, strolling up the winding path leading to the fifth level. They had started at the bottom of the gardens hours ago and Roger estimated it would take them hours more to reach the top at the demigod's leisurely pace. "She disliked the flat plains of Babylon and yearned for her home in the Median Hills.

"It took ten thousand slaves working day and night fifteen years to complete the project. Located at the peak of the gardens was a huge reservoir that fed the streams and ponds that dotted the landscape. Whenever the water level dropped below a certain mark, hundreds of huge vats filled with liquid were rolled up the terraces to replenish the tank."

Roger yawned. His interest in gardening began and ended with lettuce in salads. To him, the fabled hanging gardens were nothing more than a haven for annoying insects.

"If you study the plant formations very carefully," continued the demigod, "you will notice that the darker foliage forms a series of wedge-shaped patterns and letters. That is the lost secret of the hanging gardens. Viewed from the windows of the king's palace, the entire tableau creates a cuneiform love poem to Nebuchad-nezzar's fickle wife."

The demigod laughed, a disconcerting sound. "Beware of demanding women, my disciple. They are like a cancer eating at your vitals. Nebuchadnezzar was Babylon's greatest king. He practically rebuilt the city, revitalized his nation, and erected the Hanging Gardens. Yet Amyitis was never happy. Her whining drove her husband to drink. Many were the times I advised him to throw the nag to the lions. But he would rather face an army of Persians blindfolded than confront his wife."

The Crouching One paused. His eyes narrowed and his hairless brow crinkled in concentration. "It cannot be them, but it must," he declared, sounding shocked. "The Raging Women.

"Behind me," commanded the demigod, jerking a hand at Roger. "Quickly. Close your eyes and keep them closed no matter what you hear. Hurry. The horrors approach."

Roger had no idea what the demigod was talking about, but he also understood that now was not the time to ask questions. He did exactly as he was told. Whoever or whatever sparked such a reaction from the Crouching One was serious business.

Their smell preceded them. Roger hated animals and avoided zoos, but having been raised in the Far West, he recognized the smell of snakes. And the hissing noise they made.

"Remain silent and do not open your eyes," warned the Crouching One. "Otherwise, you are a dead man. The Raging Women are extremely vain and extremely ugly. If you see their features and speak of it, it will go hard on you."

"Nergal," said a new voice, female but definitely not human. "We heard you returned from limbo. How appropriate to encounter you here in these re-created gardens."

"Sisters," said the Crouching One, his voice polite. "This meeting is as unexpected as it is a pleasure." Then his tone turned harsh. "Your prey . . . ?"

"Is human this night," said another voice, equally inhuman. "*Was* human. You have nothing to fear from us. Our mission here is complete. We were exiting this place when we caught a whiff of your scent. My sisters and I thought it only appropriate to say hello after these many centuries."

"Very touching," said the Crouching One sarcastically. "A card would have been enough. We never were particularly close. Your kind and mine never did get along. Be gone. Your presence disturbs my meditations. I have plans to consider."

"Your thoughts concern death and destruction," said the first speaker again. Roger needed no prompting to scrunch his eyes closed. If the features matched the voice, the Raging Women were ugliness personified. "We serve justice. You defile it. Your plans have been altered."

"A human hides behind you," declared a third sister. Fingers of fear ran down Roger's spine.

"My servant," said the Crouching One. "He worships and serves me in the modern world. Surely you would not deny me one disciple?"

"We do not kill without reason," said the first sister. "That would be cruel, and we are never cruel."

"I remember," said the Crouching One, chuckling. "You are the Kindly Ones. If that is the case, be so kind as to leave me and my servant in peace."

"As you wish," said the first. "Have a nice day."

Then they were gone. However, five minutes had passed before the Crouching One told Roger he could open his eyes.

"We must return to the hotel at once," said the demigod. "The terrible sisters said something about changing my plans. As unstoppable avengers, their presence in Las Vegas bodes ill for tomorrow's auction."

"Who were they?" asked Roger, not sure he wanted the truth.

"Busybody contemporaries of mine from Greece," said the Crouching One. "Insufferable moralists, all the immortals hate them. Though not true gods, they control powers that can threaten even one such as I. Forget them."

"They're forgotten," said Roger.

Hurrying behind the Crouching One to the resort, Roger cheerfully concluded that events were progressing from bad to worse. Which was fine with him. The more confusion, the better. Hopefully, Jack Collins was close at hand and had some mischief plotted for tomorrow night. It actually didn't matter much. Whatever occurred at the auction, Roger was ready. Long hours of secret deliberations at his computer terminal had finally paid off. The answer to his problems was carefully transcribed on a sheaf of papers in his pocket. He was going to be in charge again. And this time, no one could stop him.

21

"Who the blazes," asked Hugo, thirty minutes later in their suite, "is *The Man*?"

"He's the ultimate modern-day evil authority figure," said Jack wearily as he pulled off his shoes. "Over the past three decades, poor people living in the inner city have constantly blamed their troubles on him. Sometimes they mean the government, sometimes the police, sometimes the local crime lords. But they all believe that this unseen power broker is the real force behind many of society's ills."

Jack paused to pull off his socks. "Enough human beings believing in *The Man* gave him life. In a sense, they brought their worst nightmare to life. When you birds told me that Hasan al-Sabbah owed money to some fearful, unnamed figure in the loan shark business, I immediately guessed it had to be him. Merlin verified my deduction. He's heard stories about *The Man* for years. None of them good. You know the rest."

"Except," said Mongo, "the identity of the One Without a Face? Who's he?"

When Jack shook his head, the raven turned to Cassandra. "How about you, Lady Death? The name strike any chords? You've been awfully silent since Jack returned."

"I never heard of the One Without a Face," said Cassandra slowly. There was a strange, unreadable look on her face. Something was bothering the Amazon.

"Describe to me again," she said to Jack, "the smell in the office."

"I told you," he replied, "it stank like the alligator pit at the zoo. Or the room where they keep the snakes. It wasn't pleasant."

He sighed as he wrenched off his necktie. It had been an incredible day, filled with more than its share of thrills and chills. The supernaturals hardly needed any sleep but he was exhausted. His eyes burned and his head throbbed. He craved rest.

"Don't ring no bells with me," said Hugo. The two ravens had remained with Cassandra when Jack left with al-Sabbah. After depositing his winnings, the three supernaturals had returned to their rooms to await Jack's return.

"Me neither," said Mongo. "What's the story, sis? You seen a ghost? Never saw you so pale before."

"Karsnov betrayed his own country, didn't he?" asked Cassandra, her voice muted, her eyes closed. "In a sense, he murdered people who were his kith and kin."

"I suppose you could put it that way," said Jack, wondering why she asked.

"I thought them vanished in the sands of history," said Cassandra softly. She sounded almost philosophical. "I should have realized their breed never retire."

"Mind clueing the rest of us into what you're talking about?" asked Hugo.

"Karsnov is dead," said the Amazon. "Of that, I am quite sure. He was slain, while those unlucky enough to be in his vicinity were neutralized through fear and hypnosis, by three contemporaries of mine. A trio of terrible supernatural sisters, the Greeks called them the Eumenides, meaning the Kindly Ones."

"The Kindly Ones," repeated Hugo. "I got no problem with a monicker like that."

"Mortals used the title," said Cassandra grimly, "because they feared repeating their true names aloud."

Jack shivered and it wasn't from the cold. The lights in the room seemed to dim as the ancient Greek words rolled off Cassandra's tongue. "They are Megaera, the Rager; Alecto, the Endless; and Tisiphone, the Retaliator." Each name resonated through the chamber like the beat of a giant drum. "Ugly beyond measure, with living snakes for hair, they dispense final justice for the betrayers of parents or kin. They are the Furies."

"Hell's bells," cawed Hugo. Flapping his wings, he flew up to the ceiling. "And you call them the Kindly Ones, huh? You think they're still in the hotel?"

"No," said Cassandra. "Once they complete a responsibility, they depart at once. You are quite safe, my fine feathered friend."

"I wasn't scared," protested Hugo, dropping onto Jack's shoulder. "But snakes for hair? Ugh."

"Well," said Mongo, "their unexpected interference helped our cause. No way al-Sabbah's running an auction with his prize plague master ripped to ribbons."

"I'm not convinced of that," said Jack, stretching out on the bed. With the two ravens sitting on the pillows and Cassandra relaxing cross-legged on the edge of the mattress, it was impossible for him to sleep. "A few more minutes, then you characters better leave. I'm ready to collapse."

"You think the Old Man of the Mountain has a sample of the anthrax virus hidden away for emergencies?" asked Cassandra, ignoring Jack's last remarks. The Amazon thought more than two hours of sleep a night was a sign of weakness.

"It makes good sense to me," said Jack. "We know Karsnov used a batch to kill those people Mongo mentioned. Al-Sabbah strikes me as being too shrewd not to obtain a specimen for insurance purposes. Using it, any competent scientist can deduce the proper formula. Dead or not, the Russian's grisly legacy lives on. And will be offered for sale tomorrow, or should I say since it's nearly morning, this evening."

"Enough complaining," said Cassandra, with a laugh. Rising from the bed, she gathered the two ravens in her arms. "We'll leave you alone for your beauty rest. Tomorrow will be a busy day."

"Tell me about it," said Jack. "First, I visit Paradise. If all goes well, I'll locate Megan there and figure out a method to set her free. Once that's accomplished, it's off to the auction. Where I have to destroy a world-threatening plague culture, defeat an indestructible genie, and outwit his immortal master."

"Don't forget the Crouching One," said Hugo. "He's going to be at the auction. As is Loki. And those terrorist fanatics. We can't ignore them. They might be nuts, but they're dangerous nuts."

"Too many problems and not enough solutions," murmured

Jack, trying to keep his eyelids open a few seconds longer and not succeeding. "Maybe being this close to Megan, the spell disrupting dream communication won't work. She always has great suggestions."

Unfortunately the barrier held. Jack slept like a log.

22

The insistent ringing of the telephone dragged Jack from slumberland. Groggily, he rolled over and stared at the clock. It was nearly ten in the morning. Flopping across the mattress, he grabbed the phone receiver.

"Whozzit?" he asked, barely able to speak.

"Jack, Jack?" came Merlin's worried tones. "Are you in trouble?"

"Other than suffering from sleep deprivation?" retorted Jack, shaking the cobwebs out of his head. "I'm fine. At least, I'm surviving as best can be expected considering the circumstances." His brain cleared rapidly. "Did you make those inquiries I asked about?"

"Yes," said Merlin. "That's the main reason I called. The situation's exactly as you described. I've spoken to my Japanese friends and they are definitely interested. The wheels have been set in motion. The only problem is that their representative will not arrive until eleven in the evening."

"That fits in fine with my timetable," said Jack, mentally rubbing his hands together. He loved sneak attacks. Grinning, he relayed to the mage the day's schedule. "I'll phone if whatever happened last night postpones the auction. Otherwise, proceed as planned."

"I'll notify our associates as soon as I hang up," said Merlin. There was no disguising the anxiety in his voice as he asked, "No luck finding Megan?"

"Not yet. But I'm scheduled to take a trip to Paradise at noon. The ravens will accompany me. Together, we'll locate her. Don't worry. She's continually on my mind. Rescuing her is my first priority."

"Sorry to be a pest," said Merlin. "I realize you're equally concerned about her safety. But Hasan al-Sabbah has such a nasty reputation. And Megan's always been very special to me."

"No need to apologize," said Jack. "She's special to me, too. Don't worry. I'll save her. Remember, I'm the Logical Magician."

"Any luck dealing with the genie?" asked Merlin, changing the topic. "Have you discovered any frailty you can exploit?"

Two fireballs of black feathers bulleted into the bedroom, coming to rest on the headboard. "See," said Hugo to Mongo, "I told you he was awake."

"I heard him, too," said the other bird. "My ears are the equal of yours. It merely occurred to me that, being on the telephone, Jack might like some privacy."

"Nah," said Hugo. "Jack's not like that. Who's on the phone, Johnnie?"

Jack groaned. Cassandra, he expected, was outside somewhere, exercising. Leaving him alone with the two blackbirds for company.

"It's Merlin," he answered. "He's curious if we've found a method to deal with the Afreet."

"No such luck," said the raven. "He's a major pain."

"Hugo's right," said Jack, trying to regain control of the conversation. "I've had the opportunity to watch the genie in action several times now. He presents a real challenge. The creature displays the capacity to change nearly instantaneously from a mist to a solid. In a gaseous state, he's incredibly quick, faster perhaps than even the ravens."

"I protest," interrupted Mongo. "No entity in the material world flies faster than us. We are lean, mean, flying machines."

"Perhaps," said Jack, trying to maintain two distinct conversations at the same time. "But it would be a close race."

"He cannot be invulnerable," declared Merlin. "No supernatural is without some flaw. Basic human nature demands imperfection in any creation, good or evil."

"I agree," said Jack. "The problem is that the Afreet's vulnerable only to glass. His powers are neutralized by it. The one method of defeating him is to trap him in a bottle. Unfortunately, without Solomon's signet, there's no means of effectively sealing the container. Even using a glass stopper won't work, because there's a microthin layer of air between the two pieces. In his gaseous form, the genie could slide through that easy. There's no bottle in the world that can hold him."

"Too bad," said Hugo, "they don't make containers with openings on the outside but none on the inside."

Jack's brow knotted in concentration. "Say that again."

"I said it's too bad they don't make . . . ," began Hugo.

"You have an idea?" asked Merlin.

"Perhaps," said Jack. "Just perhaps. Manipulating the circumstances might take some effort, but I believe they could be arranged. The one thing going for us is that the Afreet's not very bright. He obeys Hasan's orders without question. Neither of them strike me as being mathematically oriented. I doubt that they would recognize the trap I'm contemplating."

"Mathematics?" squawked Hugo. "You're planning to use algebra to capture an Afreet?"

"Not algebra," said Jack. "A subject a tad more complex." Speaking directly into the receiver, he asked, "Is Fritz available? And Witch Hazel?"

"Both of them are here," said the magician. "Like me, they hunger for news. And want to help."

"Well, I've got a special object for them to construct," said Jack. "It requires his building skills and her talent for magic. Together, I think they can make it happen. The big problem is whether or not they can complete the job in the next few hours. And transport the finished product to me before the auction tonight."

"If they succeed," said Merlin, "you will have it. And I am certain they will not fail."

"Neither do I," said Jack. "Put the dwarf on the phone. Describing what I want him to assemble is going to be difficult. And I'm due downstairs shortly for my trip to Paradise."

When Cassandra entered the suite thirty minutes later, Jack, otherwise fully dressed, was pulling on his shoes. Munching on the last remnants of a room-service breakfast, he was humming the third movement from *Scheherezade* by Rimsky-Korsakov.

"You're in remarkably fine spirits," the Amazon remarked, "considering the odds we're facing."

Jack grinned. "Why shouldn't I feel good? I'm about to experience the joys of Paradise.

"More significantly," he continued, "I recalled an important lesson learned during our fight with Dietrich von Bern and his minions."

"Which is?" prompted Cassandra, as Jack paused to swallow a gulp of Coke.

"In our contemporary world, old techniques no longer work against the forces of darkness. If monsters evolve, so must the method of combating them. We can't use outmoded ideas to defeat modern menaces. Changing times require changing solutions. We'll overwhelm the Old Man of the Mountain and his genie not with King Solomon's ring or some other ancient relic, but by utilizing today's science and technology. As long as we don't forget that, we can't fail."

"Brave words, Johnnie," said Mongo, gravely. "But talk is cheap. Are you sure you can back them up with solid results?"

"I'd better," said Jack, rising to his feet. "If not, civilization is in big trouble. Not that we'll be around to watch it collapse. I doubt if the Old Man of the Mountain grants second chances."

"What do you want me to do while you're visiting sin city?" asked Cassandra.

"Go out and buy me an inexpensive pocket camera and film," said Jack. "I need a miniature tape recorder also. Afterward, come back to the room and wait for the arrival of a package from Merlin. He promised it would be delivered here this afternoon. It's the key to our success tonight at the auction. Guard it carefully."

"With my life," said Cassandra solemnly.

Jack nodded. He wasn't worried about anyone stealing his precious secret weapon. No one other than a mathematician would have any idea what it was. However, his instructions gave Cassandra a sense of purpose and kept her from being bored. A good general, he understood the importance of maintaining the morale of his troops. Even if his entire army consisted of a solitary Amazon and a pair of sarcastic blackbirds.

"You two ravens turn transparent," he instructed, "and take your positions on my shoulders. Remember, I'm counting on you locating Megan in Paradise. Don't disappoint me."

"Failure isn't part of our vocabulary, Johnnie," said Mongo. "If Megan's a prisoner in this place, we'll find her. I promise."

"We never fold under pressure," said Hugo. The bird's voice dropped an octave and took on an peculiar inflection. After a few seconds, Jack realized the raven was imitating Humphrey Bogart. Badly, with a Swedish accent. "After all, we're blackbirds. *We're the stuff dreams are made of.*"

Speechless, Jack shook his head in dismay. His mother was definitely letting the ravens watch too many classic detective films on TV.

∞

23

Years before, Jack read a story titled, "To Heaven Standing Up." The title flashed through his mind as he stood patiently waiting for the elevator behind the Colossus of Rhodes in the hotel atrium. Unless he was mistaken, he was heading for Paradise, straight down.

His party consisted of six other guests, all men, and their female tour guide. An attractive dark-eyed young lady, she wore a no-nonsense skirt that descended to her ankles and bright blue blazer with the resort's name on the pocket. That she was of supernatural origin did not surprise Jack in the least. He suspected the secrets of Paradise were not for mere mortals. Stationed by the lift door, the woman checked off each visitor's name as they arrived against a master list. None of the men seemed anxious to talk, and they waited patiently in complete silence.

Curiously, Jack studied his fellow travelers. He estimated they ranged in age from his own mid-twenties to well over sixty. Nothing about them struck him as particularly exceptional. Tall and short, fat and thin, bearded and clean shaven, they shared nothing in common other than an expensive taste in clothing. None of these men were middle-class tourists. Evidently, only high rollers received invitations to Paradise.

At five minutes to twelve, their guide pressed the call button for the elevator. When it arrived, she ushered them inside. Lining the walls of the spacious interior of the car were fifteen seats, similar to those found in upscale movie theaters. As soon as they were all seated, the door to the outside world slid closed.

"Please make yourself comfortable," the woman said in a voice that tinkled like fairy bells. As she spoke, a gentle gust of cold air, with a bare hint of orange blossoms, announced the presence of an unseen air-conditioning unit in the car's ceiling. At the same time, the lights dimmed to a gentle, golden glow. "My name is Sharon. I'll be your hostess on this marvelous journey to a point beyond harsh reality, a place that heretofore existed only in your wildest dreams."

She chuckled, a deep, throaty, sexy sound, at odds with her austere, businesslike appearance. As if in response to that thought, Sharon removed her jacket and casually let it fall to the floor. Beneath it, she wore a wispy top made of a transparent gauze that left nothing to the imagination. Her firm, melon-shaped breasts, capped with large red nipples, were unencumbered by a bra. For an instant, seven men stopped breathing.

"That feels better," said Sharon. She stretched her arms over her head, shifting Jack's heartbeat into overdrive. "Paradise delivers physical substance to your most intense erotic fantasies. No matter what you imagine, it can happen here. That is more than a slogan. It is a promise."

"It sounds like a canned advertisement for a theme park aimed at oversexed adults," said Hugo, its beak in Jack's right ear.

"Notice that it's aimed only at men," said Mongo in Jack's left ear. "In early Muslim doctrine, only men are eligible for admission to Paradise. Obviously, Hasan is a believer in the old-time religion."

The ravens' caustic remarks jolted Jack back to reality. The birds were right. Sharon's byplay, though remarkably sensual and visually stimulating, appeared rehearsed. She acted as if she were carefully following a well-plotted script. Which did not prevent Jack's breath from catching in his throat when she unbuckled the belt to her long skirt and slid the garment down to her feet. With a kick, the skirt joined her blazer.

Her baggy pantaloons were as transparent as the thoughts of every man in the elevator. Smiling seductively, Sharon twirled around on her toes like a ballet dancer, proudly revealing every inch of her incredible body. "In Paradise," she intoned, as if praying, "sexual diseases are nonexistent. As is conventional morality. Every woman matches my beauty. And their only aspiration, like mine, is to fulfill your every desire."

Jack brushed the sweat off his temple. There was no mistaking the genuine lust in the supernatural's voice. While he felt sure Sharon conformed to a scripted dialogue, the emphasis she put into the words made it quite clear she meant exactly what she stated.

"There are no rules in Paradise," said the woman, gathering her outer garments together and dropping them on a nearby chair. "The houris truly want to satisfy your wildest cravings. You need merely ask to make your most secret fantasy come to pass. The word shame means nothing to us. We welcome variety. If your dreams require two women, three women, or even five or six, speak and it shall be done. Nothing is forbidden. Remember, though, you have only three hours of pleasure. Make the most of your visit."

Jack blinked. His eyelids drooped. Despite his physically aroused state, he felt drowsy. Near him, several men yawned. "Sleep gas in the air," said Hugo. "It doesn't affect us but you're about to visit dreamland, Johnnie."

"Rest now," said Sharon. Her voice came from a million miles away. "When you awaken, you will be strangers in Paradise."

24

The sound of a woman giggling woke Jack. Eyes still closed, he inhaled deeply. The air smelled like perfume. Something soft and delicate tickled the bottom of his feet. Another woman giggled. Contentedly, Jack stretched his arms lazily over his chest. Then, with a start, realized where he was.

Eyes open, he scrambled into a sitting position. He was resting on a huge stack of pillows on the floor of a gilt-decorated chamber. He still wore the same clothes as when he had entered the elevator, except for one thing. His shoes and socks were missing. Two stunning young ladies, supernatural in origin and dressed in the same transparent outfit worn by Sharon, had been caressing his soles with long ostrich feathers.

"Welcome, master," said one of the women, her hair and eyes jet black. "You may call me Alis." She pointed to her companion, a redhead with green eyes. "My friend is Candi. We are here to serve you. In all ways."

Jack gulped. The two girls possessed incredibly lush bodies shamelessly revealed by their thin gauze clothing. Concentrating in Paradise was going to take vast amounts of willpower.

"Hugo, Mongo," he whispered, hoping the two ravens were close at hand. He could use a dose of the blackbirds' sarcasm. Perhaps even a peck or two on his ears. But they didn't answer.

"No, silly," said Candi, scrambling over to Jack's side. Pressing herself against his shoulders, she began unbuttoning his shirt. "Candi and Alis."

"Stop that," he commanded hastily, trying to ignore the heat of the girl's barely clad body. Alis, reaching for his belt buckle, paused and pouted. Then she smiled wickedly.

"The master prefers to remain dressed while we engage in delightful acts?" she asked. She wiggled, setting alarm bells ringing inside Jack's head. "That would be a novelty."

"Wait a minute," said Jack, closing his eyes to avoid distractions. He raised one hand and pointed in a direction past his toes. "Go sit over there. Both of you. Right now. Then we'll talk."

"Talk?" questioned Candi, a few seconds later. While their near nude figures still had Jack sweating, he could at least keep his eyes open while he spoke. "We displease the master?"

"There are fleshier women for those who prefer their houris with more substance," said Alis. "We can summon them if the master is unhappy with us."

"Please be quiet," said Jack. He wished he knew what had happened to the ravens. Finding Megan without them would be impossible. Especially if Paradise consisted primarily of rooms like this one, and was populated with women like his two companions. Even his encounter weeks ago with the mall nymphs had not prepared him for the houris. He had never met women so willing to satisfy his every command.

That thought broke the numbness gripping his mind. He was letting his emotions override his intellect. The solution to his problems sat a few feet away. He merely had to switch directions.

"You're here to please me?" he asked.

"Yes, master," answered both girls happily, rising to their feet. "Any way you desire."

"Then sit down," said Jack, rubbing his eyes to erase his latest vision. "I want to ask you some questions. Understand? Questions. And I desire for you to provide me with, to the best of your knowledge, complete, truthful replies."

"Questions?" said Alis, wrinkling her nose. "The master prefers to talk about sex rather than engage in it. I've heard of this new style of oral sex but never engaged in it before."

"Oh, give me a break," said Jack, his temper flaring. "I'm not interested in any kind of sex at the moment. I require information and you two sexpots are going to provide it."

"Whatever turns you on," said Candi, with a shrug of her beautiful shoulders. Gone was the humble servant motif. "But you're passing up a once-in-a-lifetime opportunity. I'm really special."

"I don't doubt it," said Jack, frowning. The houri's statements triggered a long-forgotten memory. He stared at the girl closer. "Didn't you say those exact words in an X-rated film, *Bimbo Sluts from Los Angeles*?"

"Yes," said Candi excitedly. "You saw it? I made my screen debut in that movie."

"They showed it at a bachelor party I attended," said Jack. "Everyone there commented on your acting abilities." He saw no reason to mention the remarks focused primarily on Candi's lack of any such talents. The attendees had agreed she exhibited a greater command of body language than the spoken word. Jack groped for an appropriate compliment. "You showed lots of enthusiasm."

"Thanks," said Candi. Jumping to her feet, she tugged off her top and pantaloons. Totally naked, she bent over and grabbed her ankles with her hands, her buttocks thrust in Jack's direction. "This pose look familiar?" she asked, cheerfully. "I'm thrilled you recognize my features. I've starred in seventeen other films. But in most of them my face isn't on the screen."

"Please take your seat," whispered Jack, squeezing his eyes tightly closed. Watching a porno flick rarely turned him on. Being in the same room with one of the stars ready, willing, and able was another story. "Immediately."

"Your wish is my command," said Candi, dropping to the floor. "But I promise, you'll regret wasting the opportunity."

"Hey," said Alis, "cut the commercial. I'm no slouch, either." She winked at Jack. "On my day off, I work as a private dancer for hotel guests. I'm sure you've noticed the ads in the phone book and in the newspapers."

Leering, she folded her arms beneath her chest and squeezed her breasts tightly together. "Strangely enough, my legs rarely bother me. But my back aches terribly."

Jack swallowed a deep breath. While prostitution was legal in several Nevada counties, it was against the law in Las Vegas. However, business travelers and gamblers expected to find sex for sale in the city. Resourceful hookers managed to subvert city ordinances by advertising themselves as "private nude dancers for hire." No mention was made of any extra services they might provide for customers. A large section of the telephone directory featured hundreds of such services and there were even free advertising newspapers distributed on street corners with phone numbers and provocative nude photos of the "entertainers" included.

"Then you're not full-time inhabitants of Paradise?" asked Jack, trying to regain his equilibrium. "I assumed the houris never left this place."

"Are you kidding?" said Candi. "It's actually kinda dull down here. Only two types of men visit us. There's the high rollers the boss wants to entertain so they'll keep coming back to the casino and drop more money. They're okay, though most of them have bigger dreams than they can handle, if you get my meaning."

Jack nodded. Most males fantasized of being surrounded by a bevy of breathtaking, eager women. But dealing with the actual situation was another matter entirely.

"The second bunch come late at night," continued Candi. "They're the idiots who sincerely believe this hideaway is Paradise. As you can imagine, brains aren't their strong suit. They arrive doped up to the eyeballs, so keeping them entertained isn't difficult. Most of them pass out long before time's up."

"I prefer your crowd, handsome," said Alis, licking her upper lip with her tongue. "While fraternizing with clients on our off days is strictly forbidden, I've been known to make exceptions."

Jack shook his head. "Sorry, but I don't think my fiancée would approve."

Alis smiled seductively. "What she doesn't know won't hurt her. Besides, you might learn a few new tricks."

"Wow!" said a familiar voice in Jack's right ear. "That's some hot potato."

"Hugo," said Jack, sighing with relief. "Where the hell have you been?"

"Hell describes it, Johnnie," declared Mongo in his other ear. "Rescuing Megan is going to be a lot more difficult than you imagined."

"Hey," said Candi. "Are you talking to yourself?"

"Don't tell me he's nuts," said Alis. "I kinda liked the guy."

Weighing his options, Jack decided honesty was the best policy. If what Mongo said was true, he needed all the help he could muster. Snapping his fingers, he commanded, "Make yourself visible, boys."

The two ravens flickered into existence on Jack's shoulders. Hugo, with his flair for dramatics, flapped his wings and cawed. Mongo, more reserved, merely bowed his head once in greeting.

"How neat," said Candi, otherwise unperturbed.

"Cool," said Alis, equally undisturbed. Magical beings themselves, it took more than a pair of transparent ravens to shock them.

"Alis, Candi," said Jack, "meet Hugo and Mongo. The birds are my assistants. We're here to free my girlfriend, Megan, who's held prisoner down here."

"Pleased to meetcha, girls," said Hugo. Though it was physically impossible for a bird to leer, he leered. "I love your outfits. We spotted a bunch of your associates while flying through the walls, but we were in too much of a hurry to catch more than a quick glimpse of what they were doing. It's amazing the positions you humans are capable of assuming."

"Charmed," said Mongo, as Jack turned beet red.

"I'm a movie actress," declared Candi. "Maybe you've seen some of my films: *Hot and Ready, Twice Is Not Enough.* . . ."

"Sure," said Hugo. "I thought you looked familiar. When things get boring at home, Mongo and me fly over to the local X-rated theater for a few laughs." The bird cawed. "Now that you mention it, wasn't that Lola Landru in the garden five rooms from here? She was doing her special number on this one old guy. His face was so red I thought he'd pop his buttons."

"Lots of us houris moonlight as adult film stars," said Candi. "It's a quick way to make a few bucks."

"Hold on," said Jack, sensing that he was swiftly losing control of the conversation. "Let's start from the beginning. The very beginning.

"Obviously, none of the supernaturals here are really houris. By definition, they live in heaven and this place doesn't exactly fit that description. Who are you girls?"

"Well," answered Candi, "for a mortal you seem pretty well informed. There's nearly seventy of us working here for Mr. Hasan. We're wood nymphs, sea sprites, and assorted other classical beings with an appetite for uninhibited sex. Most of us drifted to Las Vegas because of its reputation as a wide-open city.

When Mr. Hasan opened this resort, he placed a coded advertisement in the newspaper, specifically looking for women like us."

"Sure," added Alis. "The pay's good, the hours aren't bad, and we get to indulge in our favorite pastime with a nice variety of partners. Mr. Hasan insists we pretend we're houris and this facility is Paradise, but the only ones fooled are the dimwits he sends here at night. The rest of our customers don't mind playing along with the gag. They're usually occupied with other matters."

"Where exactly are we?" asked Jack.

"One floor beneath the lower level of the resort," said Alis. "It was built the same time as the original hotel, supposedly as an underground storage area.

"The long elevator ride is a sham. Most of the time you're in the car is spent developing the proper mood. It only takes a few seconds to arrive at the gates of Paradise. The doors remain closed until your tour guide finishes her spiel and puts you to sleep. Then the visitors are delivered to chambers like this room throughout the complex. The sleeping gas wears off pretty quick and you awake in heaven. When three hours are up, we spray you with the same formula and you're returned to the surface. It's easy and effective."

"With so many supernaturals working here," said Jack, "I expect there are other passages to the surface than the elevator."

"Naturally," said Candi. "There's a number of stairways connected to the mausoleum level. That's how we enter and leave Paradise. The doors are marked No Admittance: Building Personnel Only." She giggled. "Of course, the doors require a key to use them. Otherwise, we'd be overrun with tourists looking for bathrooms."

"Incredible," said Jack, trying to digest everything he had heard. "Hasan's established this mini-Paradise beneath his own hotel for two purposes. During the day he entertains his wealthiest high rollers with a sexual fantasy playground catering to their wildest dreams."

"You'd be surprised at the number of repeat visitors," interrupted Candi. "We're a popular attraction."

"I'll bet," said Jack. "Then, late at night, he uses the same surroundings and nymphs to brainwash his recruits for the Assassins League. It's a slick operation."

"Cost effective, too," said Mongo. "I'm impressed. Al-Sabbah might be a bloodthirsty, inhuman fiend, but he's a good business-man."

"The dollars dropped by the millionaires anxious to visit this spot probably cover the overhead with money to spare," said Jack. "Which leads me to the question of the day. How much are you ladies paid for working here?"

"A thousand a week," said Candi. "With two weeks' paid vacation a year. We've got a contract. And a union."

"Besides," said Alis, "while the official Paradise guidelines forbid making outside contacts with our visitors, nobody enforces the rules. Lots of the girls moonlight on their days off." She smiled. "Some of us don't charge anything for fellows we really find fascinating. Guys like you, for instance."

"Watch it, sister," said Hugo, as Jack stammered an unintelli-gible answer. "He's taken. His girlfriend has a nasty temper. And her father's an awfully powerful wizard who does anything she asks."

"Just making casual conversation," said Alis, half turning her face so Hugo couldn't see, and winking at Jack. Though he remained true to his fiancée, his toes still curled.

Commanding his hormones to calm down, Jack asked, "How would you girls like to make twenty-five thousand helping me? It wouldn't require you to participate in anything dangerous. Merely open a few doors, provide a couple of costumes, things like that. No one would ever learn of your participation."

"Twenty-five grand," said Candi. "That's a half year's salary. I could finance my own movies with that bankroll."

"You sure we couldn't get in trouble with Mr. Hasan?" asked Alis. "I'd hate to lose this gig. And the boss didn't strike me as the sort of person who forgives and forgets."

"All I want to do," said Jack, "is rescue my girlfriend. Supply me with two costumes like the ones you're wearing and a key to the next floor and I'll be set. A female friend of mine can dress up in one of the outfits. She and I will sneak down here in the evening and recover Megan. Disguising her in the proper accoutrements, we'll escape before anyone notices she's missing."

"Uh, boss," said Hugo, "there's a major flaw in your maneu-vers."

"Which is?" asked Jack.

"Megan's being held a prisoner on an barren stone island at the center of Paradise," said Hugo. "The place is surrounded by a moat of burning lava. She's guarded there by an incredibly ugly creature. It has the head and breasts of a woman, the wings of a bird, the tail of a serpent, and the paws of a lion. It's not your usual run-of-the-mill warden, Johnnie. This creature means business."

"The monster was playing Trivial Pursuit with Megan," added Mongo. "The entire time we were there, it never missed a question. Not one."

"Now for the *really* bad news," said Hugo. "There's only one bridge across the river of fire. It's patrolled by a well-known beast from Cassandra's milieu. We recognized it right away. It looks hungry. Real hungry."

"A beast," repeated Jack, his spirits sinking faster than a punctured balloon. He had naturally presumed that Megan was guarded by the Old Man of the Mountain's Assassins. His background in game theory should have warned him not to make unwarranted assumptions. A monster and a legendary beast introduced unexpected variables into his rescue equation.

"It's a seven-foot-tall dog with three heads and the tail of a serpent," said Mongo. "I believe his name is Cerberus, Guardian of the Underworld."

"Hell," said Jack.

"Exactly," said Mongo.

$$\infty$$

25

"The creature in the middle of the lake of fire is the sphinx," said Alis a few minutes later. She dropped down next to Jack. He was sprawled across the cushions, lying on his chest with his hands folded behind his neck, trying to devise an alternative method for rescuing Megan. As he had told Merlin earlier in the day, without Megan free, he dared not risk confronting Hasan al-Sabbah and his genie. But rescuing his girlfriend was not going to be easy.

"I recognized the monster from Hugo's description," replied Jack. He was so disturbed that he didn't raise any objections when the nymph casually started to massage his back. "I thought the sphinx committed suicide when Oedipus answered its riddle."

"No such luck," said Alis, kneading the flesh beneath her fingers. Jack sighed as the tension drained out of his aching muscles. Megan, he decided after a moment's hesitation, wouldn't mind a perfectly innocent rubdown. Especially when it helped him focus his thoughts on their dilemma.

"The sphinx threw herself off her rock," said Alis, her breath hot against his neck. "But that didn't kill her. She was so upset that someone guessed the answer to her question that she went into seclusion. Remained there for centuries. If I looked like her, I'd wall myself up in a cave, too."

The nymph paused to tug his shirttails free of his pants. "Mind removing your top? I can't do this properly through the cloth. I promise to be good. Word of honor."

"Okay," said Jack, permitting the nymph to pull off his shirt. He resumed his position on the pillows, his hands tucked beneath his chin. Shutting his eyes, he tried to relax as Alis's warm hands expertly manipulated the sinews of his shoulders and upper arms. "Remember, keep it clean."

"I wouldn't think of trying anything bad," said Alis innocently. The tips of her fingers tiptoed gently along his spine. "Your skin is so nice and white. You can't imagine how tired I get of entertaining the bronzed Adonis types that frequent this resort."

"Mathematicians don't have a lot of free time for the beach or tanning salons," said Jack, defensively.

"Don't misunderstand me," said Alis, her hands toying with his belt. "I find intellectuals fascinating. They think of such inventive . . . ideas."

She rested her palms on his waist. "Any objections to removing your trousers? You're wearing shorts, so it's not sinful. I can sense there's a lot of tension built up in your calves."

"What about Hugo and Mongo?" asked Jack. "I wouldn't want them to get the wrong idea."

"Those two birdbrains went hunting for chocolate syrup with Candi," said Alis, her hands busy with Jack's pants. "We keep some in the other room for a few of our kinkier guests. I doubt if they'll return soon."

It took the nymph only a few seconds to strip Jack of his slacks. For some unknown reason, his lack of clothing didn't disturb him. Nor did he worry about the nymph keeping her promises, even though he knew such beings were notorious liars. Smiling happily, he luxuriated on the thick cushions. "The air in here smells terrific," he remarked, as Alis massaged his lower legs.

"It's scented," said the nymph. She scrambled around so that her head was facing his feet, putting her in a much better position to massage his calves. "They lace it with a subtle but amazingly powerful aphrodisiac. It works wonders."

"That's interesting," said Jack, dreamily. He hated admitting it, but Alis's silky caresses were getting him aroused. Very aroused. He smothered a yawn. Meanwhile, the peaceful surroundings were lulling him to sleep.

"Tell me more about the sphinx," he said, trying to steer the conversation toward his problems.

"I'm not positive when she finally emerged from hiding," said Alis, "but the old girl was singing a new song. Instead of asking questions, she was answering them. Evidently, she spent most of her years in solitude reading and memorizing facts. I guess she wanted to establish herself as some sort of oracle. But the ugly buzzard soon discovered that no one liked a know-it-all."

"I'm familiar with that phenomenon myself," said Jack, thinking of his friend Simon. He wondered what the changeling was doing lately. Hazily, he wondered what Alis was doing at that moment.

"What *are* you doing?" he asked, momentarily alarmed.

"The waistband of your shorts is stifling the natural flow of blood to your thighs," said Alis patiently, hooking her thumbs beneath his underwear. In one quick motion, she slid the garment off, leaving Jack completely naked. "Now, doesn't that feel lots better?"

"I guess so," he admitted, yawning again. His mind was filled with cobwebs and he was having difficulty thinking straight. He still felt quite aroused, though it no longer seemed very important. It obviously didn't bother Alis. "How did the sphinx end up working here?"

"She held a job in a Coney Island sideshow for years," said Alis, "running a memory scam. When Mr. Hasan opened this resort, he hired her as his special assistant. She oversees operations in Paradise from Hell. And she guards special prisoners when the necessity arises."

"Sort of a den mother and warden combined," said Jack. "Is she still obsessed with information?"

"You bet," said Alis, rising from the cushions. "Excuse me while I remove my own clothing."

"No problem," said Jack, completely at peace with the world.

"That damned sphinx brags constantly how nobody can ask her a question she can't answer," remarked Alis, wiggling out of her pantaloons. She dropped them in a heap on top of her jacket. "Talking with her is a real drag."

"If she comes from ancient Greece," said Jack, languidly, "and like all supernatural beings is true to her nature, she doesn't know lots of things. Facts aren't answers."

"Whatever," said Alis. "Enough discussion. I'm interested in intercourse of another nature."

Sensuously, the nymph straddled Jack's lower back, her naked thighs pressing against his. The entire weight of her extremely hot, extremely desirable body rested on his buttocks. Alis was right, he decided. No more verbalization. Fully relaxed, he inhaled deeply, filling his lungs with the marvelous air. Free of worry, his mind soared. Barely conscious, he floated in a state of absolute bliss.

"Roll over," murmured Alis, her voice fuzzy and indistinct. "Show me what a nice big boy you are."

The nymph was stronger than she looked. Moaning in anticipation, she wrenched Jack over onto his back. Eyes closed, he vaguely sensed her large breasts pressed against his chest. Her long, very sexy tongue licked his left earlobe. The heat from her body enveloped him completely.

"Now, we'll address a few of my questions," she chuckled. Her hands roamed freely across Jack's naked body. The nymph moaned in anticipation. "I think you'll answer them in fine fashion. Just leave me in complete control, lover, and relax. I'll do the asking from now on."

Dreamily, Jack released his last hold on reality. And drifted into fantasyland.

26

Two hours later, Jack sat on the bed in his suite, describing his visit to Paradise to Cassandra.

"Then, after the birds departed with Candi to hunt for chocolate, you interviewed Alis and learned what you could about the sphinx," said the Amazon.

"Right," said Jack. He saw no reason to mention his own vague recollections of that session or the following half hour entirely missing from his memory. He remembered questioning the nymph while she massaged his back, then waking up from a sound sleep right before it was time to depart. He was sure there had been some talk about removing his shirt, but he and Alis were both fully dressed when he awoke. Shrugging his shoulders in dismissal of the whole incident, he continued.

"We made a deal right before I was rendered unconscious by sleeping gas for the elevator ride upward. The two nymphs agreed to meet us at a door to Paradise at six tonight. That's when they get off work. Alis gave me her extra set of harem garb already. I concealed it under my shirt on the trip up. You can put it on before we leave. When we contact them later, she'll have another outfit for Megan—to wear as a disguise once we set her free. The girls will also provide us with a key for the doors. Fortunately, one passkey fits every lock in Paradise."

"Six P.M.," said Cassandra, glancing at the clock. It was nearly four. "That's going to be cutting it close. Which reminds me. There's a message on our telephone answering machine from our buddy, Hasan. It's about the auction tonight."

"I gather, then, the event's not canceled," said Jack, studying the complex phone system on the endtable. Like most modern hotels, their suite featured a message center for missed calls. The orange light signaling a recording was flashing orange. After carefully reading the small print several times, Jack finally discovered the correct button to push.

"Mr. Green." Heard over the telephone, Hasan's voice was definitely not human. "I regret to inform you of the untimely passing of Professor Karsnov. We found the body of our late guest in the rear chamber of the security floor. His remains were not a pretty sight and I thought it best to cremate them at once."

The blood drained from Jack's face. Incidents like this murder helped remind him that they were not engaged in a game. The principals engaged in this auction meant business. And their business was death and destruction.

"In any event, I call to assure you that the auction is still scheduled for tonight at ten o'clock. While the dear doctor is no longer with us, I was wise enough to keep a set of his notes on the virus in my personal safe. Along with those papers, I have a vial filled with a small sample of the actual plague virus. Together, the two items should fetch a tidy sum. Karsnov's execution is a minor inconvenience. Nothing more. I will see you tonight. Have a nice day."

Jack grimaced. "A minor inconvenience."

He stood up. "That package from Merlin arrive?"

"Right here," said Cassandra, patting a padded airline bag at her feet. "It came about an hour ago by special messenger. Merlin reeled in a few favors to get it here today." The Amazon lifted the bag to her lap. "I didn't look inside. It's not very heavy."

"It shouldn't be," said Jack, unzipping the bag. "Where are the ravens? I thought they'd be swarming over me to see what's inside."

"They left a short time ago," said the Amazon. "Hugo mentioned something about visiting some old friends that are in town for the weekend. It was while you were taking a shower. They didn't say when they would return, but I'm sure they'll be back in time for tonight's festivities."

"I'm not worried," said Jack. "They probably stopped off somewhere looking for chocolate bars." For some reason, the mention of chocolate brought a smile to his lips. He had no idea why.

Carefully, Jack removed a glass bottle from the travel bag. Less than a foot long, it was made of light blue glass that glistened in the artificial light. The neck of the container twisted at a very unusual angle. After staring at it for a few seconds, Cassandra shook her head and turned away.

"I can't look at that thing," she declared. "It gives me a headache."

"It should," said Jack, grinning. Gently, he lowered the vessel back into the bag. Though he had instructed Fritz to use the strongest glass possible, Jack was taking no chances. "This bottle combines mathematics and magic in a unique manner. I think King Solomon would have approved."

"That's for tonight," said Cassandra. "But what are we going to do about this afternoon? Notably, concerning the rescue of a young lady in distress. The sphinx is a deadly opponent. As is Cerberus. That trio of heads on him think independently, making him the equivalent of three enemies. Only Hercules ever defeated the hellhound. I'm afraid I'm not in his class."

"His heads act on their own," said Jack, his brow creased in thought. "Talk about a split personality. I think we should be able to exploit that disorder to our advantage."

He extracted a Coke from the refrigerator. Other than a minor, unexplainable ache in his hips, Jack felt terrific. It was amazing, he concluded, what a good nap accomplished.

"You have the card Big John left us?" he asked Cassandra, sipping his drink.

"It's here on the dresser," said the Amazon. "You want me to give him a call?"

"Right away," said Jack. "Keep your fingers crossed that he's free. We require someone familiar with Las Vegas to drive us to a big pet store. Our visit to Paradise necessitates the purchase of a few special items. And in the meantime I'm aiming to persuade him to assist us once we extricate Megan. We could use his help."

"He struck me as the type who doesn't like getting involved," said Cassandra as she dialed the chauffeur's answering service.

"His ingrained character, as defined by his song, forces him to assume that attitude," said Jack. "Basically, he's a good man. He won't refuse a lady in distress."

The relay service contacted Big John just as he was dropping off a passenger at the Empress Casino. "He's less than a mile from our hotel," said Cassandra, after a brief conversation. "I told him we'd meet him at the lobby door in fifteen minutes—if nobody gives me a hard time in the elevators."

Jack sighed. Most guests at the resort studiously ignored the Amazon's outrageous outfits. A few loudmouths spewed forth lewd remarks that, to Jack's immense relief, Cassandra shrugged off with a nasty laugh. However, one obnoxious drunk made the mistake of trying to fondle the Amazon while in the elevator returning from her morning exercise routine.

The unfortunate soul was resting peaceably in the Las Vegas hospital, nursing two handfuls of broken fingers, several bruised ribs, and a minor concussion. After examining the drunk's injuries, the police labeled the beating a professional job and concluded the man had been lucky to escape with his life. No one connected the thrashing with Mr. Green's beautiful companion, Ms. Saman'ta Jones.

At present, Cassandra wore a pair of white twill stretch cotton pants that laced up the sides of both legs from her ankles to her waist. Matching it was a white cotton Lycra top with molded cups that left most of her back, chest, and stomach bare. Few women possessed the figure and posture to do the outfit justice. Oddly enough, Cassandra Cole, Amazon warrior, was one of them. To Jack, it didn't make sense.

"I thought Amazons were repulsive," he remarked, writing a note for the ravens. He didn't want the birds worried if they returned to find nobody about. "Most mythology books describe them as hideous, scarred women with haglike features. In fact the only trait you share in common with the legends is your love of battle."

"You're confusing fantasy with reality, Jack," said the Amazon, laughing. "Maybe there were real Amazons once, as described in *The Iliad,* but I'm not them. Humanity's shared subconscious mind brought me to life. I'm the creation of many thousands of mortals' dreams. The real Amazons may have been gruesome crones, but not the imaginary species. Men fancied taming our cold, imperious loveliness. Women thought of us as the embodiment of female power. They wanted us strong but desirable. We were shaped by both sexes. My companions and I were always beautiful."

"That's why supernaturals talk so dramatically," said Jack, nodding in comprehension. "And act with such flair."

"Definitely," said Cassandra. "People dream in Technicolor, not in black and white. That's why the good guys are so good and the bad guys are so bad. We're created with panache. Hugo wasn't kidding when he quoted Shakespeare and Bogart, Jack. We *are* the stuff dreams are made of."

27

The elevator trip to the lobby of the hotel proved uneventful. However, as they were crossing the atrium, heading for the entrance, they were waylaid by Hasan al-Sabbah. The Old Man of the Mountain, the Afreet in attendance, was escorting a pair of visitors through the casino.

Both of the men wore light tan suits, brown shirts, bloodred ties, and dark sunglasses. One was tall and thin, the other short and broad. Each had swarthy skin and jet black hair. The short man had a mustache, while his companion was clean shaven. Hasan introduced them as Mr. Smith and Mr. Wesson.

"Pleased to meet you," said Jack, with a polite nod. He had no desire to shake hands with either man. These were without question the representatives of the Brotherhood of Holy Destruction. Jack did not think highly of terrorists.

Smith grunted in reply. Wesson didn't make a sound.

The Old Man of the Mountain shrugged as if in apology.

"Mr. Green represents one of my major backers. He is here to witness the auction tonight." Al-Sabbah waved a hand and smiled at Cassandra. "He is accompanied by the charming Ms. Saman'ta Jones."

Both terrorists turned and stared at Cassandra through dark

lenses. Smith grunted again. Wesson's face twisted in an expression of disgust.

"In my country, a woman wearing such an outfit would be flogged," he declared coldly. "Decadent, capitalist bitch."

"Depraved lackey of the sex-crazed bloated warlords of the Great Satan," added Smith.

"Gentlemen," said Hasan al-Sabbah, his white features ashen. Jack's relationship to Cassandra was unclear and the Old Man of the Mountain feared offending *The Man*'s emissary. Equally worrisome was the possibility that Cassandra herself might be a confidant of the diabolical vice lord. "Ms. Jones is my guest. Please apologize at once."

Wesson laughed harshly. "Never."

The Old Man of the Mountain frowned unhappily. He was caught in a vise. He dared not push Smith and Wesson too hard. He was relying on their participation at the evening's auction. Yet he was equally loath to allow them to insult agents of his major creditor. As if sensing al-Sabbah's dilemma, Cassandra resolved Hasan's predicament.

"You gentlemen represent the Brotherhood of Holy Destruction, I believe?" she asked rhetorically, her voice cool and calm. If anything, Cassandra sounded amused. "I pray, for your sake, that you come fully prepared to bid extravagantly for the prize offered tonight. Because I suspect you were instructed to return with the virus or not return at all. Groups like the Brotherhood do not tolerate excuses. Which would thus leave you at my tender mercies."

Finishing her short speech, Cassandra's hands flashed quicker than the eye could follow. Steel glistened then vanished. Smiling, the Amazon handed each man the remnants of his crimson tie, sliced off an inch below the knot. "An expert can prolong the death by a thousand cuts for weeks," she declared, the tone of her voice making it quite clear she was such an expert.

"Time for us to do some sight-seeing before dinner," said Jack, taking Cassandra by the elbow. "We don't want to be late for tonight's proceedings."

He nodded again at the Old Man of the Mountain and the two terrorists. Smith and Wesson stood frozen in place, their slashed ties dangling from petrified fingers. Jack couldn't resist a parting dig. "We're cutting it close already."

They struggled to maintain straight faces until they exited the casino. Once outside, spotting Big John's limo at the curb, Jack and Cassandra exploded with laughter. "You know how to cut off a conversation, Ms. Jones," Jack declared in mock serious tones. "Talk about castration nightmares."

"Do you think I wounded their pride?" asked Cassandra, her eyes glowing with a mixture of laughter and rage.

"You definitely cut them down to size," said Jack. "I bet they're fit to be tied."

"I don't mean to break up your party," said Big John, coming up behind them, "but your car is waiting, folks. Pet store closes at six sharp."

Still chuckling, they followed the giant chauffeur over to the limo. Politely, he opened the rear door of the automobile. As Cassandra slid inside, Big John whispered, "Didn't mean to rush you, but a couple of gents back there were giving you the eye. They didn't look like the friendly type."

"Where are they?" asked Jack once they were all in the car. The dark glass enabled them to look out without anyone looking in. "Can you point them out?"

"Sure," said Big John. "That's them over by the cab stand. The two huge albino dudes and the slick operator standing between them. I've seen some pretty bad operators in this burg, but that mean mother beats the rest six ways to Sunday."

"It's Loki," said Jack to Cassandra. "Along with your two friends, the frost giants."

"They're here for the auction," said Cassandra. "Hopefully, our disguises fooled them."

"Maybe, maybe not," said Jack. "I don't think it matters. Mom struck me as reading Loki right. He'll keep his mouth shut until there's a clear winner in the game. And with Karsnov dead, that could be anyone, including us."

"Karsnov?" said Big John. Once Jack identified their adversaries, the chauffeur had steered the limo out onto the road leading to downtown Las Vegas. "I heard that name today."

"You did?" said Jack. "When. And from whom?"

"Another big dude," said Big John. "Not the size of those white-haired wonders, but plenty large. Reminded me of one of those trained bears in the circus. Guy in his mid-fifties, he spoke English with a thick accent. He asked me if I ever heard of this scientist, Karsnov, and where he might be staying. When I told him I never heard of his buddy, he switched subjects and queried if there had been any unexplained deaths in town lately. When I mentioned the rash of pneumonia cases the past month, he got real excited. Cursed like a sailor in some foreign language."

"How did you know he was swearing if it was in another tongue?" interrupted Jack.

"Curses is curses," said Big John. "No hiding those words."

"The words are unimportant," said Cassandra. "What matters is where this new player in the game is staying."

"Why, at your hotel, of course," said Big John. "I dropped him off there a few hours ago. I heard him say to the doorman he had reservations for the night. His name's Bronsky, Boris Bronsky."

Jack digested the name in silence. He was certain the Old Man of the Mountain had not mentioned another bidder. Bronsky was an X factor.

"Was he mortal or supernatural?" asked Jack.

"Definitely mortal," said Big John. "You folks involved in some kind of secret mission or whatever?"

"Why do you ask?" replied Jack, winking at Cassandra.

"Oh, just curious," said the driver. "You got me wondering, with this talk of an auction and the like. Why are we heading for a pet store? You scheduled for a secret strategy conference with some spies there?"

"No such luck," said Jack. "I need a few treats for a special dog."

"It must be special if you're in such a hurry," said Big John. "You got this pet of yours up in your hotel room?"

"He's no pet," said Jack. "His name is Cerberus, the Hound of Hell."

"Cerberus?" said Big John. "Ain't he an aardvark?"

"You're thinking of the comic book character," replied Jack. "This monster lives beneath the Seven Wonders of the World Resort and is guarding my kidnapped girlfriend."

"Girlfriend?" Big John's shoulders hunched together and his voice dropped an octave. "Kidnapped. And you're planning to rescue her?"

"You got it," said Jack. "Tonight."

"Those three hoodlums at the hotel involved in the scam?" asked Big John.

"Definitely," said Jack. "It's too complicated to explain all the sordid details in a few minutes, but the gist of it is simple enough. There's a major auction of dangerous drugs taking place at the casino office tonight. Attending it are a number of major crime lords. My partner and I work for a secret agency trying to break up the operation. The bosses knew they couldn't buy me off, so they kidnapped my sweetheart. One move on my part and she's history."

"Our task force hijacked two high-level couriers to the meeting," said Cassandra, smoothly taking up the fable when Jack paused for a breath. "They disguised us to take the messengers' place. Thus far, we've avoided detection. Loki's the only member of the organization we've dealt with in person, and until this afternoon, we managed to stay clear of him and his goons."

"What's the sting?" asked Big John.

"We have to free Jack's girlfriend before the auction," said Cassandra. "Once she's safe, we're prepared to bust apart the entire organization."

"I'm in," said Big John, parking the limo in front of a huge pet supply warehouse. "The one thing I can't ignore is a woman in peril. If you want my help, you've got it."

"We want it," said Jack, grinning. "And I know exactly what I want you to do."

28

Persuading Big John to cooperate proved to be relatively easy. Convincing Cassandra to wear a houri's costume was not nearly as easy. The Amazon refused to don the transparent outfit.

"Why bother?" she asked angrily. The clock in their room read five thirty-five. They had less than a half hour till their scheduled meeting with Alis and Candi on the resort's lower level. Jack fretted they might not make the rendezvous on time. Or at all. Cassandra adamantly rejected his pleas that she change clothes. "You can see right through the material. It's degrading and sexist and totally unacceptable."

"It looks good on the nymphs in Paradise," said Hugo. The two ravens had been waiting for them when they returned from the pet store. Neither bird offered to explain his absence and Jack was too busy with other concerns to pry. "Those girls ain't afraid of displaying their charms."

"Bird," said Cassandra, an edge to her voice, "beware comparing me with those wantons. I am a true Amazon, not a common trollop. I do not take such insults lightly."

"Sorry," said Hugo. "I didn't mean no offense. It's just that there's a lot riding on your dressing the part."

"Honor," snapped Jack, the brief exchange between the Amazon and raven inspiring him. "On the blade of your knife, you pledged your sacred honor that this effort would succeed. Are you prepared to compromise the entire mission because of your modesty?"

The Amazon scowled. Jack breathed a sigh of relief. He recognized the signs. Cassandra was trapped by her own pledge. Honor was her life. She was bound by her word. Grabbing the outfit, Cassandra exited into the bedroom. "Watch your tongues," she warned before closing the door, "if you value your lives."

The arrived at the scheduled rendezvous point exactly at six. Taking a cue from Sharon, the elevator operator to Paradise, Cassandra wore one of her few respectable outfits, a slacks-and-coat combination, over her harem gear. Jack was casually dressed in a sport shirt and slacks. He carried a leather attaché case under one arm. The two ravens, silent and transparent, sat on his shoulders.

Turning the corner at the end of a corridor to the washrooms, they soon came upon a pitch black door engraved in red letters, Employees Only No Admittance. Softly, Jack knocked three times on the unyielding metal.

The door swung open immediately. Standing on a narrow landing fronting a long series of steps leading downward were Candi and Alis. The two nymphs were dressed in their street clothes. According to the information they had provided Jack, there was a locker room and changing area at the base of the stairs. That it was patrolled by three members of Hasan al-Sabbah's security force troubled Jack not in the least. In her present mood, Cassandra hungered for a melee.

The two houris' taste in clothes reflected their personalities. Both of them wore apparel that looked as if it had been painted on. Candi favored a knit red cotton tank dress that barely covered her breasts and thighs. Alis preferred black, sporting a shimmery leather skirt and bustier along with black seamed stockings.

"Welcome, pilgrims," giggled Candi, beckoning them inside. She closed the door, ensuring that they wouldn't be seen by any curious tourists. "Here's the key and the second set of clothes. No one's in the locker area and the guards are eating supper. We're the last girls to leave. The other shift arrived a half hour ago. No one's due till midnight. It's a quiet night in Paradise. Those invisible birds around to guide you to your lady love?"

"We sure are," said Hugo, his voice seemingly coming out of thin air. "Bring any chocolate with you, babe?"

"Not tonight, sweetie," said Candi. "Sorry."

Jack handed the nymph a white envelope. "The money's inside. Don't spend it all in one place."

"Retirement fund," said Candi. She opened the letter and divided the money into two equal shares. After giving Alis her half, Candi tucked the balance into her purse. "That's the only spot the police don't touch when they search me," she declared, laughing.

Alis winked at Jack, causing him to blush beet red. "This has to be the most I ever earned," said the dark-haired nymph, "not flat on my back."

"What should I do with the passkey?" asked Jack, anxious to change the subject. "Won't somebody miss it?"

Alis handed Jack a small white card. Printed on it were the words, *Alis in Wonderland, Private Dancing for Discriminating Gentlemen*, along with a phone number and a post office box. "Mail it back to me," said the nymph. "It's a spare but I might need it someday."

She licked her upper lip, a motion that inexplicably caused Jack to tremble. "Besides, who can tell what the future holds? Call me if you're in Vegas again. We can get together and have a drink. Maybe even discuss shared dreams."

"Uh, sure," said Jack, not certain what the nymph meant. Cassandra, busily removing her outer garments, chuckled at his obvious discomfort. He carefully stuck the card in his wallet. While he couldn't imagine ever contacting Alis again, these days anything was possible.

"Give us five minutes' head start before you descend into Paradise," said Candi. "I want to be well away from the hotel before the fireworks start."

"Don't worry," said Jack. "If my plan runs smoothly, nobody will realize Megan's gone for hours. By then, Hasan will have other difficulties on his mind."

"Time for us to go," said Candi, reaching for the door. "Good luck."

Catching Jack completely off guard, Alis twined an arm around his neck and kissed him gently on the lips. "Stay safe, lover," she whispered, then followed her companion out the exit.

"Sweet girl," said Mongo. "A truly caring individual."

"Yeah," said Hugo, "but take my advice, Johnnie. Mentioning her to Megan would be a big mistake."

Jack, still recovering, silently nodded his head in agreement.

29

"Tonight," declared the Crouching One, "the world is mine."

"Aren't you a tad premature in reaching that conclusion?" asked Roger. He peered over the top of the novel he was reading to stare at the pacing demigod. For the past two hours, the Lord of the Lions had done nothing but march to and fro in their suite, rubbing his hands together in anticipation of the night's events. His constant gloating was driving Roger crazy. "I recall you saying almost the exact same words the night of von Bern's aborted human sacrifices."

"A God learns from his mistakes," answered the Lord of the Lions. "Last month, that thrice-damned Logical Magician interfered with my schemes. I seriously underestimated Collins's abilities. However, al-Sabbah has successfully neutralized our worst enemy. Without him present, my plans should proceed like clockwork. There is nothing anyone can do to stop me."

Roger smothered a smile. The demigod was completely unaware of his own plans. Tonight, it was going to receive an unexpected jolt. As were Hasan al-Sabbah and any other supernatural beings present. Nor was Roger convinced that Jack Collins and his allies were not nearby. The mathematical magician had displayed an astonishing talent for turning up at the right place at the right time. As before, the Crouching One was underestimating Collins's abilities.

"What about the representatives from the Brotherhood of Holy Destruction?" he asked. "And Loki and his frost giants?"

"Annoyances, nothing more," said the Crouching One, dismissing his competition with a wave of a hand. Blue sparks flickered from his fingertips. "I have a score to settle with the Brotherhood. They rescued Karsnov using my information, but afterward they refused to deal directly with me. Instead, they went to the Old Man of the Mountain. Their mistake shall cost them dearly."

The demigod laughed, an unnerving sound. "As to Loki, I know him from olden days. He is still the same sniveling coward, hiding behind brainless henchmen. I have nothing but contempt for the Sly One. He is a worm. If he stumbles into my path, I will crush him beneath my heel."

Roger placed his book on an end table. Like most murder mysteries, he found it too contrived for his tastes. Normally, he read computer manuals for relaxation. But he had been unable to find one in the resort's newsstand.

"Hasan al-Sabbah won't be pleased if the auction flops," he remarked. "The Old Man of the Mountain is counting on generating a fortune to pay off his bet. I gather a representative of his major creditor flew in specifically to observe the proceedings."

"Then he wasted a trip," said the Crouching One. "The plague virus will be mine. At the price I set."

"Why do you want the stuff anyway?" asked Roger. It was rare that the demigod was this talkative. Inadvertently, it might reveal some important information. Roger understood the importance of taking advantage of the moment. "How can a plague virus reestablish your power?"

"The greatest power in the world, my befuddled human servant," said the Crouching One, "is fear. Though the last of my worshipers died thousands of years ago, the same terrors that frightened them continue to haunt mortals today. I ruled ancient Babylon as the God of Death and Destruction. Plague served as my loyal servant, chastising those who disobeyed my commands. A small amount of pain, properly applied, worked wonders. What I accomplished then I can do again, once I am equipped with the proper tools."

"But people won't worship a disease," protested Roger.

"No," said the Crouching One, "but they will bow down to the one who controls that disease. They will worship me or perish. Do not mistake cynicism for intelligence, sophistication for knowledge. Civilization is a thin shell, with barbarism lurking close beneath the surface. The wars raging right now in Africa and Eastern Europe demonstrate how easily mankind reverts to savagery."

The Lord of the Lions chuckled. "To use your own terminology, I am an expert at pushing the right buttons. Using the plague virus selectively, I will undermine the basic tenets of your society. Darkness will descend upon the Earth. And as darkness engulfs the world, I shall emerge once again as the supreme master of everlasting night. Nergal, Lord of Death, will reign supreme."

"Very dramatic," said Roger, shaken more than he cared to admit. "But it all hinges on you obtaining the anthrax germs."

Blue sparks crackled like fireworks over the Crouching One's forehead. "In a few hours, the Old Man of the Mountain will discover my will is not easily thwarted. He will deliver the plague virus to me, or suffer the consequences."

The demigod's fingers curled like claws. Sparks leapt from one digit to another. Remembering the deadly spots on his elbow, Roger shivered. He muttered a silent prayer to the printout in his pocket. If it didn't work tonight, he was doomed. And from the sound of the Crouching One's threats, the entire world was doomed with him.

30

Cassandra led the way descending the steps. Though the nymphs had assured them that the three security guards were occupied with their dinner, the Amazon didn't believe in taking unnecessary chances. "A true professional assumes nothing," she declared. "One man with heartburn, searching the locker room for antacid pills, could ruin our entire venture. With me in front, he'll never have a chance to alert the others."

Jack wasn't about to object. He fought to the best of his ability when necessary, but he was not in Cassandra's class. As the Logical Magician, he was content to play his role as the master planner. To him, being a hero meant using his brains. Conan the Conqueror had his place in the universe, but battling fiends in the neon jungle of Las Vegas was not it.

It was nearly a hundred steps to the bottom of the stairwell. Jack, walking a few steps behind the Amazon, kept his gaze fixed to Cassandra's neck. Early on, she had made it quite clear that if he looked anywhere else, he would be very, very sorry. Though temptation gnawed at him, Jack kept it at bay by concentrating on the vision of an angry Amazon handing him his eyeballs on a platter. It worked wonderfully well as a deterrent.

The locker room was empty. Lining the walls were nearly fifty brightly lighted dressing tables, like those used in nightclubs. Behind them were a series of a hundred metal lockers. One door led off to the powder room and shower. A second consisted of a steel frame and two pieces of frosted glass. Next to the door, engraved in the brick wall, were etched the words, Entrance to Paradise. Best Behavior, Please. The Customer Is Always Right. Especially Here.

"Evidently, not everyone agrees with the sentiments," whispered Cassandra, pointing to a line of graffiti scratched directly below the company motto. "The difference between heaven and hell is merely a matter of perspective."

"Beyond this portal," whispered Jack, "is the guard post. Once you've taken care of them, we're free to enter Paradise and find Megan. Can you handle it?"

Cassandra grinned. "Three humans against one Amazon? Those aren't odds, they're a sure thing. Give me two minutes. Since I'm not carrying any weapons, I want to be positive that none of them are—"

Without warning, the door to the inner chamber opened, cutting off Cassandra in midsentence. A big, husky figure, nearly seven feet tall and dressed in a black-and-gold uniform, stared at Cassandra in surprise. "What are you doing here?" he growled, in a deep bass voice. "You're twenty minutes late."

Then the giant's features knotted in bewilderment. "Wait a minute. Who the hell are you? We don't got no tall, dark houris working here." The guard's eyes widened in astonishment. "And who the hell is that guy? No humans are allowed in the locker area for any reason. That's against the rules."

"Rules are made to be broken, big boy," said Cassandra, and grabbed the guard by the collar of his shirt. In one smooth, continuous motion, she jerked him forward and dropped her body to the floor. Her feet lanced up, caught the shocked sentry in the chest. Shrieking in disbelief, he flew over Cassandra's head and crashed into the metal lockers behind them.

"Take care of him," she said over her shoulder as she darted into the next room. "I've got to stop the other two before they set off the alarm."

Jack whirled. Amazingly, the guard was climbing to his feet, shaking his head more in surprise than in pain. Obviously, Hasan al-Sabbah stationed his most dependable servants at the entrance to Paradise. Grimly, Jack noted the giant had no aura. He was supernatural in origin.

"What the heck is he?" he muttered to himself, forgetting the two invisible ravens sitting on his shoulders.

"A ghul," said Mongo, calmly. "We've encountered several of their kind during our wanderings. Powerful brutes, they eat human flesh. They have incredibly alert senses that enable them to hunt unwary travelers in the desert."

"Spare me the lecture," said Jack, backing up to the wall. The ghul was looking straight at him, its eyes the color of glowing coals. The monster grinned in anticipation, displaying a mouthful of yellow fangs. A dribble of saliva ran down its jaw as it took a giant step forward.

"You birds remember any special weakness I can use against this monster?" Jack asked queasily.

"Sorry," said Mongo, "not a thing. They're tough, really tough."

"You want us to slow him down a mite?" asked Hugo. "We could try the old double-beak-in-the-ears routine."

"Do it," said Jack, sliding along the wall as the ghul advanced another step. "Hurry."

"Men can't come in the locker room," said the ghul, spreading open his huge arms. "The boss would be angry with us if he learned you was here. But he's never gonna ever find out. 'Cause there won't be any evidence left."

There was no mistaking what the ghul meant. Anxiously, Jack circled a nearby dressing booth. His gaze swept the counter, hunting for a weapon. Unfortunately, there wasn't even a nail file present. The only things on the table were a half dozen atomizers filled with perfume and a powder puff.

Desperately, Jack pushed a chair into the ghul's path. Laughing, the giant kicked it aside. "You can't get away from me," the monster declared. "I can smell you a mile away."

"I bet you can," replied Jack, inspiration striking. As did the two ravens.

The ghul shrieked and slammed his hands to his ears. "That hurt!" he bellowed. Swinging his head to and fro, he hunted wildly for his invisible assailants. "That hurt my ears bad."

"See if you like this any better," said Jack, pushing an atomizer as close to the giant's nose as he dared and spraying. Suddenly, the locker room smelled like roses. Bushels and bushels of roses. It was an extremely potent perfume.

The ghul sneezed explosively. Once, then again, and again. Jack grabbed another atomizer. "Didn't care for that fragrance?" he asked mockingly, squeezing the trigger. A overwhelming mix of orange blossoms and hyacinths filled the air. He grabbed a third, then a fourth, and a fifth. "How about this? Or this? Or this?"

Eyes tearing, hands waving about frantically, the ghul stumbled into the metal lockers. Its head rocked back and forth with one gigantic sneeze after another. Jack continued to empty atomizer after atomizer at the fiend. Its painful howls mixed with sneezes as it sank to the floor, trying to escape the overwhelming mixture of perfume.

"There's a hot plate on the third table that should perform wonders," said Mongo in Jack's ear. "Try knocking him on the head a few times with it."

Jack didn't need to be told twice. It required eight smashes to the ghul's skull before the creature finally collapsed unconscious. Panting, Jack dropped the metal appliance to the floor. "Thank God," he declared. "My arms were tiring out."

"Smart idea, realizing the ghul's overdeveloped sense of smell would make him vulnerable to perfume," said Mongo. "That was quick thinking."

"Thanks," said Jack. "Anybody check on Cassandra?"

"Did I hear my name mentioned?" asked the Amazon from the doorway. She caught a glimpse of the motionless ghul spread-eagled on the floor. "Sorry I left that one for you, but the other two proved to be more difficult than I expected. Ghuls are rough customers. Looks like you managed fine on your own. I told you that training in unarmed combat would pay off."

The Amazon's nose wrinkled, noticing for the first time the overwhelming smell of perfume. "What happened? Did he overturn one of the tables when he fell?"

"Not exactly," said Jack. "I'll explain some other time." He shook his head, dismayed with his carelessness. "Remind me next time I make a deal with nymphs to press them a little harder for pertinent details. Alis never mentioned ghuls in her description of the guard post. She probably didn't think it mattered."

Bending over, he rolled the motionless giant onto its stomach. "This goon should be out for hours, but let's tie him up to be on the safe side." He glanced at his watch. "Then off to rescue Megan. We're running out of time."

∞

31

Jack's scheme called for him to use the uniform of one of the security guards as a disguise. The notion made perfect sense until their actual run-in with the security force. Jack had never thought to explain his full plan to Alis and Candi. He now realized that had been a major mistake.

Cassandra, walking casually beside him, her arm linked with his, stifled a giggle as he tripped over his pants for the third time. All three of the ghuls had been giants. Their pants rolled down past Jack's shoes while their jackets stretched to his knees. In a hurry, without any sort of sewing equipment, he managed the best he could, rolling up and tucking in. But he couldn't walk more than a dozen steps without one garment or another betraying him.

His companions found his predicament endlessly amusing. Cassandra, forced to endure the entire weekend in garments she found degrading, took particular pleasure in gently mocking Jack's efforts. Gritting his teeth, he stumbled along, trying not to attract attention.

Fortunately, that didn't prove to be very difficult. Invisible on his shoulders, the ravens provided directions through the maze of linked chambers that led to the solitary bridge across the moat of fire. Approximately half of the rooms were occupied by two or more nymphs. None of them expressed the least interest in Jack or Cassandra.

Keeping his mind on his destination was the hard part. In keeping with the traditional trappings of Paradise, modern means of entertainment such as TVs, radios, or CD players were not allowed. Instead, the women in the chambers were forced to amuse themselves in other fashions. A few played chess or checkers. Most of the rest indulged in procedures that had Jack gasping for breath and averting his eyes. There was only so much a man could bear to watch.

"Are we almost there?" Jack muttered after staggering through a chamber occupied with six nymphs engaged in a complex act he would have sworn impossible to accomplish. He wiped the sweat off his forehead. "Otherwise, I might have to put on a blindfold."

"Two more rooms," answered Mongo. "Do you find the sexual practices of the female of your species disturbing? Strange. Hugo and I consider their actions extremely fascinating."

"We view them from different perspectives," said Jack. "Take my word for it."

"If you insist," said Mongo. "Birds don't engage in orgies. I think that is why we find them so intriguing."

"Just find the damned moat," said Jack. "And cut the chatter."

"I was merely trying to keep you from getting nervous," said Mongo, sounding miffed. "The entrance is through that portal."

"Thank the Lord," Jack said, and pulled open the door. And found himself staring at a vision of hell.

The center of Paradise consisted of a crater eighty feet in diameter. It was circled completely by a narrow rock rim four feet in diameter. Unlike the rooms surrounding it, the crater was not covered by a roof. Instead, the stone ceiling of the cavern was visible thirty-five feet from the floor. The walls of the chambers stretched half that distance, forming a natural amphitheater. The only break in the brick surface was the door from which they had emerged.

A sea of fiery lava bubbled and fizzed fifteen feet below the crater's rim. Jack gasped for air. The ravens hadn't exaggerated when they described the place. It was hot as Hades in the crater.

Directly in the middle of the molten rock was a circular finger of stone twenty feet across. Sitting on it was a small cinder-block cottage. "That's where the sphinx is holding Megan prisoner," said

Mongo unnecessarily. "Which is your second obstacle. The first one is sitting on the bridge over there."

"Over there" was thirty feet around the rim of the crater. A white marble bridge, ten feet wide, extended from the edge of the pit to the island at its center. Chained to the foot of the span by two massive chains waited Cerberus, the three-headed guardian of the gate.

"You birds positive you know exactly what to do?" asked Jack. "One mistake and Cassandra and I are dog chow."

"I'm set, Johnnie," said Mongo.

"Me too," answered Hugo. "Let's do it."

Drawing in a deep breath, Jack started walking toward the immense hound. All three heads growling faintly, the huge beast rose to its feet. Adamite steel links rustled with its every movement. Six saucer-size eyes glared at them as they approached. Jack, never a dog person, forced one foot after another. He felt as if he were walking right into the mouth of Hell. The three mouths of Hell, to be exact.

"He won't hinder our passage across the bridge," said Cassandra. "The hound is trained to let people enter the infernal regions. Coming back is when we'll experience problems. Crossing should be a snap."

"I know that," said Jack. "You know that. I'm praying that the big, nasty dog knows it."

Step by step, they advanced until they stood directly in front of the beast. While it glared ferociously at them, the monster otherwise made no move to halt their progress.

"Get out of my way, hound," commanded Jack, trying to keep his voice from trembling. Dogs sensed your fear and reacted to it, he recalled someone once telling him. Act unafraid and they would step out of your path. "We want to cross the bridge."

Snarling in triplicate, the three-headed monster shifted position to let them pass. Gaze fastened on the cottage that was their final destination, Jack slid by the hound. It wasn't just the heat rising from the pit making him sweat. The bridge was littered with smashed and broken bones. Human bones. According to Alis, the Old Man of the Mountain disciplined unruly followers by leaving them in Hell for a few days. Evidently, more than a few had unsuccessfully tried to escape.

Fifteen feet beyond the beast, Jack started breathing again. They had gotten past the first obstacle. The sphinx was next. Mentally,

Jack reviewed his trivia question. Though it had been years since he taught elementary calculus, he nevertheless remembered Zeno's paradox perfectly. Some problems were too good to forget.

The door to the building stood wide open. As they drew closer, two figures emerged. Jack's heart leapt for joy when he spotted Megan. His girlfriend was still dressed in her red silk nightgown. She looked a bit frazzled but otherwise unharmed. Unfortunately, she was not alone. Standing next to her, watching them with suspicious eyes, was the sphinx.

If Cerberus was a zoologist's bad dream, then the sphinx was his worst nightmare. The monster combined body parts of human, lion, reptile, and bird into a bizarre living jigsaw puzzle. Though it possessed the head of a beautiful woman, Jack noted that when the sphinx opened its mouth to speak, it had the teeth of a lion. They worked better, he concluded grimly, when it devoured its victims.

"Who are you and what do you want?" asked the sphinx. It spoke with a woman's voice, but there were hints of a reptile's hiss, a bird's trill, and a lion's roar in its tone. "I expected no one for another day."

"Plans have changed," announced Jack. Megan, watching without much interest, stiffened in shock. She hadn't recognized Jack or Cassandra, with their disguised features and unusual outfits, until she heard her fiancé's voice. Her smile of relief vanished almost instantly as she looked at the sphinx, then at Jack, then again to the monster. She obviously realized that Jack had come to rescue her but had no idea how. She was about to find out.

"I heard of no change," said the sphinx, staring at Jack and Cassandra with undisguised hostility. "Hasan always telephones me if there is a change."

"Telephones you," repeated Jack, his mind racing for a reply. "Well, the phone company is working on the lines today. The Old Man of the Mountain sent me here to get the girl. He wants her right away."

"Nonsense," said the sphinx. "She stays. . . ."

"I've heard that you brag that you know the answer to nearly every question in the world," interrupted Jack hurriedly. "I find that difficult to believe."

"You do?" said the sphinx, unfurling its wings. There was a nasty edge to its voice. "Why is that, human?"

"Because my friend Zeno has been hunting the solution to his riddle for years and hasn't been able to find it. And he's remarkably intelligent."

"Zeno?" growled the sphinx. "A common Greek name associated with several ancient philosophers. Tell me this conundrum, mortal, and it better be an interesting one. I don't take kindly to being insulted. Brag, indeed."

The sphinx's display of teeth made it quite clear what she did to those who disappointed her. Jack hardly noticed. He had hooked his fish. Now it was time to reel her in. It had taken mathematicians over two thousand years to resolve Zeno's paradox. He doubted that the sphinx could solve it in less time.

"I'll state the question in simple terms," said Jack. "Achilles and a tortoise decided to have a race. The famous hero, feeling sorry for his slow-moving opponent, decides to be fair and gives the turtle a head start. But according to my friend, Zeno, this simple act of charity leads to the conclusion that no matter how fast Achilles runs, he is unable to pass the tortoise."

"Are you sure this question has an answer?" asked the sphinx warily. "It isn't one of those stupid riddles about barbers and shaving?"

"Let the Kindly Ones tear the flesh from my bones if I lie," declared Jack solemnly. Cassandra had suggested the oath, one not given lightly, in view of recent happenings at the resort. "This question is asked and answered in high schools throughout the United States."

"Continue," said the sphinx. "I've read plenty about the state of education in this country." The monster contemplated the claws in one gigantic paw. "If your wretched students can unravel this riddle, then so can I. Ask and I will answer."

"Since Achilles gives the turtle a head start," continued Jack, "he first has to reach the point where the turtle starts, which we will name A1. However, during this time, the tortoise has advanced further, to point A2. Thus, Achilles must cover the distance from A1 to A2. But, while he does that, the turtle continues on to point A3. Each time Achilles crosses the distance to the next point, the turtle has inched on to yet a further point."

The sphinx frowned. "But Achilles must pass the turtle sooner or later."

"Must he?" asked Jack. "To pass the turtle, Achilles must complete an infinite number of acts in a finite amount of time. Since traversing each distance takes some time, traveling an infinity of them will take an infinite amount of time. Thus, while Achilles draws nearer and nearer to the tortoise, he never overtakes him." He spread his arms in bewilderment. "How can such things be?"

The sphinx scratched its head. The expression on its face was indescribable, though Jack had seen it many times before on the faces of his students. The monster was lost in a mathematical wilderness. "I need a moment or two to think things through. Give me a second."

"Why not," said Jack. "Take your time. Maybe draw a diagram. That might help."

"Good idea," said the sphinx. Claws sharper than steel scratched a line into stone. Eyes narrowing to points, the monster stared at the picture as if confronting an enemy.

"If Achilles starts here," the sphinx muttered, marking off one point, "and the turtle starts here . . ."

Cautiously, Jack stepped a foot closer to Megan. The sphinx didn't notice. It appeared mesmerized by its drawing. Jack tiptoed closer, at the same time beckoning to his sweetheart to circle the monster. A few seconds later, their hands closed in a brief embrace.

"While Achilles moves from A10 to A11," declared the sphinx, shaking its head in annoyance but otherwise remaining captivated by the diagram, "the turtle advances from A11 to A12. The distance between them continues to shrink, but it nonetheless remains." The monster snorted in disgust. "When he moves to A12, the turtle is at A13. . . ."

The sphinx never saw them leave. If it was like most of the fanatic Trivial Pursuit players of Jack's acquaintance, nothing short of the island sinking into the lava would tear it away from the enigma. The sphinx was trapped by a paradox that had confounded philosophers and mathematicians for twenty centuries.

"What would you have done if the beast knew calculus?" Megan whispered in one ear, kissing him delightfully as she did so. Among her many charms, his fiancée was an accomplished mathematician. "Or studied the theory of limits?"

"I held Cantor's theorem proving that the infinity of the irrational numbers is larger than the infinity of the integers in reserve," replied Jack, grinning. "I came well prepared."

"I hope so," said Megan, shuddering. "Because Cerberus looks hungry. And he's not interested in trivia."

They had advanced halfway across the marble bridge. Only a few yards separated them from the three-headed dog. This time, it did not step aside to let them pass. As Cassandra had remarked, Cerberus was trained to admit people into hell. It did not allow them to leave.

Jack crossed his fingers and reached into the small bag he carried beneath his shirt. His hand emerged with a fistful of dog biscuits. "Be ready to run," he advised Megan as he raised his arm.

"You don't really think that monster will be distracted by dog food?" she replied anxiously.

"Not in the least," said Jack, flinging the biscuits forward. They landed at the monster's feet. Sniffing, one of the hound's three heads bent over to examine the food. "That's just the signal."

"Signal for what?" asked Megan.

Cerberus howled. Two of its heads jerked upward into the air, snapping at things not visible to the naked eye. The third head, caught unawares, was pulled along. The path to the outer rim was momentarily clear.

"For that," shouted Jack. Grabbing Megan by the hand, he hurtled past the baying hound. Cassandra followed close behind. They were on the ledge, nearly at the door, before Cerberus ever noticed they were gone. A few seconds later, the trio crowded into the empty chamber on the other side of the portal.

"Neat trick," said Megan, hugging Jack passionately. Cassandra tactfully stared in the other direction. "How did you manage it?"

"Not me," said Jack, disentangling his girlfriend's arms from around his waist. Kissing Megan was one of life's great pleasures, but they were running on a tight schedule. "The birds did it."

"The ravens?" said Megan.

"Yeah, the ravens, sweetie," said Hugo, flashing visible for an instant as it landed on Jack's right shoulder. In one claw, the blackbird held a slender piece of metal. Cawing, the bird waved the instrument about. "Us and these marvelous things called high-frequency dog whistles."

"It occurred to me," said Jack, "that three heads on one body presented a major dilemma in mental mechanics. Coordinating movement among a trio of separate entities is difficult enough under ordinary circumstances, much less when they're linked together by muscle and bone. I merely overloaded Cerberus's capacity for synchronized action."

Jack patted Hugo on the head fondly. "Hugo and Mongo flew

around two of the hound's heads blowing their ultrasonic whistles. You saw Cerberus's reaction to the racket. The shrill noise drove the dog crazy. It had to attack the cause. But, the hound couldn't physically direct three entirely distinct motions at once. As we were the least painful distraction, the monster ignored us and concentrated on the birds."

"My Logical Magician," declared Megan cheerfully. "I knew you would rescue me. I never gave up hope, even after losing thirty-one games in a row of Trivial Pursuit. What's next on the agenda?"

"First," said Jack, "you have to take off that nightgown . . ."

"Jack," giggled Megan, "don't you think we should wait till we have more time?"

". . . and put on this costume I brought with me," Jack concluded, his face red as Megan's lingerie. His girlfriend wasn't as raunchy as the nymphs in Paradise, but she tried. "Dressed like a houri, you'll blend in with the rest of the girls as we make our escape."

"Prepare yourself to be exposed to scenes of utter depravity," warned Cassandra as Megan, not the least bit self-conscious, stripped off her nightgown and pulled on the transparent harem garments. Jack, gentleman at heart, turned his head while she changed. Though afterward, seeing Megan's stunning figure totally revealed in the wispy material, he wondered why he bothered.

"I'm a big girl," Megan declared. "Living most of my life in the big city, I doubt if anything can shock me."

The two ravens clearly took Megan's statement as a challenge. They steered Jack and his two female companions on a completely different path to the locker room. On this trip, none of the rooms were empty. And each chamber provided a scene more scandalous than the one preceding it.

After a few minutes, Jack mentally dubbed their route the "orgy circuit." Chess and checkers were nowhere to be seen. Instead, the nymphs were engaged in much more stimulating games. Their behavior added new meaning to the word *outrageous*. Jack concentrated as best as humanly possible on searching each room they entered for the door. He preferred retaining a few private sexual fantasies, and the nymphs' conduct left absolutely nothing to the imagination.

Fortunately, Jack's uniform gained them clear passage through the byways of Paradise. Most of the nymphs ignored them completely. The few that were physically able to stare in their direction did so for an instant, then returned to their other pursuits. No one questioned their presence as they journeyed from one chamber to another. Making idle conversation was not something that concerned the nymphs. They were too busy using their mouths in other ways.

Megan's reaction to their first orgy was a muffled "oh." Five nymphs engaged in a clearly impossible sexual position elicited an even quieter "oh, oh." When they were forced to weave their steps between a dozen women moaning simultaneously in pleasure, Megan's "oh, oh, oh," was nearly inaudible.

To Jack's relief, the door leading out of that particular room brought them to an empty chamber. Which, in turn, exited into the guards' retreat. Too much of a good thing, Jack decided, thankful to be free of Paradise, was too much.

While Cassandra checked the ghuls, carefully ensuring they were securely bound and remained in dreamland, Megan changed into the skirt and blouse Jack had brought for her. "I take back everything I said," she declared somberly when she was finished. "I guess I'm not as worldly as I thought. I still can be shocked."

"Which," replied Jack, "is nothing to be ashamed about. That's one of the things that makes us human."

Megan grinned. "That's also one of the things I love about you, Jack Collins. You have a wonderful talent for saying the right words at the right times."

She reached out and drew Jack's face to hers. He didn't resist. Life was too short not to pause a few instants to enjoy a kiss. Especially with the most dangerous events of the evening yet to come.

32

Big John met them in the front of the resort lobby at eight-thirty. Relief flooded the giant chauffeur's face when he spotted them approaching. "I was beginning to worry," he admitted, squeezing Jack's hand in a grip of steel. "You said eight o'clock."

"We encountered an unexpected surprise or two," said Jack. "Megan, this is Big John. John, my fiancée, Megan Ambrose. She's the love of my life. Please take good care of her."

"You can count on me," said Big John. His massive hands curled into fists the size of coffee cans. "I won't let nobody lay a hand on her."

"Wait a minute," said Megan, indignantly. "I'm not going anywhere. That auction's tonight. You can't send me scurrying off to safety while you take all the risks. I want to help."

Jack nodded. He had anticipated exactly this reaction from Megan. And was prepared to deal with it.

"As I explained climbing the stairs, I deceived Hasan al-Sabbah into inviting me and Cassandra to the auction. We're attending as his honored guests. However, I doubt that I could explain your presence there. There's no way you can attend."

He paused, preparing himself for the big lie. "Besides, Cassandra and I won't be in any danger until the event's nearly over. That's when my scheme goes into effect. Before, we'll act as observers, nothing more.

"When the action starts, I've mapped out our precise moves. I'm not going to minimize the danger. There's an element of risk in my plan, but with Cassandra there to protect me, I'm not very concerned. We'll destroy the anthrax virus and neutralize the genie using advanced mathematics. Loki won't interfere once he realizes there's no profit to be made. Nergal, judging by his past attempts, prefers working behind the scenes. The only ones who worry me are the representatives from the Brotherhood of Holy Destruction. Fanatics can be remarkably unpleasant, especially when their dreams go awry."

"I'll handle them," said Cassandra, rubbing her hands together in anticipation. "Don't forget Mr. Wesson called me a decadent bitch. I owe them one."

"There," said Jack. "Another worry put to rest."

"You studiously avoided mentioning the Old Man of the Mountain," said Megan. "He's the mastermind directing this whole operation. Maybe Hasan al-Sabbah's not a demigod, but he's centuries old, impossible to kill, and plenty mean. Meeting him the night I was kidnaped, I could feel the evil force oozing out of him. He's no pushover."

"I'm well aware of that fact," said Jack. "Which is why you can't stay here with me. I need you elsewhere. When you leave the resort with Big John, he's driving you directly to the airport. The two of you are meeting a very important surprise guest flying in for tonight's auction. His plane is due at eleven sharp. Your father and I arranged his appearance this evening. Your job is to make sure he shows up at the auction before Hasan leaves. All of my plans hinge on his arrival."

"Who is this mystery man?" asked Megan.

"I'll leave that for you to discover," said Jack. "Merlin assured me that you've met him before. That's why I particularly want you to greet him at the airport. He's a wary, exceptionally cautious gentleman, and your familiar presence will put him at ease."

"I'm not certain I understand what you're planning," said Megan.

"Neither am I," said Jack. "But I'm convinced this conspiracy is our only chance of permanently dealing with the Old Man of the Mountain."

He consulted his watch. It was less than twenty minutes to the hour. "Convinced?"

"Not one hundred percent," said Megan. "I suspect you're trying to shield me from danger. That's typical of you. But there's no time to argue about it now. I'm stuck following orders and I know it."

She grabbed him by the collar and kissed him hard upon the lips. "Take care of yourself, Jack Collins. Life without you would be dreadfully boring."

Megan turned to Big John. "Come on, my chauffeur. Let's get moving before I start bawling. You know any good songs to chase away the blues?"

"Miss," declared Big John, starting to hum his theme, "I *am* a good song."

Watching them walk away, Jack wondered if he would live to see Megan again. He had deliberately minimized the danger he would face in the auction. Cassandra was incredibly tough. But even she couldn't defeat stupendous odds. If their surprise visitor didn't arrive exactly at the right moment, things could get awfully grim.

"Let's make a quick stop at our suite," said Jack. "We can change clothes and collect our special package. Then it's off to the races."

"Cheer up, Jack," said Cassandra brightly as they headed for the elevators. Faced with the prospect of imminent battle, the Amazon was bubbling with good spirits. "Whether we succeed or fail, it will be a glorious fight."

"I just hope it's not our glorious funeral," said Jack. "I sort of looked forward to spending the next few years enjoying my life."

"That's the trouble with you mortals," declared Hugo, invisible as usual on Jack's left shoulder. "You worry too much about living dull lives and not enough about dying magnificent deaths."

"That's easy for you to say," declared Jack. "You spent centuries preparing for Götterdämmerung. I'm not ready yet for the Twilight of the Gods."

"Hmm," said Mongo. "That image raises an interesting notion. Hugo, fly with me for a minute. I want to ask you something."

"Ravens with secrets?" said Cassandra. "That's a novelty."

The birds returned to Jack's shoulders as he boarded the elevator to their suite. "Don't fret too much about tonight,

Johnnie," said Mongo, mysteriously. "Hugo and I promised your mom we'd take care of you. And we aim to keep our word."

"Would you mind explaining exactly what mischief you birds are plotting?" asked Jack, bewildered.

"Sorry," said Hugo, chuckling. "If you can keep secrets from Megan, we can do the same with you. Trust us."

As Jack saw it, he didn't have much choice.

33

Jack blinked, then rubbed his eyes as he stepped off the elevator into the Old Man of the Mountain's third-floor throne room. The ravens had briefly described the immense chamber but their report had not done the palatial room justice. It was a scene right out of *The Arabian Nights*.

Fifty feet square, the room was lavishly decorated with gold-and-ivory murals, depicting famous historical battles. The ceiling stretched forty feet over their heads and consisted of a huge mosaic pattern of colored glass. Located in the center of the chamber was a massive obsidian throne. Next to it was a small folding table, on which rested a tiny glass vial and a thick wad of notebook paper held together by rubber bands.

Arranged in a semicircle ten feet away from the throne were a dozen high-backed chairs. Scattered on the floor were several dozen large cushions. Though there was no visible source of lighting, the chamber was brightly illuminated.

Further to the left was a long table with a fancy display of finger sandwiches and an elaborate punch bowl filled with ginger ale and melting sherbet. A small group of men stood there engaged in conversation. Several houris, dressed in their transparent outfits, acted as hostesses. Jack was relieved that he didn't recognize any of the nymphs' faces. Or figures.

Oddly out of place in the Arabian Nights setting was a butler's folding table in the far corner of the chamber. On it was a plain black telephone. It was the Old Man of the Mountain's lone link to the outside world, and seeing it gave Jack a boost. The phone increased his chances of survival a thousand percent. Or so he thought at the time.

"Mr. Green, Ms. Jones," exclaimed Hasan al-Sabbah, rushing over to greet them. The Old Man of the Mountain wore a simple white robe belted around the waist by a black sash. The simple outfit suited his ascetic features perfectly. Hasan glowed with the force of his personality.

"Welcome to my humble abode," he declared, inclining his head in a bow of respect. Carefully looking around to make sure none of his other guests were nearby, he lowered his voice before continuing. "My sincerest apologies for the crude behavior of those camel-scum members of the Brotherhood of Holy Destruction. In more civilized days I would have ordered their tongues ripped out for uttering such insults to my honored company."

"The gentlemen had other neckties in their luggage?" asked Cassandra primly.

The Old Man of the Mountain smiled. "An impressive display," he declared. "I wondered if your presence here with Mr. Green reflected more than mere decoration. Your demonstration proved my suspicions well grounded."

"*The Man* prides himself in using his personnel to their best advantage," said Cassandra, smiling in return. Jack couldn't decide which of the two had a more threatening expression.

"If you ever find yourself interested in changing jobs," said al-Sabbah, "please think of me. I could use a woman of your skills in my organization." He paused. "Are you truly an expert in the death of a thousand cuts? It always has been my favorite torture."

"I learned it from Dr. Fu Manchu in Limehouse during the 1920s," said Cassandra. "He was an excellent teacher."

"The recognized master in the field," said Hasan al-Sabbah, nodding. He turned to Jack. "Your companion is a rare gem, Mr. Green. I commend you for your good taste."

He sighed heavily. "Please excuse me. I must circulate among my other guests, lest they feel slighted. We are impatiently waiting the arrival of Nergal, the Lord of the Lions, Master of Death and Destruction, and chief pain in the ass. These demigods are always late. They relish making a grand entrance. Once he is here, we will begin the auction."

Bowing again, the Old Man of the Mountain returned to the hors d'oeuvres table. Jack, not anxious to socialize with the other attendees, especially Loki and his frost giants, steered Cassandra in the other direction.

"You met Dr. Fu Manchu?" he asked the Amazon as they walked. "I thought he existed only in novels."

"Enough people read those books and believed them true," said Cassandra, "to give him life. Talk about a melodramatic character. Though created with a brilliant mind, the poor doctor spoke mostly in clichés. He had a terribly difficult time adjusting to postwar England. The last I heard, he was operating a Chinese restaurant in Soho called the House of Si-Fan."

"What about Sherlock Holmes?" asked Jack, overwhelmed by what he was hearing. "Millions of fans assumed he actually existed."

"Never met him," said Cassandra. "But Jack the Ripper told me years ago that the great detective was writing mystery novels. I forgot what pen name he was using."

"Enough," declared Jack. "My brain is overloading." The more he learned about the supernatural community, the more he realized how little he truly knew. "I notice that Hasan didn't say a word about your outfit."

"The Old Man of the Mountain strikes me as the type of man not interested in women," said Cassandra. "Like most brilliant but evil masterminds, he considers females as sexual playthings and nothing more. He's a typical male chauvinist megalomaniac, albeit a polite one."

Jack shook his head. It was hard to conceive anyone not being stunned by Cassandra's latest costume. The Amazon wore a black bodysuit made of cotton and Spandex, with a skin-baring scalloped neckline. Over it she had on a quilted crop-length jacket in a bright tie-dyed polyester print. Black stretch cotton denim jeans, a pair of calf-high cowgirl boots, and a wide leather belt with silver decorations completed the picture. If looks could kill, Cassandra was lethal tonight. As was her clothing.

Tucked in the lining of her boots were a pair of switchblade knives. The metal decorations on her belt were miniature throwing stars, small but absolutely deadly in the hands of a professional. A dozen poison darts formed the bracelets she wore on her wrists.

Concealed within her jacket were two pair of thin brass knuckles. And the length of dark ribbon knotted in an exotic pattern through her hair was steel wire that doubled as a strangler's cord. The Amazon had come prepared for war.

Jack, who was well aware of his limitations as a fighter, was armed with a padded airline bag containing his blue bottle. Nestled in one corner were the pocket camera and tape recorder Cassandra had purchased that afternoon. Those few items and his quick wit were his only weapons against a horde of supernatural foes. He hoped they would be enough.

Sitting transparently on his left shoulder, unusually quiet thus far, was Hugo. Mongo had flown off immediately after they reached their suite, on his secret mission. He swore to return before the evening's events were concluded.

"A big guy's coming over," warned the bird. "Somebody I never saw before. Damned if he don't remind me of a bear."

The newcomer did resemble a huge, furry circus bear. He stood well over six feet tall and weighed nearly 350 pounds. He was dressed in a dark brown suit whose seams were pushed to the limit by his massive barrel chest. A thick tangle of brown hair covered his head and peered out of his collar and sleeves. His face was clean shaven, with a wide bulb nose and bright red cheeks. Beneath big bushy eyebrows, his dark black eyes, piercing and direct, stared at Jack and Cassandra with undisguised curiosity. Remembering Big John's story, Jack concluded that he was about to encounter the mysterious Boris Bronsky.

"Goodt evening," said the stranger pleasantly, in a rumbling voice that furthered his bear comparison. His accent was as thick as molasses. He extended a huge hand in greeting. "My name is Boris Bronsky, of the Russian KGB. I'm pleased to meet yous."

"Jack Green," said Jack, remembering at the last instant not to use his real name. "My lady friend is Saman'ta Jones."

Cassandra dipped her head slightly, acknowledging the stranger. Then she frowned, as if confronted by an unpleasant memory.

Wondering what was bothering his companion, Jack shook hands with the newcomer. Bronsky had a firm, unyielding grip. Though the Russian looked soft and flabby, Jack surmised that he labored hard to maintain that image. There was a core of steel beneath the outer layer of paunch.

"I have heardt of you from our host, Mr. al-Sabbah," continued

Boris. "He tells me that you are here merely as observers. I gather he owes you a lot of money?"

"Not us," said Jack. "Our employer. Are you here to bid in the auction, Mr. Bronsky, or also merely to watch?"

"Call me Bear," said Bronsky. "Everyone does. It is a goodt nickname. As to why I am in attendance, I am most definitely anxious to place bids in this auction. When my government learned of this event, they flew me here on a special jet to represent our interests. Russia wants Professor Karsnov's formula destroyed, my friends. And we are willing to pay lots and lots of money to assure that happens."

"You're the one," said Cassandra unexpectedly, "who hired the Eumenides to eliminate Karsnov."

Bronsky tilted his head and stared at the Amazon in astonishment. "The Unseen Three? That is their title? The Eumenides? In twenty-five years, they never once mentioned it."

"You've dealt with the Furies for a quarter century," said Jack, astonished, "and didn't know their proper identities?"

The Russian shrugged. "It hardly seemt important. Year after year, I was given termination assignments from my superiors. Every one of them I passed on to the mysterious trio for completion. They never failed. Their payment came from a secret KGB slush fund controlled by my office. Since no one other than me knew of their existence, I received full credit for the kills. It made for an easy life. Until this Karsnov business arose. What a mess."

"The Furies killed the scientist but they didn't destroy his sample virus or notes," said Jack, guessing the Russian's plight.

"You comprehended the situation perfectly," said Bronsky. "I sent the Unseen Three out on their mission of vengeance several weeks ago. Since nobody suspected the possibility of a new batch of plague virus, I gave no orders to my agents to destroy it. When I learned a few days ago of this auction, I realized immediately that even if the Unseen Three succeeded in eliminating Karsnov, the danger would still exist. That's when I made arrangements to fly to Las Vegas. Whether the traitor was alive or dead, I had to attend this event to make sure his legacy did not survive. When I arrived, I learned that the Unseen Three had done their job. Now I got to do mine. Is a lot of extra work, but that's life.

"My country wants to make absolutely sure that all traces of the infernal plague are destroyed. That is why I am here. My instructions are to spend whatever is necessary to obtain the items."

The Russian paused. He stared at Cassandra. "How did you divine my association with the Three? I had hardly mentioned my assignment before you spoke."

"The smell," said the Amazon, wrinkling her nose. "The Eumenides possess a distinct odor. A trace of it clings to you."

Boris sniffed, then shook his head. "You have a strong nose," he declared. "It was nice talking widt you. I think before the bidding starts I will grab me another drink. All this excitement, it makes me thirsty."

The Russian shuffled off in the direction of the punch bowl. Jack turned to Cassandra, smiling faintly. "What do you think?" he asked, raising his eyebrows. "A possible ally?"

"Perhaps," said Cassandra. "I've encountered men like our friend Boris before. They give the impression of being stuck in situations far beyond their capabilities. Yet somehow they always come out on top. Ineptness is a perfect disguise. Oh, damn."

"What's wrong?" asked Jack, swinging his head in the direction of Cassandra's vision. He immediately spotted her cause for concern. Loki, trailed by his two ice giants, was approaching.

"What a pleasant surprise," murmured the Norse deity. "Freda Valkyior's son, Jack, and his darkling companion. I didn't expect to run into the pair of you at this gathering. But I should have known better." Loki laughed nastily. "After all, you are the Logical Magician."

Jack didn't bother denying his identity. A master of treachery and deceit, Loki wasn't fooled by the simple disguises they employed. Remembering his mother's evaluation of the trickster's character, Jack instead went on the offensive.

"Hasan al-Sabbah told me you were scheduled to attend the proceedings," he said casually. "I'm glad to see you here."

"You are?" said Loki, confused. "Why is that?"

"I want the Old Man of the Mountain's downfall tonight reported far and wide," said Jack. "His fate is meant to serve as an object lesson to others considering plotting against me. Obviously, if Cassandra tells the tale, certain supernaturals would doubt its validity. But none will question its truth if you're the witness."

Jack tried imitating Cassandra's nastiest smile. "Watch closely, Loki. You'll learn quite a bit before the evening ends. You might even discover how a demigod can be returned to the outer darkness."

The Norse deity licked his bloodless lips. His jet black eyes flickered uneasily. "You . . . you . . . are lying. The means do not exist."

"Maybe not before," said Jack, confidently. He knew he had the trickster frightened. "But I've developed a technique I'm confident will do the job. If you don't believe me, look into my soul. Go ahead, I won't stop you."

"No," said Loki. Anxiously, he gestured for the two frost giants to close around him. "As the prince of lies, I can easily tell when a mortal is bluffing. You're not."

Loki's eyes narrowed. His voice turned mellow. "Please recall that despite our differences, I've done nothing to meddle in your affairs. My position has been one of strict neutrality. Any disagreements you have are with Hasan al-Sabbah and the Crouching One. I see no reason why our truce should not continue through the evening."

"Precisely my feelings," said Jack. "I'm glad we see things eye to eye. Otherwise, the results could be exceedingly unpleasant."

"I think," said Loki, nervously, "that I need another drink before the auction starts."

Cassandra chuckled as Loki, trailed by his two frost giants, headed for the punch bowl. "Too bad Hasan isn't serving spiked drinks." She glanced at Jack. "Your remarks scared Loki out of his wits. Have you actually solved our impossible riddle? Can you vanquish a God?"

"Perhaps," said Jack. "Unfortunately, it's a method that will take weeks to work. Which means we have to survive tonight's festivities to learn if I guessed right."

"Elevator's coming up," said Hugo in Jack's ear. The raven's sense of hearing was incredible. "The show's about to get on the road."

34

"Finally," said the Crouching One, as the elevator stopped at the third floor. "Vengeance is mine."

"Where did you pick up that line?" asked Roger, astonished. "Reading the Bible?"

"No," said the demigod, "Mickey Spillane. You had several paperbacks by him in your library. I found his work eminently entertaining."

The elevator door slid open. Slowly, dramatically, the Crouching One shuffled out of the lift into the throne room. Roger sighed. The Lord of the Lions was capable of walking at a brisk pace when necessary. Tonight, it was deliberately slowing down to a crawl. The demigod had an overwhelming passion for the melodramatic. It enjoyed making everyone else wait.

"Ah, my honored guest," said Hasan al-Sabbah, the annoyance in his eyes belaying his pleasant greetings. "We have been eagerly awaiting your arrival. The auction is scheduled to begin in minutes."

"Very good," said the Crouching One, smugly. "I'm glad we are not late."

Rub it in, thought Roger.

As his mentor and the Old Man of the Mountain sparred verbally, he visually swept the room, trying to place the other participants in

the auction. Roger disliked the unexpected. His master spell was
aimed at the supernaturals in the chamber. He wanted a good distance
between himself and any mortals present. Once the magical beings
had been put in their place, the gun in his pocket would ensure the
obedience of his fellow humans. If they were all in his line of fire.

The first group he spotted was Loki and his two frost giants
standing in front of the punch bowl. The dark-haired Norse deity
looked nervous. Roger wasn't very surprised. According to the
Crouching One, Loki put up a brave front but was a coward at heart.
He was acting as an agent for an Eastern European nation that wanted
the plague virus for "ethnic cleansing." Among mortals, Loki
commanded fear and respect. In the presence of Hasan al-Sabbah and
Nergal, Ruler of the Underworld, the Sly One shrank to insignifi-
cance. The frost giants were immense but had the brains of snowmen.
Roger dismissed Loki and his icy companions as unimportant.

Close by the trickster, a massive middle-aged man dressed in a suit
several sizes too small waited passively, arms folded across his barrel
chest. He looked bored. Roger guessed that this was the Russian
emissary, Boris Bronsky. He didn't know much about the new player
in the game, but it seemed very unlikely that Bronsky could do much
to affect the outcome of the evening's events. He was too late on the
scene to have any major influence on the scenario Roger had
carefully constructed. The sight of a gun would probably turn him
into a quivering lump of Jell-O. Besides, big and fat, the man
resembled a ponderous old bear. Roger, no fan of animals, discharged
Bronsky as a minor annoyance.

Roger's gaze drifted to the center of the chamber. Located next to
Hasan al-Sabbah's gigantic obsidian throne was a small folding table.
It was covered with a jet black tablecloth. Displayed there was a
small glass vial and a stack of papers bound by several rubber bands.
The infamous legacy of Sergei Karsnov. Behind the table stood
al-Sabbah's neon red Afreet. The ferocious guard watched the two
treasures with unwavering eyes. The genie's presence at the auction
supposedly guaranteed the integrity of the affair. Patting the folded
paper in his pocket, Roger thought otherwise.

Actually, the Afreet was the only supernatural entity present who
worried him. The genie moved incredibly fast. Roger's spell froze all
magical beings in place after the first two lines were read aloud. He
planned to distance himself far enough away from the Old Man of the
Mountain and the Crouching One so that neither of them could reach
him before he uttered the necessary words. But the genie could.

Working in Roger's favor was the fact that the genie possessed the intellect of a stone. It never acted without orders. Unless al-Sabbah commanded him to stop Roger, the Afreet wouldn't act. Roger counted on the notion not striking the Old Man of the Mountain until it was too late.

Loitering not far from the display were the two representatives from the Brotherhood of Holy Destruction. Preferring anonymity, they hid their identities behind the ludicrous aliases of Smith and Wesson. The Old Man of the Mountain had introduced them to Roger earlier in the evening. He had not been impressed. Typical fanatics, they acted as if the world revolved around their mission. Sneering, they had called him "a bloated, capitalist warmonger." Roger didn't mind. He had been called worse by business rivals. Once he controlled the plague virus, their tune would change quickly enough.

The final pair of guests at the auction he had never seen before. These were the representatives of *The Man,* the villainous loan shark who frightened even the Old Man of the Mountain. Roger studied the mismatched duo with growing comprehension. A tall, slender young man and a stunning black woman, their appearance confirmed his earlier suspicions. Hasan might think the two spoke for the crime boss, but Roger knew the truth. His postcard had done the trick. There was no doubt in his mind that he was looking at Jack Collins and Cassandra Cole. They were attending the auction as honored guests of their most dangerous foe.

Roger drew in a deep breath. As expected, Collins hadn't disappointed him. But the Logical Magician's presence at the event no longer mattered. Roger had complete control of the situation. He chuckled and tilted his head slightly in Collins's direction.

"You find this occasion amusing?" asked the Crouching One, as al-Sabbah departed to inform his other guests that the auction was about to begin. "That is the first time I have heard you laugh in weeks."

"I'm just relieved that the Old Man of the Mountain isn't forcing everyone to sit on cushions," said Roger. "My back still aches from our previous visit."

"Hasan wants his guests comfortable," said the Crouching One. "As if it matters."

Roger grinned. For a change, he was in complete agreement with the Lord of the Lions. It didn't matter what Hasan wanted. It didn't matter at all.

35

Jack stared at the demigod talking to the Old Man of the Mountain. Nergal, Lord of the Lions, Master of Death and Destruction, resembled a short, elderly man, crippled by age. Barely five feet tall, the Lord of the Lions had a back arched so badly that its hands nearly touched the floor. Looking like a vulture hovering over its prey, the ancient entity truly was the Crouching One.

Completely hairless, lacking even eyebrows, the demigod had skin the color and texture of aged parchment. In deference to its surroundings, Nergal wore a dark blue pinstripe suit. The Lord of the Lions seemed nothing more than a wizened old business executive—except for its eyes. They glowed with an inner yellow fire, harsh and unblinking, cruel and utterly inhuman. Glimpsing those orbs, Jack knew for sure he finally faced his ultimate foe.

Behind the demigod, shifting about impatiently, was a tall, slender man with thinning hair and a scraggly beard. He was dressed in a pair of old jeans and a faded black sweatshirt. The stranger seemed unperturbed by the company he kept, leading Jack to suspect that here was the person responsible for Nergal's reappearance in the modern world.

The man's gaze methodically circled the room and came to rest on Jack. A brief smile lighted up the newcomer's face and he nodded imperceptibly to Jack. The man laughed, drawing a comment from the Lord of the Lions.

"Our mysterious postcard person?" asked Cassandra quietly.

"Probably," said Jack. "Who is he, Hugo?"

"Hasan al-Sabbah called him Roger Quinn," the bird whispered in Jack's ear. "Earlier this afternoon, while you and Cassandra were out buying pet supplies, Mongo and I visited a few old friends in the city. Returning, I stopped in the casino and eavesdropped on the Old Man of the Mountain as he escorted Smith and Wesson through the casino. It must have been shortly after your confrontation with the pair. The fanatics were still pretty steamed about Cassandra's remarks. Hasan tried to distract them by introducing Quinn. According to the Old Man of the Mountain, Roger owns a major computer consulting firm in California. Smith and Wesson weren't impressed. That pair learned diplomacy from Attila the Hun."

"Dale Carnegie they're not," Jack murmured in agreement. "Anything more about Quinn?"

"Roger was the human present during the conversation between the Old Man of the Mountain and the Crouching One I told you about on your arrival in Las Vegas," said Hugo. "He was the guy who said they shouldn't underestimate you, and referred to Dietrich von Bern. I got the impression he worked for Nergal."

"If that's the case," said Jack, "it plays havoc with my earlier theory that he sent the postcard as a warning. Unless Mr. Quinn is playing both ends against the middle. We better keep a close watch on him this evening."

Jack shook his head in amazement. In most of the fantasy novels he had read in the past decade, the mortals involved with faeries and demons were always liberal arts majors. Numerous series' books featured rock musicians, artists, and poets. Nobody wrote about scientists or engineers encountering the supernatural. Yet here in the real world, the two human agents working for the forces of light and darkness both specialized in mathematics.

In an odd fashion, it genuinely reflected an important truth. Just because artists and musicians dealt with emotions and feelings didn't mean they would accept without question the existence of supernatural beings. In fact, most artistic people of Jack's acquaintance, faced with the bitter realities of contemporary existence, were hard-headed cynics. Heartache and suffering had burned the dreams out of them. In their minds, they understood the world perfectly and refused to let themselves be contradicted by facts.

He doubted if any of them would adjust easily to the notion that magical entities shared man's world.

Mathematicians, however, dealt with abstractions. Accepted beliefs meant nothing to them. Abstractions governed the universe. Prove a statement true and it was true. Thus, when Merlin originally demonstrated that magic worked, Jack accepted it as truth. He merely adjusted his frame of reference. As would any mathematician. It was all, he reflected, perfectly logical.

Hasan al-Sabbah interrupted Jack's thoughts by clapping his hands together sharply three times. Immediately, all conversation in the room ceased. "My friends," announced the Old Man of the Mountain, "we are ready to begin. Please be seated. The proceedings will commence in a few moments."

"Wait," said the Crouching One, raising one gnarled hand in protest. The demigod spoke with a surprisingly mild voice. "Before we start the bidding, I want to personally thank the representatives from the Brotherhood of Holy Destruction for rescuing Professor Karsnov from certain death in Russia. If it was not for their swift action, none of us would be here tonight. They are true heroes."

Smith and Wesson appeared astonished. Jack couldn't blame them. According to Hugo, the demigod had been livid with rage over the fact that the terrorists double-crossed him and delivered the scientist to the Old Man of the Mountain. The Crouching One did not strike Jack as a God who forgave and forgot.

"A commendable attitude," said Hasan al-Sabbah, his voice betraying his own bewilderment at the demigod's unexpected shift in opinion.

"Come," said the Lord of Lions, stepping over to the two fanatics, "let me congratulate you both." The demigod thrust forward its hand. "Gentlemen, I salute your courage."

Hesitantly, Smith reached out and grasped Nergal's outstretched hand. When nothing unusual occurred, the tall man grinned, revealing a mouthful of yellowing, broken teeth. Moments later, his companion also accepted the demigod's commendatory handshake.

"Wonderful," said Hasan al-Sabbah. "Let bygones be bygones. Now may we begin?"

Only Jack noted that Roger Quinn's face had turned a sickly shade of green. He wondered what was behind Nergal's actions. Somehow he suspected it wouldn't be a lengthy wait before he found out.

36

Jack sat at the end of the semicircle of chairs farthest from the table. Gently, he laid his bag outside the ring of furniture. Bending over, he pulled open the zipper and examined the bottle inside. It looked fine. Carefully, he stood it erect so that the mouth of the container stuck out the top of the canvas grip.

"You understand the plan," he subvocalized to Hugo, sitting invisible on his shoulder.

"I know what I'm supposed to do when you give the signal," the bird muttered in his ear, "but I sure the hell don't understand why. I ain't complaining, mind you. The All-Father sent us on plenty of missions without explaining the reasons. That was his style— brooding, mysterious, *incomprehensible*. I'm just kinda curious how you're gonna trap the genie, destroy the virus and save the world using a bottle with a funny neck."

"I'll explain after it happens," promised Jack. "I was hoping Mongo would take care of the notes during the confusion, but since he's not here, we'll have to improvise."

"He'll be back," said Hugo. "With the cavalry."

"I hope so," said Jack. "The odds are definitely stacked against us tonight."

Cassandra sat next to Jack. The Amazon was relaxed and loose.

Her hands rested on her lap, close to the knives in her boots and throwing stars in her belt. She was ready and anxious for battle.

Beyond the Amazon were Loki and his two frost giants. The Master of Lies, sitting between his massive bodyguards, studiously avoiding meeting Jack's gaze. Loki desperately wanted the plague virus. But, more important, the Sly One wished to be on the winning side.

Positioned directly past the farther frost giant was Boris Bronsky. The big Russian sat with his arms folded across his chest, his eyes closed and head bent as if in deep thought. Or in deep sleep. With Bronsky, it was hard telling.

To the right of the Russian were Smith and Wesson. The two terrorists chatted in low, guttural voices while they waited. Like all of the guests, they were anxious for the auction to start.

Roger Quinn sat slumped in the chair next to the fanatics. His right hand was thrust deep in his jeans pocket, as if clutching a life preserver. There was a frightened yet determined look on his face.

At the other end of the ring waited the Crouching One. The Babylonian demigod appeared remarkably cheerful. It sat cross-legged on the chair, supporting its head with its hands. Every few seconds, its gaze shifted from the vial of plague germs to the Muslim extremists. Blue sparks flickered across the Lord of the Lion's fingertips, sputtering in the silence.

"I will now state the rules of the auction," declared Hasan al-Sabbah, perched like a vulture on his obsidian throne. "If there are any questions or remarks, please save them until I am finished."

The Old Man of the Mountain glared meaningfully at Nergal, but the Crouching One didn't make a sound. Jack snatched a quick peek at his watch. It was ten-thirty. Even if the plane carrying his mysterious guest arrived right on time, the trip from the airport would take at least thirty minutes. He had to stay alive for an hour or more. He hoped Hasan had a lot of explaining to do.

"Since there are only four parties involved in this event, we will keep formal procedures to a minimum," said the Old Man of the Mountain. "I see no reason why we should spend the entire night involved in this business. To the victor belongs the spoils. For the rest of you, I have arranged magnificent entertainment in appreciation of your participation."

"Faugh," said Mr. Wesson. "Get on with it, already. The sooner we depart this salacious den of iniquity and sin, the better."

Hasan's narrow, bony fingers curled into fists. Master of his domain, the Lord of Assassins was clearly growing weary of the terrorists' insults. "The joys of Paradise are available for those of you who care to indulge in such pleasures." The Old Man of the Mountain's thin lips narrowed into pencil lines. "For those who prefer to mate with camels, that too can be arranged."

There was no mistaking the animosity in Hasan's tone. Wesson's jaw dropped as the full implication of the veiled threat hit home. His mouth slammed shut and remained tightly closed as the Old Man of the Mountain continued.

"The bidding will start at ten million dollars. As the Lord of the Lions bears prime responsibility for discovering this treasure, he will be given the honor of starting the proceedings. We will continue in the semicircle, excluding of course my guests, Mr. Green and Ms. Jones. To expedite matters, minimum raises will be ten percent of the previous bid. Thus, if Loki bids twenty million, Nergal will either respond with twenty-two million or drop out. Bidding will continue until all bidders but one have passed. That final participant will be the winner."

"The exact prize?" asked Loki.

"Karsnov's notes on the development of the virus," said Hasan, pointing to the stack of papers on the table. "Using those, any capable scientist should be able to duplicate his formula. Not that it matters. In the vial is an actual sample of the plague serum. If used properly, there is enough material in that container to kill several hundred thousand people."

"What assurances do we have that you didn't photocopy the notes and plan to sell them to the losing participants in the weeks to come?" asked Smith.

"My word," said Hasan curtly. "That is guarantee enough. Are you implying otherwise?"

"Of course not," said Smith hastily. "I was merely checking. No offense intended."

"Good," said Hasan viciously, obviously no longer in absolute control of his temper. "My female camels are extremely lonely. They are starved for affection."

The Old Man of the Mountain laughed nastily. "Any other questions? Or comments?"

"What about delivery?" asked the Crouching One.

"At your convenience, to wherever you wish," said Hasan.

"Arranged by the winner and my Afreet. No safer method of transportation exists."

"What about payment?" asked Loki. "When do you need the money?"

"Within the week if not sooner," said Hasan. "Payable in cash. Large bills are fine, but no checks."

He bowed his head slightly in Jack's direction. "My note to Mr. Green's employer comes due in seven days. I am anxious to be free of that obligation."

The Old Man of the Mountain rose to his feet. "If there are no more—"

"I have a comment," said Boris Bronsky, unexpectedly. "May I speak a few words before the auction commences?"

"Go ahead," said Hasan. "But please keep it short."

"Idt is not much to say," declared the Russian, "so it will not take long."

Bronsky climbed to his feet. His mild voice rang with surprising authority. "This stuff is very evil. I am filled with great disgust that some of you plan to make use of idt. The virus should be destroyed. My government intends to do just that if we win this auction."

Boris paused. Loki yawned. Smith and Wesson sneered.

"This plague virus was developt on Russian soil by a Russian scientist. Thus, idt belongs to the Russian people. If you buy it here, you are receiving stolen property and will be liable to criminal prosecution." The Russian hesitated for a second, frowning at the smiles forming on several of his listeners' faces. "Laugh at me if you like. Karsnov, that traitor, thought he was above the law, too. He paidt the price for his arrogance. Maybe I'm not so threatening. But I got some friends who aren't as nice. Dey think poorly of those who betray a trust."

"Enough lecturing," said the Lord of the Lions. "I am a God. My purposes are my own. I refuse to be bullied by a mere mortal. Bring on the Kindly Ones. Once I control the plague virus, the Three Sisters will be helpless against me." The Crouching One extended a clawlike hand. Dramatically, he jerked his fingers closed. "I will crush them to dust if they dare interfere."

"We are not afraid of anyone associated with the rotting carcass of your depraved Communist empire," declared Wesson. He spat on the floor then rubbed a shoe in the wetness. "We spit on the bankrupt running dogs of the Great Satan."

Loki shrugged. "I'm simply acting as a middle man for other parties," he stated lazily. "Talk to them if you want. They live pretty close to your borders."

Hasan al-Sabbah raised his hands in mock astonishment. "It appears that you are the lone altruist at this auction, Mr. Bronsky. Why am I not shocked? Please take your seat. If the Russian government wants the plague virus returned, bid for it."

Hasan clapped his hands together twice. Instantly, the Afreet, stationed behind the table, swelled to twice its size. The suit it had been wearing fell in shreds at its feet. The genie, glowing neon red, nude and sexless, glared at its audience. "I guard this treasure!" the creature bellowed in a voice that crackled like thunder. It flexed its immense, octopus arms. "Touch it without permission and die."

"Impressive," murmured Jack. "What do you think, Hugo?"

"He's fast but I'm faster," replied the bird. "I can steal the vial right out of his hands. Keeping it more than a few seconds is what worries me."

"I'll handle that," said Jack confidently. He glanced at the blue bottle at his feet. "Mathematically."

37

The Old Man of the Mountain lifted the vial of anthrax spores over his head. As if drawn forward by a magnet, everyone present leaned forward. It was the scene, Jack realized, observed in the crystal ball by Sylvester the Cat. The start of Hasan al-Sabbah's auction.

"Sergei Karsnov's legacy," declared the Lord of Assassins in a sonorous voice. "Silent, invisible, painful death. What am I bid for this marvelous toy?"

"I offer ten million dollars," answered the Crouching One. The auction had begun. Jack glanced again at his watch. He dared not make his move yet. There was too much time left. He needed a distraction to delay the auction. Mentally, he crossed his fingers and prayed for a miracle. It materialized sooner than he expected.

"The Brotherhood of Holy Destruction," announced Mr. Smith, arrogantly surveying the room, "financed by the deep pockets of certain exceedingly wealthy, devotedly faithful Islamic nations, laughs at the parsimonious bid from the so-called God of the thrice-cursed Babylonians. We raise the amount to twenty million."

"Thank you," said Hasan, returning the vial to the tabletop. "It would be greatly appreciated if in future rounds, you keep the insults to a minimum and merely state your bid."

"The Russian people," declared Boris Bronsky, "though officially on record as protesting that this auction is illegal and immoral, offer thirty million U.S. dollars in the interest of international peace and brotherhood."

"Thirty-three million," said Loki, a faint smile crossing his lips. "My clients hired me to obtain the virus at the best possible price. No ten-million-dollar raises for me."

"Nergal," said Hasan al-Sabbah, "the bid returns to you."

"I find this bargaining repulsive," responded the demigod. "I am Lord of the Lions, Master of Death and Destruction. The plague should be mine by right."

"Does this mean you are dropping out?" asked Hasan, patiently.

"Forty million," answered the Crouching One. Blue sparks circled its forehead.

Smith laughed. "An insignificant raise from an insignificant god. Your days are past, forgotten one. Return to the dust from which you arose. The Brotherhood of Holy Destruction bids fifty million dollars."

"Sixty million," said Boris Bronsky immediately.

"Impossible," said Wesson, turning to face the Russian. "The Russian pig is lying. His country's economy is in shambles. They can barely manage to feed their stupid peasants. Their foreign debt is staggering. This bid is a sham."

Hasan al-Sabbah scowled. "My apologies, Mr. Bronsky, but the point is well taken. Russia's problems are well publicized. How do you intend to pay?"

Boris smiled. "With foreign aid, of course. Matching America's defense spending the past few decades ruined my nation's economy. Faced with complete collapse of our government, we turned to those most responsible for our plight. And as the world's only remaining superpower, they responded. The United States has pledged billions to help rebuild my country. A few tens of millions diverted from the total will never be missed. Redirecting funds has always been a KGB specialty. Idt is satisfactory answer?"

The Old Man of the Mountain nodded. "Quite satisfactory. Loki, the bidding continues with you."

"Sixty-six million," said the Norse deity. He paused for a second, then continued speaking. "Might not the same query be raised for the Lord of the Lions? He is not financed by an independent nation. What is his source of funds?"

"They're starting to aim for the jugular," whispered Hugo in Jack's ear. "Watch for the fireworks. Nergal ain't the type of God who takes insults well."

"Mr. Quinn's business enterprises are worth in excess of one hundred and fifty million dollars," snarled the Crouching One through clenched teeth. "And I have access to the secret treasure vaults of the kings of Babylon, filled with riches beyond measure."

"Such wealth, *if it even exists*," declared Wesson sanctimoniously, "no longer belongs to you, O creation of diseased minds. It is the property of the revolutionary councils that govern those lands today."

"Seventy-five million," said the Lord of the Lions. "And mastery of the state of Nevada when I regain my powers. California," it added, "is already promised to my faithful assistant."

"Nonsense," said Smith. "I protest. We are not ignorant children, to be bribed by the sugarcoated promises of this disgusting old pile of horse shit."

Cassandra leaned close to Jack. "Smith and Wesson are overplaying their roles. They're acting too obnoxious. It has to be a ruse. Be ready for trouble."

Jack nodded. The terrorists had deliberately attacked the Crouching One's every statement. They wanted to enrage the ancient demigod. And had succeeded.

Slowly, deliberately, the Crouching One rose to its feet. The demigod trembled with fury. Blue sparks sizzled along its fingertips. Dramatically, the Lord of the Lions lifted an arm and pointed at Smith and Wesson.

"It is time to put an end to the insults," declared the Crouching One. "Forever."

"Agreed," cried Smith, leaping out of his chair. "But not the way you plan, spawn of the devil."

With a flourish, the terrorist ripped a compact machine-gun pistol from inside his jacket. Laughing ruthlessly, Smith waved the gun in Nergal's face. "Thank you for rising to the bait," he declared. "We needed a short diversion to free our weapons. Your timing was perfect. Especially since I was running out of insults."

Wesson, a sadistic grin on his face, was also on his feet. Back to back with his partner, he held two of the deadly weapons. One was aimed in the general direction of the other participants in the auction. The second he pointed directly at the shocked face of Hasan al-Sabbah.

"If anyone dares move a muscle, including that miserable genie," said Smith, "we will shoot. At this distance, the bullets' impact will rip your stupid heads right off."

The terrorist grinned. "This farce has lasted much too long. The Brotherhood of Holy Destruction honors no pact with infidels. Our instructions were painstakingly clear. Promise them anything, we were told, but do not leave the auction without the plague germs. We intend on doing exactly that. Anyone foolish enough to try stopping us will be executed."

"Gentlemen, I am very disappointed," said the Old Man of the Mountain calmly. "Your leaders promised me their honest participation in this event."

Wesson laughed. "They lied. Fool—did you actually think they would hand over any of our hard-earned terrorist dollars to a major competitor? You should know there is no honor among thieves, or assassins. Now, give me the vial and be quick about it. Or pay the price of disobedience."

Out of the corner of an eye, Jack saw Cassandra reach to her boots and slip a switchblade knife into each hand. The Amazon had no intention of letting the two terrorists leave the room with the plague virus. Jack shook his head, nearly impaling an ear on Hugo's beak.

"Sorry," said the bird. "I was concentrating on Wesson's hands. They look funny to you?"

Jack's eyes widened. Hugo was right. The terrorist's fingers had turned charcoal gray. Like water being absorbed by a blotter, the color gradually crept up the man's hands, heading for his wrists.

"Damn," said Hugo. "His skin is crumbling to powder."

Wesson shrieked as he made the same discovery. His two guns dropped to the floor as the digits holding them vanished into a cloud of dust. Jack gasped in horror as a dribble of fine ash trickled out of the terrorist's sleeves. The killer was melting away before their eyes.

"What is . . . ?" began Smith, whose question likewise turned into a scream. His weapon followed the others to the floor. Sobbing in fright, he dropped onto his chair. Dropped and continued falling, as his body dissolved into a dark mist. In seconds, all that remained of the two terrorists were their empty clothes.

"They paid the price for insulting a god," said Nergal. "My touch of death never fails."

The demigod stared at Hasan al-Sabbah. "I warned you that pair could not be trusted."

"I took a calculated risk," said the Old Man of the Mountain. "You win some and you lose some. They will not be missed."

Al-Sabbah motioned to the genie. With a roar of noise, the dust and clothes disappeared. Seconds later, the Afreet returned to its position behind the table.

"Would anyone care for a drink?" asked the Old Man. "A short break is in order. Then, we will continue with the auction. The Crouching One retains the high bid, at seventy-five million dollars and the state of Nevada. It is Mr. Bronsky's turn to make an offer."

"Remind me," murmured Jack to Cassandra, as they walked over to the refreshment table for cups of punch, "never to shake hands with the Lord of the Lions."

38

"These people," said Boris Bronsky quietly, "isd not very pleasant."

"Considering their background," replied Jack, "that's not particularly shocking. The Crouching One is an ancient demon God of Death and Destruction. Hasan al-Sabbah, the Old Man of the Mountain, is the immortal leader of a cult of assassins. And Loki is the evil trickster from Norse mythology. None of them qualify for good citizenship awards."

The two of them were alone at the end of the refreshment table. Loki, backed by his frost giants, was examining Karsnov's notes. Al-Sabbah and Nergal, standing in front of the Old Man's throne, were discussing the pros and cons of dissolving enemies into powder. Cassandra paced the floor like a caged tiger. Patience was not one of her virtues. Roger Quinn, his face tinged green, had wandered off in search of a bathroom.

"I was thinking," said the Russian, "dat if any of them buy plague formula, it will lead to a big disaster. Maybe for the whole human race. We should not let that happen."

"We?" asked Jack. "What exactly are you proposing, Boris?"

"Yous and me join forces. Working as a team, we stop the others. And destroy the virus and the notes tonight."

"I have certain responsibilities . . . ," began Jack, not wanting to step out of character.

"My government will pay your boss the money lost," interjected Boris. "You godt responsibilities to your human race, too."

Jack grinned. There was no arguing with the Russian. "My real boss would be glad to hear you say that."

The Russian's eyes widened immeasurably. "Your real boss?"

"We're fighting on the same side for a change," said Jack, feeling very James Bond-ish. "I've a surprise planned near midnight. So take plenty of time bidding. Stretch out the auction for as long as possible. Then, when I make my move for the vial, you grab the notes. In the confusion, destroy them. Okay?"

"I will follow your orders to the letter," said Boris. "Dis is very exciting. And very dangerous, too."

"All in a day's work," declared Jack, stoically. On his shoulder, Hugo shook with silent gales of laughter.

They returned to their chairs a few minutes later. Quickly, Jack informed Cassandra of his conversation with the Russian. "He evidently thinks I'm with the CIA or FBI," said Jack. "I saw no reason to persuade him otherwise."

"Good move," said the Amazon. "Why confuse him with the truth."

Frowning, Cassandra surveyed the room. "Did you notice that Roger Quinn is still missing? I wonder what's keeping him?"

"Here he comes now," muttered Hugo. "Over there, by the elevator. He's unfolding a piece of paper."

"Mr. Quinn," called Hasan al-Sabbah from in front of his throne, "please be seated. We are about to continue the auction."

"One second," Roger said, and staring down at the document in his hands, began reading in a loud voice.

"O spirits of darkness, who are wicked and disobedient, hear my commands and obey. Let those who are named Nergal, Master of Destruction; Hasan al-Sabbah; Loki, the Sly Trickster; and any others present of lesser rank but supernatural origin, heed my words and obey. The Curse of the Chains binds you to me forever and aye. By the glorious and incomprehensible names of the true God and creator of all things, by the irresistible power of those same names, I curse thee into the bottom of the Bottomless Pit. There thou shall remain until the Day of Judgment unless thou heed my each and every command and do my will."

"Oh, brother," murmured Hugo in Jack's ear as Quinn paused

for a breath. "The Curse of the Chains. I haven't heard that clinker in centuries. I wonder if he's mastered the correct pronunciation of the holy names. That's the section that separates the magicians from the apprentices."

Jack quickly scanned the room. Loki, Hasan al-Sabbah, and Nergal appeared frozen in place. The Afreet hovered above the table with the plague vial, looking puzzled. As did Boris Bronsky. Cassandra, standing absolutely motionless, winked.

"Obey me now," continued Roger, sweat dripping down his forehead, "in the mighty names of Adonai, Zebaoth, Amioram, Tetragrammaton, Anexhexeton, and Primematum. Obey me always in the names of Baralamensis, Baldachiensis, Paumachie, Apolorosedes, and Liachide. Obey me, now and forever, amen."

No one moved. No one spoke. For an instant, time stopped. Reaching into his pocket, Roger pulled out a revolver. "Now, I'm in charge," he declared, cheerfully.

"Not really," said Loki, shaking his head. He applauded politely. "But you did recite that spell nicely."

"An excellent job," agreed Hasan al-Sabbah. "One rarely hears that many sacred names invoked with the proper accents. It must have taken many hours of study."

"But . . . but," stuttered Roger, sounding confused, "you're bound by the Curse of the Chains. You can't move or talk without my permission. I uttered the spell perfectly. It had to work. You're my slaves."

"These fools never learn," said the Old Man of the Mountain. He clapped his hands. "Guards, take charge of this idiot before he accidentally does some real damage with that toy gun."

Mentally, Jack groaned when three gigantic ghuls emerged from a sliding door in the wall. He had hoped Hasan employed cult members in his chambers. Cassandra could hold off a horde of ordinary humans for hours if necessary. She was no match for dozens of ghuls. Timing remained critical if they hoped to survive.

"Don't kill him," said Nergal, shaking its head in disgust. "Despite Roger's faults, he normally performs his tasks adequately. He can't help being greedy. Training a new assistant would be tiresome."

"But why didn't the spell work?" demanded Quinn, struggling helplessly in the arms of his captors. "The summoning spell I originally used to raise you from the outer darkness functioned

perfectly. All the spells I recited summoning demons ran
smoothly. What went wrong with the Curse of Chains?"

Supernaturals couldn't resist a question, no matter who asked it.
They loved to talk. It was part of their nature.

"The answer is obvious," said Loki. "We supernaturals have
been closely involved with the publishing industry since its
beginnings. Didn't you ever hear the phrase, 'printers' devil'?
While we see nothing wrong with issuing books containing
summoning spells, we are not foolish enough to permit any
binding spells to be published intact. That would be suicidal. You
pronounced the incantations perfectly, foolish mortal. However,
the spell itself, as written, is gibberish. As are all magical charms
and enchantments of that category available to the general public.
Your attempted rebellion was doomed from the start."

"Take him below," commanded Hasan al-Sabbah, waving a
hand in dismissal. "He can share the rock with the sphinx and
Collins's girlfriend. They will welcome the company."

The ghuls, dragging a befuddled Roger Quinn, disappeared into
the elevator. "Now," said the Old Man of the Mountain, "we can
continue the auction in peace."

Reaching over, Jack unzipped his bag completely, revealing the
blue bottle within. He lifted it out and placed it on the floor
between his and Cassandra's chairs. The bag containing the
camera and tape recorder he pushed off to the side. No one paid
him any attention.

Casually, he peeked at his watch. It was exactly eleven. If the
airlines could be trusted, his secret weapon was now in Las Vegas.
In approximately thirty minutes, Hasan al-Sabbah was going to
receive a highly unwelcome phone call. At that precise moment,
Jack planned to steal the plague virus. And all hell would break
loose.

It did, but not in the manner Jack had imagined.

39

"I am confused about the last bid," said Boris Bronsky, as the auction resumed. "My government authorized me to spend lots of U.S. dollars on Karsnov's secret. However, I cannot offer control of a section of my country as part of the deal. Maybe we could discuss some land in Siberia, but no people. Under the old system, you could probably get terms. But we are a democracy now. Trading people for merchandise is forbidden."

The Old Man of the Mountain sighed heavily. He was starting to look older than his centuries. It had been a tiresome evening for the Lord of Assassins. "A strictly monetary bid will suffice for now. We can discuss extra incentives later. What is your bid, Mr. Bronsky?"

"Uh," said the Russian, "I forget where we are. It is a high of seventy millions?"

"No," said Loki. "I bid sixty-six, then Nergal raised the ante to seventy-five. You're at eighty-three."

The Russian frowned. "What happened to eighty-two million, five hundred thousand? Five hundred thousand dollars is a lot of money to round off. I offer eighty-two, five. No people."

For the first time since his arrival in al-Sabbah's throne room, Jack relaxed. With Bronsky slowing the action to a crawl, the auction could drag on for hours. Which meant that his scheme would proceed like clockwork. All was good with the world. For about fifteen seconds.

That was when the phone in the far corner of the room rang. Startled, Jack checked his timepiece. It was only five minutes past the hour. It could not be his call.

"Use that spectacular hearing of yours to eavesdrop on this conversation," he whispered to Hugo as Hasan al-Sabbah hurried over to the telephone.

"Yes," said the Old Man of the Mountain curtly. His sunken eyes shrank to the size of pinpoints as he listened. "What? They're what? They will pay for that mistake—pay dearly. Yes, you did right to continue. The girl is missing? How can that be? What does the sphinx say?" Hasan's voice had risen with each question until he was nearly screaming. "Well, tell the dolt to forget the puzzle and answer you!"

"The guards escorting Roger to Hell found the other ghuls unconscious," whispered Hugo. "Instead of reviving them, they rushed over to Hell. They're calling from the phone in the sphinx's home. You can fill in the rest."

"Son of a bitch," said Jack, disgusted by the unexpected turn of events. "Toss my schedule out the window. It's history."

He tapped Cassandra lightly on the arm. "Ready for action? We're changing plans. Hasan's discovered Megan's missing. We can't risk the possibility that he'll stop the auction. When the Old Man hangs up the receiver, Hugo, that's your signal. The plan starts right then."

Cassandra grinned and reached for her knives. The Amazon never looked happier. She loved impossible odds.

"The dog can't talk, you idiots!" Hasan screamed into the phone. His white features were bloodred. If the Old Man of the Mountain wasn't immortal, he would have died centuries ago from high blood pressure. Even his eyes were tinged with crimson. "Awaken the incompetents in the guard room. Set their feet on fire if necessary. Call me when you have some explanations!"

Hasan slammed down the receiver. Instantly, Jack's left shoulder went numb. Hugo had launched himself at the vial. Everyone's gaze was fixed on the Old Man of the Mountain as he stormed back to his throne. Thus, only Jack saw the raven materialize as if out of nowhere directly on top of the plague vial. But the bird didn't remain unnoticed long.

"Hey, stupid," cawed Hugo, flapping his black wings in the Afreet's face. "I've got your dumb vial. And you can't catch me."

"Stop it!" shrieked Hasan. "Save the virus."

No one saw the race. Both supernatural entities moved at speeds faster than the eye could follow. In a larger room, they would have broken the sound barrier.

In the space of a heartbeat, Hugo rocketed across the room to Jack's mysterious bottle. The Afreet, a red blur, was less than a microsecond behind. But that barely measurable tick of the clock was all the time the raven required. It dropped the vial into the mouth of the light blue container and then vanished through the chamber wall. With an odd popping noise, the tiny vessel tumbled into the heart of the twisted glass figure.

The genie didn't hesitate. It never disobeyed direct commands. The raven wasn't important. The virus was what mattered. Air whooshed as the neon red figure shrank into a swirling red cloud. With the same popping noise, the Afreet followed the vial into the bottle.

Immediately, the entire container glowed bright crimson. It rattled violently for a few seconds then stopped. Fritz Grondark built bottles to last for an eternity. It became even more difficult to look at without getting a headache. The genie did not reappear. Nor did the vial.

"That's that," said Jack, cheerfully, after trying fruitlessly to stare into the mouth of the container. He knew better but couldn't resist the temptation of attempting the impossible. "Scratch one Afreet and one plague virus. They're prisoners of the fourth dimension."

"Explain yourself, mortal," demanded Hasan al-Sabbah angrily. The Old Man of the Mountain glared at Jack from the safety of his obsidian throne. Behind him stood the Crouching One, and behind them both were Loki and his front giants. Boris Bronsky sat balanced on the edge of the small table where Karsnov's manuscript, momentarily forgotten, resided. "What nonsense are you babbling?"

Jack smiled at Cassandra. The Amazon smiled in return. She was the reason the others maintained their distance from Jack and the blue bottle. The Amazon gripped a knife in her right hand and a handful of throwing stars in her left. Stuck point first in the floor at her feet were her other knife and a half dozen poison darts.

Cassandra was ready, willing, and anxious for a melee. None of the immortals she faced appeared anxious to challenge her.

"It's a Klein bottle," declared Jack, dipping his head as a signal to Boris Bronsky. The Russian nodded in response. "Supposedly, it can't exist in our physical universe. But, then, neither can immortal demigods, genies, and sphinxes. So I asked a few friends with magical powers to see if they could construct one. And they did."

Faced with a puzzle they did not understand, the supernaturals acted exactly as Jack expected. Like legendary rogues and villains throughout history, they stopped reacting to the situation and instead started asking questions. They couldn't do anything else. It was part of their basic nature.

"What is a Klein bottle?" asked Hasan al-Sabbah. "And why, since it is not capped by the seal of Solomon the Wise, hasn't my Afreet emerged from inside it?"

"A Klein bottle is the three-dimensional equivalent of a Möbius strip," explained Jack, slipping into his graduate student lecturer mode. "It's a bottle with only one surface—the inside and outside form one continuous plane. It doesn't require a cap because the contents are within and without at the same time."

"Impossible," declared the Old Man of the Mountain. "That makes no sense. Everything has two sides."

"Really?" replied Jack. "What about a Möbius strip? Surely, you've seen one. Take an ordinary strip of paper. Give it a half twist then connect the ends to form a closed ring. It becomes a surface with only one side. If you take a paintbrush to it, you can paint both sides on the strip without ever lifting the bristles from the paper. Though it appears to have two sides, it verifiably has only one. An ant crawling along the strip will never come to the end."

Al-Sabbah grimaced in mental pain. Jack recognized the expression. He had seen it for years on the faces of countless students. The Old Man of the Mountain had gone into math shock. "What about this magic bottle?" he demanded. "How can a container have no inside?"

"Raise the concept of a Möbius strip one dimension," said Jack. Out of the corner of his eye, he saw Boris Bronsky casually lean over and pick up Karsnov's manuscript. No one noticed. Their attention was fixed on Jack, the blue bottle, and his explanation.

"Take a thick glass tube, open at both ends," said Jack, repeating the instructions he gave Fritz Grondark. "Stretch one end into the neck. The other open end is the base. Twist the neck in a semicircle and pass it through the fourth dimension, thus making no hole, into the side of the tube. Connect the open mouth to the open base and you have a Klein bottle. As it utilizes a curve transversing the fourth dimension and we live in a three-dimensional world, it's impossible to visualize. Which is why staring at the bottle gives you a headache. Our minds can't cope with curves outside the universe."

"You speak gibberish," said the Old Man of the Mountain. "I hate mathematics. I've always hated mathematics. This must be a trick. Genie, return to me. Now. I command it."

Other than the bottle glowing brighter red, nothing happened. Jack shook his head. "Sorry. He can't do a thing. There's no exit from a Klein bottle."

"But there's no seal," said Hasan angrily.

"This bottle doesn't need a plug," said Jack. "When the genie chased the vial into the Klein bottle, he pushed himself into a four-dimensional curve. The Afreet is inside and outside the container at the same time. The entrance and exit form a continuous loop. Departing and returning are synonymous. He finds himself coming and going at the identical instant. When he leaves, he enters and vice versa. Like the ant on a Möbius strip, the genie can never find an exit. The bottle is a topological nightmare. And he's trapped by it."

"Destroy the bottle," whispered the Crouching One. "Shatter it to a thousand pieces. That will free your servant."

Jack shook his head, grinning. Behind his spellbound audience, Boris Bronsky had retreated to the elevator. The Russian held a Zippo lighter in one hand and was carefully incinerating Karsnov's manuscript a few pages at a time.

"I don't think that would be a good idea," said Jack. "If you slice a Möbius strip along the center, it forms one long two-sided loop. But if you cut it a third of the distance from the edge, the scissor makes two complete trips around the strip in one continuous trip. The results are two strips intertwined—a two-sided hoop and a new Möbius strip.

"Cutting a Klein bottle down the middle, which would require passing your knife through the fourth dimension, would produce two mirror-image Möbius strips. And, probably a genie divided into two parts. Perhaps. No one can say for sure since no one has had the opportunity before to deal with such a construction. Equally possible, the genie and the vial instead might disappear into the higher plain of existence.

"If you don't slice the bottle exactly in the middle, the results defy speculation. Shatter the container into forty or fifty pieces and you could end up with bits and pieces of the Afreet scattered throughout the universe. Or create four-dimensional sinkholes that would swallow nearby objects like black holes. In any case, the Afreet and plague virus would definitely not survive the separation."

Hasan al-Sabbah howled in frustration. Loki grimaced. Nergal, Lord of the Lions, scratched his head in bewilderment. Boris Bronsky finished burning the last pages of Karsnov's notes and strolled over to the baffled supernaturals.

"Why?" asked the Old Man of the Mountain despondently. "Why did you do this? Obviously, it took advance planning. You came here specifically to thwart my plans. What reason prompted *The Man* to order this punishment?"

"You pompous, overconfident moron," snarled the Crouching One before Jack could launch into a lengthy discourse on the Old Man of the Mountain's supposed infractions. "Haven't you yet comprehended the truth? These two owe no allegiance to the one you fear. What proof did they offer? You accepted them on their word and they took advantage of your stupidity."

"But," said Hasan, confused, "if they are not associated with *The Man*, who are . . ."

"Mathematics," spat out the Crouching One. "Deliberation and rationality. Face the facts, you incompetent executioner. He's Jack Collins, the Logical Magician."

Jack, knowing the time for pretense was finished, inclined his head in acknowledgment. "At your service. Assisted and abetted by the lethal Ms. Cassandra Cole."

Hasan al-Sabbah's bony fingers clenched into fists of rage. "The Collins figure my agents had been shadowing in Chicago the past few days?"

"A doppelganger, of course," said Jack.

"The so-called Master of Treachery and Deceit deceived," declared the Crouching One, more than a hint of mockery in its voice. "At least Dietrich von Bern didn't provide food and lodging for his foe." The demigod raised its hands skyward. "Why am I singularly cursed to be served by incompetents and fools?"

"Is goodt question," replied Boris Bronsky.

The Russian had positioned himself between and slightly behind Loki's twin frost giants. Reaching up with massive ham-sized hands, Bronsky grabbed the two leviathans by their outside ears and slammed their heads together. The crack of skulls echoed like a gunshot through the chamber. "You is not the only one who has complained about the same difficulty."

Ponderously, the Russian stepped over the unconscious frost giants. "There is plenty of ineptitude close by," continued Bronsky as he marched past a stunned Loki and joined Jack and Cassandra. "It is a common plague. People have suffered from its effects for thousands of years. If you could isolate and breed the germs responsible, you could conquer the world in a week. Maybe less."

Boris grinned at Jack. "I did good, huh?"

"Exceptional," said Jack. "I thought the extra touch with Loki's bodyguards was inspired."

"They forget sometimes," said Boris, "that big, friendly bears have claws, too."

Shaking his head in frustration, a distraught Old Man of the Mountain sank into the center of his obsidian throne. Arms folded in disgust, the Crouching One stared daggers at the Assassin overlord. Meanwhile, Loki walked around his helpless assistants, trying to kick them awake.

Jack glanced at Cassandra and winked. The minutes were slowly but surely passing. In the reasonably near future, the phone would ring, delivering a decisive blow to Hasan al-Sabbah. Jack was starting to think they might survive the evening without a single violent adventure.

"Well," grumbled the Crouching One, "what steps are you planning to recover your lost honor? I assume you realize that if word of this fiasco becomes known, your business will drop to nothing. Nobody wants to hire an assassin so inept he wines and dines his worst enemies. And allows his genie to be trapped in a mathematical contraption."

Hasan shifted uncomfortably on his throne. It was clear that Nergal's criticisms stung his vanity. "The deeds are done," said the Old Man of the Mountain. "How can I undo what has already taken place? The disaster is complete and cannot be repaired."

"Kill them," said the Crouching One. Jack cursed in annoyance. The ancient demigod was determined to rule the world. And it still considered eliminating a certain Logical Magician as the necessary first step in achieving its ambition. "That simple action would reverse your fortune."

"I could smash the life out of them," mused al-Sabbah. "Then claim that I decided to keep Karsnov's formula for myself. The prestige of murdering Collins and acquiring the plague virus would bolster my sagging enterprises. No one would know I was lying."

The Old Man of the Mountain shook his head. "Unfortunately, the deception disregards my most pressing predicament. My note to *The Man* comes due in less than a week. Unless that debt is paid in full, this entire plot remains meaningless."

"How much is owed?" asked the Crouching One.

"A hundred and ten million," said Hasan al-Sabbah. "Hell cost a great deal more than I anticipated."

"I will pay that sum," said the Lord of the Lions, "for the head of the Logical Magician. To be precise, only his head, neatly preserved in a metal box. Do we have a deal?"

"Yes," said Hasan al-Sabbah, straightening in his chair. "We have a bargain. Though, if you don't mind, we will dispense with the customary handshake sealing the agreement."

"Understood," said the Crouching One.

Beaming with good cheer, Hasan al-Sabbah whistled.

"No worries," said Boris Bronsky to Jack. "Me and the young lady, we defend you from these three repulsive fellows. Even if they wake up the two albinos, I don't think we have much trouble."

"It's not them who worry me," said Jack. A dozen hidden doors had opened in response to the Old Man of the Mountain's signal. Shambling out of them came a horde of seven-foot ghuls. "Those guys are the problem."

40

"You're making a big mistake," shouted Jack at the Old Man of the Mountain, as the ghuls filled the chamber. He counted nearly thirty of the monsters. Cassandra was a one-woman army, but not even Hercules could defeat a supernatural army of this size. "I'm not joking. Remember Dietrich von Bern. He underestimated me, too. Mess with the Logical Magician and you'll be sorry."

"Will I?" laughed Hasan al-Sabbah. "Somehow I doubt that. You deprived me of my Afreet, Mr. Collins. I think it only fair I take your life in exchange."

A flutter of wings, a gust of wind, and Hugo landed on Jack's left shoulder. "Sorry I skipped out after the chase," said the bird, "but I decided to check on Mongo's progress. Anything interesting happen while I was gone?"

"This and that," said Jack. "We trapped the Afreet in the Klein bottle. Nergal guessed our true identities. And Hasan al-Sabbah decided to accept the demigod's offer of a hundred ten million bucks to flatten me, Cassandra, and Boris Bronsky into pancakes. That covers the high points."

On the Amazon's advice, they had retreated, taking the bottle and Jack's airline bag, to the far wall. It prevented them from being surrounded. Unfortunately, there were now enough ghuls present in the chamber to crush them to death by sheer force of numbers.

Twenty feet distant, the Old Man of the Mountain stood upright on the arms of his obsidian throne, exhorting his army of ghuls to mash the three unbelievers to putty. At his side, the Crouching One nodded his head in approval. Loki, flanked by his befuddled frost giants, lurked far to the rear of the chamber, near the elevator.

"I burned Karsnov's notes," added Boris Bronsky, proudly. He shook a huge fist at the horde of monsters shakily advancing on their position. Cassandra and her knives made them cautious. "Now, I die a hero. Pretty busy day."

"Cheer up," said Hugo. "Help is coming."

"Kill them!" screamed Hasan al-Sabbah. "Tear the infidels to pieces!"

"Five Mississippi, four Mississippi . . . ," Hugo counted.

A ghul, braver than the rest, detached itself from the horde and grabbed for Cassandra. Her two knives flashed and the creature howled in unexpected pain. The other monsters hesitated for an instant, then continued forward.

"Three Mississippi, two Mississippi . . ."

"Better hurry," said Jack as a dozen ghuls reached for him.

"One Mississippi," said Hugo, his voice rising. "Zero!"

The cavalry arrived in spectacular fashion. The throne room exploded with a boom of thunder and a flash of lightning. A wild wind swept through the room. And six mighty figures came hurtling out of the night sky.

It took Jack a moment to realize the thunder was the sound of the glass dome in the ceiling cracking. The lightning was the room lighting reflecting off the thousands of tiny fragments of glass falling to the floor. The wind and the riders were not as easy to explain.

Like frightened children, the ghuls huddled around Hasan al-Sabbah's throne. The Old Man of the Mountain stood transfixed on his chair, an unreadable expression on his upturned face. Beside him, the Crouching One stared at the descending riders with a mixture of curiosity and hatred. Neither immortal seemed to recognize the new players in the game. But Loki did.

"The Valkyrior," he cried in a mixture of shock and amazement. "The Choosers of the Slain."

Jack swallowed. Hard. He always wanted to meet his mother's

relatives, but he had no idea it would be in such dramatic fashion. Or that their apparel would be so remarkably flamboyant.

There were six Valkyries, each riding a snow white horse the size of a Clydesdale stallion. The animals' eyes blazed with red fire. Strangely enough, they looked very familiar to Jack. His mother's horse, Flying Feet, obviously belonged to the same magical herd. That these immense beasts could fly, Jack concluded, had to be one of magic's greatest triumphs. The warrior maidens on their backs rode them with the utter confidence born from hundreds of years of experience.

His aunts, for the facial resemblance to his mother was quite apparent, were all blonde, buxom, and of Rubenesque proportions. The ancient Scandinavians obviously preferred their women in heroic dimensions. Their golden hair was braided in pigtails, their skin was white as newly fallen snow, and their eyes shone with a bright blue luster. However, their outfits reflected none of their northern heritage. Unless it was northern Texas. For the six Valkyries wore Las Vegas–style cowgirl outfits.

Suede, denim, and fringe dominated. The women were dressed in very short tie-dye buckskin skirts, beaded fringe suede halter tops, and mid-length embossed black leather boots. On their heads they wore fancy cowboy hats, decorated with turquoise and feathers. Looped around each of their saddles were lassos, and buckled to their belts were two old-fashioned six-guns. But, the guns were there just for decoration. These Valkyrie cowgirls were armed for an old-fashioned Viking showdown.

Three of them carried huge broadswords, which they swung around in the air like candy canes. The other three brandished doubled-edged steel battle-axes. All of them wore a massive leather shield on their other arm. The Choosers of the Slain were prepared for war.

Circling the chamber as they descended, the Valkyries guided their steeds in a loose ring around Hasan al-Sabbah and his ghoulish servants. Precisely at the same instant, all six horses touched the floor. As promised by Hugo, the cavalry had arrived in grand fashion.

"Hi, Jack," said Mongo, alighting on his free shoulder. "Sorry we were late, but the girls had a ten-thirty show at the Blue Lotus Hotel on Glitter Gulch. We rushed over the minute it concluded. Glad we made it before the fun started. The Valkyrior would have hated to miss the fireworks."

"You arrived in the proverbial nick of time," said Jack. "Another minute and we would have been ghul chow."

"You think the monsters will try and make troubles?" asked Boris Bronsky, a glazed expression on his face. Jack didn't blame him. He felt sort of dazed himself. "There's a lot more of them than the flying ladies."

"They'll stay exactly where they are and act as meek as kittens," declared one of the blonde warrior maidens, guiding her mount close to Jack. She swung her battle-ax in a circle over her head three times, tossed the weapon up toward the smashed skylight, and then caught it with her other hand as it descended. "No supernatural fiend picks a fight with the Choosers of the Slain, whatever the odds. We don't start battles—we finish them."

Grinning, the Valkyrie leaned over and patted Jack on the cheek. "Glad to finally meet you, nephew. I'm your aunt Gretta. Hugo and Mongo think the world of you. It's nice to hear someone in the family is making a name for himself."

"The pleasure's mine," said Jack, blushing. "Mom never talked much about you."

"We gave her a hard time for leaving," admitted Gretta. "She was the best trick-shot artist among us. We believed her departure would hurt the act. But that was years ago.

"Since then, we've managed fine on our own. Been touring the country for the past few years as the Six-Gun Sweethearts. Finally landed this contract at the Blue Lotus, runs for the summer. It's tons of fun and a change of pace, though the costumes are kinda dumb. Still, we like it better than the rodeo circuit."

Two huge gray wolves with unusually expressive features jogged over. Jack had no idea how the animals had gotten into the chamber, but he was beyond wondering.

"Johnnie," said Mongo, "these are our friends, Geri and Freki. They live with the girls."

"Odin's wolves," said Jack, remembering an earlier conversation. "Or should I say, his big, big dogs with immense teeth?"

"Yeah, that's us," growled one of the wolves. "Pleased to meetcha. Any friend of the birds is a friend of ours." The dog paused and looked up at the Valkyrie. "Hey, Gretta, we gonna rip these ghuls to shreds? The girls are anxious to spill some blood and me and Freki haven't torn anybody to bits in years. Whatd'ya say?"

"It wouldn't be much of a battle, I'm afraid," said Jack's aunt, sighing. "These desert types fold under pressure. We'd have to tie one hand behind our backs to make it a fair fight. That would take too much time. Remember, we've got a performance scheduled at midnight."

Gretta turned to Jack. "Nephew, what's your pleasure? After all, you were the one threatened by these thugs. You decide. What should we do with them?"

"Let them go," said Jack, without hesitation. "The ghuls at least. I'll deal with Hasan and the Crouching One later."

"Let them go?" repeated his aunt. "Even though they tried to murder you and your friends?"

"They're merely the hired hands," said Jack. "Why punish them for obeying the Old Man of the Mountain's commands?"

"Whatever you wish," said Gretta. His aunt had the same disappointed look he'd often seen on Cassandra's face. She would have preferred a battle to the death. "I'll go over and inform the snake of your generosity."

"Is goodt decision," said Boris Bronsky when the Valkyrie left to speak with the Old Man of the Mountain. "Enough fighting for one night. We won, no?"

"No," answered Cassandra, before Jack could reply. "Hasan al-Sabbah's immortal and close to invulnerable. The Old Man of the Mountain is a deadly foe and he won't forget this defeat. Nor will the Crouching One. You've foiled its plans twice now. Until we eliminate those two fiends, your life will be in constant danger."

Jack merely smiled. "Don't fret," he said to Cassandra. "The evening's not over. Why not say hello to the Valkyries? I'm sure they'd be happy to see you. Help them supervise the ghuls' evacuation. And listen for a phone call."

"A phone call?" repeated Boris Bronsky, as a perplexed Cassandra wandered off. "You're expecting an important message?"

"A friend I never met," said Jack, "is going to solve one of my problems in a most unexpected manner."

41

It took twenty minutes to clear the throne room of ghuls. Their departure left Jack, Cassandra, the birds, and Boris, along with the Valkyries and their pets, facing the Old Man of the Mountain and the Crouching One. To no one's surprise, Loki and the frost giants had made a quick exit immediately after the arrival of the Valkyrior. The Sly One was no favorite of the warrior maidens and he knew it.

"You win this round, Collins," snarled Hasan al-Sabbah, "but there will be other games. And you won't be able to hide behind the skirts of these women forever."

"My, he's a spiteful character," said Jack's aunt Hannah. It was difficult remembering the names and faces of six newly acquired relatives, but Jack was adjusting quickly. Plus, Hugo supplied the correct identity when necessary. "Maybe we should tie him in a sack and bury the bag in the Gobi Desert for a few years. That would teach the old goat some manners, I bet."

"It might not be a bad idea," declared Aunt Siglunda. "What do you say, nephew?"

"I'm afraid it would be an exercise in futility," said Jack. "Hasan al-Sabbah's pretty indestructible and is a master schemer. Sooner or later, he'd escape from whatever prison we employed and come after me again. There's a simpler and better means to vanquish him."

"Nonsense," said the Old Man of the Mountain. "I am implacable, vindictive, and without mercy. You will never master me, Collins. You're not ruthless enough."

As if in response to Hasan's bragging, the phone in the corner rang. Jack grinned. Perfect timing.

"Better get it," he said to al-Sabbah. "It's for you."

"Who calls at this hour?" asked the Old Man of the Mountain, puzzled. He walked over to the telephone and picked up the receiver. "Yes?"

The Old Man's face clouded in annoyance. "Can't he wait until the morning? I am busy at the moment." He paused, listening intently. "He said what? Repeat that—at once."

Hasan al-Sabbah's features turned from white to ashen gray. His harsh voice sank to a shocked whisper. "Yes, I heard you perfectly. Send him up. Immediately. I will wait here."

A shriveled husk of a man staggered back to the obsidian throne. The Old Man of the Mountain collapsed in his chair, his blazing eyes transformed to burned-out cinders.

"You," he muttered, barely able to turn and stare at Jack, "orchestrated this disaster. The one who approaches comes at your bidding."

"Merlin arranged the details," said Jack, "but I called the shots. Your history betrayed you." Jack pursed his lips, as if in deep contemplation. "Perhaps I'm more ruthless than you thought."

The elevator door slid open. Out of the lift stepped Megan, Big John, and a short, squat Asian man dressed in a conservative three-piece suit carrying a brown attaché case. Spotting the group clustered around the throne, they walked forward.

"We should be going, nephew," whispered Aunt Gretta, "but this is too good to miss. The show must go on—but a little later than usual tonight."

Megan, catching sight of Jack, rushed over and threw her arms around his neck. The following few moments blurred as his sweetheart kissed him with the intensity of an atomic explosion. When he recovered his equilibrium, Jack noted that his six aunts were all beaming with pride.

"Nice girl," declared Boris Bronsky. "Friend of yours?"

"My fiancée," said Jack. "Megan, this is Boris Bronsky, a friend and ally from Russia. And if you haven't already guessed, the

Six-Gun Sweethearts are my mother's sisters, the Choosers of the Slain from Norse mythology."

"Pleased to meet you," said Megan cheerfully. "Sorry we were a bit delayed. Toshura's plane didn't arrive until eleven-fifteen. We rushed over here as quick as possible. Big John broke nearly every traffic law on the books. I was worried we would arrive too late."

"No problem," said Jack. "I'll tell you all about it later." The oriental visitor had reached the obsidian throne. "I want to hear what our friend has to say."

"It was nice seeing him again," whispered Megan. "We met in Japan last year when Dad was working on the big Godzilla oxygenation project."

"Shhh," said Jack as the Japanese businessman began to speak.

"Mr. Hasan al-Sabbah, I presume?" he asked rhetorically. "I am Toshura Miyamoto, senior partner of Akasaka Holdings International. My company represents a number of Japanese firms interested in investing funds in valuable real estate in the United States of America. For several years, we have been anxious to acquire a casino in Las Vegas. Many of our wealthy tourists visit this city expressly to gamble. A resort catering to their special needs, operated and owned by their countrymen, would no doubt be a tremendous success."

"No doubt," said Hasan al-Sabbah, dryly.

"My friend and associate, Mr. Ambrose, contacted me the other day and informed me of the possibility of acquiring the Seven Wonders of the World Resort. Aware of the constantly shifting circumstances, Akasaka Holdings acted with all possible speed. With the cooperation of Ambrose Associates, my firm was able to purchase in the past day the outstanding stock, notes, and debts on the property. We completed the last transaction, with a gentleman known as *The Man*, only a few hours ago."

Miyamoto bowed. "I regret to inform you that this hotel no longer belongs to Hashashin Enterprises. It is now part of Akasaka Holdings International. That is why I am here—to facilitate the transfer of ownership of the property as smoothly and quickly as possible. The necessary documents are in my briefcase."

Hasan al-Sabbah drew in a deep breath. "Of course. I understand your concern, Mr. Miyamoto, and will do everything in my power to assure a swift and orderly transition." The Old Man of the Mountain hesitated for a second. "By some small chance, were any of your ancestors Mongols?"

Miyamoto stared at al-Sabbah with a curious expression on his face. "How intriguing. My friend, Mr. Ambrose, asked the exact same question the other day. My great-great-grandmother came from Mongolia. According to family tradition, she traced her ancestry back to the great khans."

"She didn't exaggerate," declared the Old Man of the Mountain sadly. "The resemblance is quite remarkable."

Hasan al-Sabbah didn't elaborate and Mr. Miyamoto was too polite to ask what he meant. The Old Man of the Mountain sluggishly raised himself from his throne. "Come," he said wearily, stepping to the floor, "I will introduce you to my senior staff."

A broken Hasan al-Sabbah stopped in front of Jack. "I salute you, Collins. Defeating me by purely economic means is both diabolical and depraved. It is a scheme worthy of the most heinous masterminds."

A tear trickled down the Old Man of the Mountain's cheek. "I hate starting over. A man my age shouldn't have to work so hard. Finding capable new recruits is such a pain. And convincing them that paradise exists in these modern times is growing increasingly difficult."

"You could retire," suggested Jack.

"Lamentably, I cannot," said Hasan al-Sabbah. "Mankind's dreams define me. I am what I am. And that is all that I ever can be."

The Old Man of the Mountain gestured to the elevator. "Come, Mr. Miyamoto. Time for us to leave."

"Care to explain to us what that was about?" asked Megan as Hasan al-Sabbah and Toshura Miyamoto disappeared in the lift.

"The Order of Assassins was destroyed in the year 1256," said Jack. "Shortly before then, the Old Man of the Mountain made a terrible mistake. Secure in his mountain fortress, he executed two foreign envoys sent under a flag of truce. That treacherous deed incensed the lord who had dispatched the ambassadors. The Old Man had insulted the wrong man. Hulagu Kha Khan, leader of the Mongol horde, swore revenge. A million men overwhelmed the Hashashin. Alamut was torn apart, stone by stone. And the Order of Assassins was annihilated."

Jack shrugged his shoulders modestly. "I merely updated the scenario. Instead of a Mongol horde razing Alamut, Hasan's original headquarters, a Japanese corporation seized control of the

Old Man's new base through a forced buyout. Different titles, different times, same results."

Megan hugged Jack. "My hero. Defeating the nasty Old Man of the Mountain without working up a sweat. Brains beats brawn again." She grinned her wicked grin. "I've a nice reward for you. When we're home alone, just the two of us."

To the vast amusement of his six aunts, Jack turned beet red.

42

The Valkyries left a few minutes later. "Are you confident you'll manage all right?" asked Gretta as she prepared to depart. His aunt pointed a finger at the Crouching One, standing alone and ignored in a corner of the room. "That one can't be trusted."

"On his own, he's relatively harmless," said Jack, "as long as you don't shake hands with him. Nergal works through agents. Don't worry about me. In a few minutes, I intend to let him withdraw also. First, though, I want to put a plan of mine into operation."

"In that case, nephew," said Gretta, leaning off her horse and pinching him on the cheek, "take care. Say hello to your mother for us. Maybe sometime in the near future, we'll come east for a visit. Or a wedding!"

"Sure," said Jack, his mind boggling with the thought of a reception hall filled with Valkyries, gnomes, witches, and elves. He wondered if Megan might consider eloping.

With a roar of wind, the six white horses bearing the Choosers of the Slain leapt up into the air and sailed gracefully out the roof of the throne room. It was an exhilarating, magical sight. Even with them dressed in cowgirl outfits and shouting "Yahoo!" as they rode off into the night.

Strolling over to his travel bag, Jack pulled forth his tape recorder and pocket camera. Beckoning to his friends to stay away, he marched across the chamber to the Crouching One.

"Well," said Jack, carefully stopping a safe distance from the ancient demigod, "I guess that leaves you as my last problem."

"Don't expect me to congratulate you on your great successes," sneered the Crouching One. "You are a worthy opponent, Collins, but in the end, I will triumph."

"Why is that?" asked Jack, casually switching on the tape recorder's built-in microphone.

"Gods are patient," said the Lord of the Lions. Like every supernatural entity, the demigod loved the sound of its own voice. "Immortal and indestructible, we can afford to take the long view of things. It doesn't matter to me if this scheme fails, or the one following, or the one after that. I can wait. Centuries mean nothing to me. No matter how many battles you win, the last triumph shall be mine. And with one victory, the war will be over."

"Why bother?" asked Jack.

"It is my destiny," said the Crouching One proudly. "I am Nergal of Babylon, God of Death and Destruction, Pestilence and Plague. As it was in ancient times, so it shall be in these modern days. I am a God. And Gods rule mankind."

"I thought you might say that," declared Jack, pressing the off button on his tape recorder. "Feel free to depart. There's nothing I can do to stop you."

"Thank you for realizing the obvious," said the demigod. "I plan to stop at Hasan's imitation Hell and rescue my foolish servant. Then the two of us will return to California. Roger is an idiot but he has his uses. I am sure you and I will meet again someday."

"Perhaps," said Jack mysteriously. He paused. "Would you mind if I asked one small favor? I know it may sound stupid, but in my numerous encounters with the supernatural, you're the only real God I've met. Could I snap your photograph as a souvenir?"

Maybe if the Crouching One understood modern technology, he would never have agreed. Or if Roger Quinn had been there, his assistant would have suspected something amiss. But Roger was stuck on an island in the middle of a sea of burning lava. And Nergal was conceited as only a true demigod could be.

"Of course," answered the Crouching One. "Take several. Would you prefer a normal pose? Or something more threatening, like the type used on cuneiform tablets?"

"How about both?" replied Jack, grabbing his pocket camera from his bag. "If you don't mind."

"My pleasure," said the Crouching One.

The demigod spent five minutes mugging for the camera. Though pompous and overbearing by nature, Nergal possessed a keen sense of the absurd. The Crouching One seized the opportunity to strike the most outlandish poses possible. Which suited Jack, focusing and snapping his photos, just fine.

Afterward, with a polite nod to Cassandra and Megan, the Lord of the Lions exited the chamber. Jack, standing alone for a second, shook his head in admiration. The Crouching One was evil and dangerous, but for a demigod, the ancient entity had style.

"Want to explain to us dumb birdies what that was all about?" asked Hugo, alighting on Jack's right shoulder.

"I don't remember you collecting photos as a youth," said Mongo, landing on Jack's other shoulder.

"And why did you want a cheap pocket camera?" asked Cassandra. "If you wanted a crisp, clear picture of the Crouching One, I could have bought a top-of-the-line model. Considering the lighting with the roof blown out, these photos are going to be all fuzzy. They're going to lack clarity and detail."

"Exactly," said Jack, cheerfully.

"Yous are definitely the most mysterious fellow I have the pleasure of meeting," declared Boris Bronsky. He grabbed Jack and gave him a big bear hug. "Sorry, but I gots to be going. My government wants to know what happened here right away. I will give them a much-edited version of the events. Maybe they even award me a medal."

"You deserve one, Boris," said Jack, wheezing. His ribs felt as if they had been crushed in a vise. "Without your help, I don't know if we would have survived. Thanks again."

"We will meet again," said the Russian. "I feel it in my bones."

The Russian kissed Megan on the forehead, shook Cassandra's hand, and winked at the ravens. And then he too was gone.

"Party's over," said Jack. "We should be going. Merlin deserves a phone call. Then sleep for all of us. Tomorrow, there'll be time to relax and do some sight-seeing. After saving the world for the second time this summer, we deserve a short vacation. The bottle gets deposited in our suite and returns with us to Chicago when we leave. When we return home, we can sink it in a chest at the bottom of Lake Michigan."

"You're not going to reveal a clue about why you took those pictures, are you?" stated Megan, sounding frustrated.

"Nope," said Jack. "Not yet. Wait a few weeks and I'll tell all. I promise."

And he refused to say another word about the subject. Despite some very intense coaxing by his fiancée.

43

"An amazing recovery, Mr. Quinn," said Dr. Philips, two weeks later. "If I hadn't examined the blemishes myself, I would swear they never existed."

"Then they're definitely gone?" asked Roger, his voice trembling with ill-concealed emotion.

"I can't find a trace that they were there in the first place," answered the doctor. "If I were a religious man, I'd say you've experienced a miracle." Philips's brows knotted in curiosity. "You haven't been visiting faith healers or charlatans like that, have you?"

"Not in the least," said Roger. "I woke up this morning and the marks were gone. That's the whole story."

"Your jaunt to Las Vegas?" suggested the physician.

"I'm not sure," answered Roger truthfully. "Near the end of the trip, I experienced a major financial setback. Fortunately, everything was satisfactorily settled the same evening. Since returning home, I've led a rather quiet life."

"Maybe," said the doctor as Roger buttoned up his shirt, "the desert air agreed with you."

"Obviously something did," said Roger. "Thank you, Doctor. I must say it was a pleasure to see you today."

Out on the street, Roger sucked in a deep breath of air and exhaled slowly. It felt wonderful to be alive and to be free. Free of the blotches on his elbow, and free of the Crouching One. For, though he had not said a word to the physician, Roger knew that the disappearance of the marks on his skin were the direct result of another mysterious vanishing. The Lord of the Lions was gone.

When Roger had awakened that morning, his home felt different. It lacked a certain sense of presence that had hovered over the surroundings for months. A quick but thorough check of the building confirmed his suspicions. Nergal was no longer present. There was no sign of the demigod's departure, but the ancient entity was definitely not on the premises. It wasn't until an hour later that Roger thought to check his elbow. That was when he realized that the Crouching One hadn't merely left, but was gone for good. Somehow, Jack Collins had sent the Babylonian deity back to the outermost dark.

"I don't know how you did it, Collins," murmured Roger as he walked along the street, "but I thank you from the bottom of my heart. Now I can try that damned spell again. This time, though, I'll get it right."

Roger cursed as the front of his nose exploded in pain. It felt as if he had been jabbed in the face by a sharp stick or bird's beak. But, of course, there was nothing there.

44

"Then the joker muttered a line about starting over again," said Hugo angrily. "So I pecked him in the nose."

"We'll have to keep a close eye on Mr. Quinn," said Merlin. "I'll dispatch a minor elemental to rain on his parade whenever necessary."

"Explain to me again how you banished the Crouching One from our world," Megan said to Jack. "I'm still kinda hazy on the details."

Their entire group—Merlin and his daughter, Jack and his supernatural friends, and the two ravens—sat in the wizard's inner sanctum, feasting on pizza and Coke. It was a victory celebration of sorts. Spread out on the floor were a half dozen copies of the latest issue of a nationally known weekly tabloid. Smeared across its front page, as seen in thousands of supermarkets throughout the country, was the headline, "Ancient Babylonian God Resurfaces in Las Vegas." Beneath the words was one of Jack's close-up photos of Nergal, snarling at the camera.

"The problem, simply stated," said Jack, "was how to convince hundreds of thousands of people to disbelieve an entity that they were unaware even existed. At first, it appeared a hopeless task. Then the notion struck me that what I actually needed to do was delineate a hoax that no one accepted as truth."

"Isn't the purpose of a hoax to fool people?" asked Cassandra.

"The best ones do," said Jack, "but lately, even the most elaborate attempts fall flat. As Hugo remarked in Las Vegas, modern man is awfully cynical. People refuse to believe anything on face value. That's what doomed the Howard Hughes autobiography, the Hitler diaries, and the recent Jack the Ripper papers. Investigators refuse to accept them as fact until they study them scrupulously. And, as with most hoaxes, the deceptions collapse under the intense examination."

"So you decided to publicize Nergal's reappearance in our world," said Megan, "assuming that everyone would treat it like an obvious sham."

"You catch on quick," said Jack, flashing a smile at his sweetheart. Megan was sharp. "At first, I wasn't sure how to proceed. I considered TV talk shows, but I rejected them as too dangerous. The demigod did possess supernatural powers and if he used them on television, he might stir up more belief than disbelief. That's when I latched onto the scandal sheets."

"Yeah," said Hugo. "I understand now. People read those papers but never believe the headlines."

"Better," said Jack. "They *disbelieve* the headlines. Which is exactly what we wanted.

"I contacted a friend from my undergraduate days who works for the biggest national weekly in the country. The interview and photos floored him. I'm sure he thought I was engaged in some bizarre practical joke, but it didn't matter. That's why I preferred the cheap camera. I didn't want the material to be too convincing. I gave him permission to run the story for free.

"And," he finished dramatically, "there are the results."

"When ten million people read that story," said Megan, "Nergal was history. The supermarket newspaper crowd disbelieved him right out of our universe. He returned to the nothingness from which he emerged."

"Speaking of returning," said Mongo, "it's time for the two of us to bid you good-bye. I'm sure your mother wants a full report on your adventures in Las Vegas."

"Yeah," said Hugo. "Freda's probably been going nuts without us." The bird cawed. "She depends on our advice for running the business. We're indispensable."

Hugging blackbirds was difficult but Megan managed. Jack settled for a hand-to-claw shake. Then, with a final squawk of good-bye, the birds rocketed through the walls of Merlin's office, bound for home.

"Why do I have a feeling," asked Jack of no one in particular, "that we'll see that pair again?"

∞

Epilogue

"Jack," cooed Megan seductively, "what do you think of this outfit?"

Jack's breath caught in his throat as he turned to face his sweetheart. It was late the same night. He and Megan had left the party, still going strong, and had returned to her condominium a half hour earlier. His fiancée had whispered something about needing to show him something important that couldn't wait until tomorrow. Gullible as ever, he had accompanied her to the penthouse. It wasn't until Megan disappeared into her bedroom to freshen up for a second that he started getting suspicious. By then it didn't matter.

"Beautiful," he managed to whisper. Megan stood in front of the sliding glass door leading to the patio. As it had once before, the bright moonlight blazed like a beacon on her stunning shape. This time, Megan wore a sheer pants-and-top combination that left nothing to the imagination.

"That costume," said Jack, "looks awfully familiar."

"It's the houri uniform you gave me in Paradise," murmured Megan. "I saved it for the appropriate moment. Tonight's the night for your reward. Come on out onto the patio. We'll be alone out there. And there's no genies to disturb us."

"That sounds wonderful," said Jack, following his fiancée into the garden. A few minutes later found them on the same large glider in the center of the sea of red and white carnations.

"Forget the small talk," said Megan, wrapping her arms around Jack's neck. "Kiss me, you fool."

He obeyed happily. And often.

"Sorry I'm not particularly seductive this evening," declared Megan, her breath coming in short gasps, "but I've been a good girl long enough. Get out of those clothes, my love, before I rip them off you."

Jack was in no mood to disobey a direct order. Especially that direct order. Hastily, he reached for his belt buckle. And froze, as he heard a rustling on the roof behind them.

"I love this part," said a familiar voice.

"Yeah, me too," answered the other. "I wonder if they'll try that position where—"

"Hey," yelled Jack, "what the hell are you two birds doing here? Why aren't you with my mother in New Jersey?"

"We're cursed," said Megan. "We're cursed."

"Your mom was glad to see us . . . ," said Hugo.

". . . for about fifteen minutes," continued Mongo. "She said the past few weeks were the first time she's had peace and quiet for the last five hundred years. Evidently Freda enjoyed the silence. She sent us back to stay with you two for the foreseeable future."

"Oh, terrific," said Jack, as his sweetheart muttered something about a recipe for raven stew. "Then when do I get to be alone, without any observers, with Megan?"

Quoth the raven, "Nevermore."

Author's Note

Zeno's famous paradox, "Achilles and the Tortoise," is based on the mistaken premise that the sum of an infinite series of numbers is infinite. It isn't.

While many of the people and events in this novel exist only in the imagination of the author, the testing of an anthrax plague on unsuspecting citizens of St. Petersburg is true. Which proves that truth is much more frightening than fiction.